NEVER
SUBMIT

The Kurtherian Gambit 15

MICHAEL ANDERLE

COPYRIGHT

DEDICATION

To Family, Friends and
Those Who Love
To Read.
May We All Enjoy Grace
To Live The Life We Are
Called.

Never Submit
The Kurtherian Gambit 15 Street Team

Beta Editor/Readers

Bree Buras (Aussie Awesomeness)
Tom Dickerson (The man)
S Forbes (oh yeah!)
Dorene Johnson (US Navy (Ret) & DD)
Dorothy Lloyd (Teach you to ask...Teacher!)
T S (Scott) Paul (Author)
Diane Velasquez (Chinchilla lady & DD)

JIT Beta Readers

Kimberly Boyer
John Findlay
Trista Collins
Alex Wilson
Bruce Loving
Ginger Sparkman
Jed Moulton

If I missed anyone, please let me know!

Editors

Stephen Russell
Kat Lind

**Thank you to the following Special Consultants
for NEVER SUBMIT**

Jeff Morris - US Army - Asst Professor Cyber-Warfare, Nuclear
Munitions (Active)

CHAPTER ONE

QBBS MEREDITH REYNOLDS, OPERATIONS AND OBSERVATION AREA

"Shit."

"Gesundheit," Maria Orsitsch replied.

Bethany Anne turned to look at the German leader. "I'm sorry?"

"What?" Maria stopped looking at the mesmerizing display of colors from the Yollin Annex Gate and turned to see Bethany Anne looking back at her, puzzled. Maria thought back to what she had just said and asked, "Didn't you sneeze?"

Bethany Anne smiled, eyebrows raised. "Noooo, I said *shit.*"

Maria made a small 'o' with her mouth. "Sorry, my mistake. But while I have you talking," she pointed at the gate on the screens, "why aren't we moving forward?"

Bethany Anne thought about that question for a second and shrugged, a glint of mischievousness in her eyes.

"Shit," Bethany Anne replied, completely straight faced.

NEVER SUBMIT

Now it was Maria's turn to stare at the young Queen, trying to figure out how, or if, she was joking. In the few weeks since those from New Schwabenland had arrived on the Meredith Reynolds, Maria had been in Bethany Anne's company quite a bit. Enough to both enjoy and be the target of her, at times, wicked sense of humor.

It was time to play twenty questions. "Is that in English?" Maria tossed out.

Bethany Anne answered. "Yes, English."

Maria put a finger to her lips before asking, "Pedantic or vulgar?"

This time, it was Bethany Anne who had to pause. "Um, let's go with a vulgar way to say a proper word."

"Okay, so waste," Maria agreed. "So, the reason we aren't moving forward is either an engineering issue or a convenience problem?"

Bethany Anne nodded this time but didn't clarify which of the two answers might be right.

"Hmmm," Maria thought a moment. "Most of the people on this asteroid are Americans, yes?" Bethany Anne smiled. "So, most of you have not used a bidet in your lifetimes?"

It was just a bit over half of those on the asteroid were American, but Bethany Anne wasn't trying to split hairs, here. She shook her head.

"I presume the engineer or team that helped design the restrooms was European?"

"South African, I think," Bethany Anne said then paused a moment and got that split-second faraway look in her eyes. "I've been corrected, they were German."

Maria Orsitsch asked, "How many rolls are you short?"

Bethany Anne smiled. "It all depends on the number of months or years we decide are sufficient to change over.

While we could certainly force the issue, I've been told there are a few things that might be wise to bend a little. Right now, I'm being informed I should bend another eleven days due to the production schedules on Earth. Apparently, that's based on how many rolls are presently shipping out across the world."

"Just how much toilet paper are we discussing?" Maria asked, finally confirming the product that was causing the Etheric Empire from passing through the Annex Gate.

"Assuming a quarter million people, an average of eighteen months, using fifty-seven sheets per person and double-ply rolls of five hundred sheets we'll need approximately seven point seven billion sheets or fifteen point four million rolls. If Earth's manufacturing capacity is thirty-four million rolls per day, I'm told we should acquire this paper over a period of time, not to just order that many for a single day delivery."

Maria blinked a few times. "How much money is that?"

"At least ten million priced in bulk, closer to fifteen million for something pulled off Amazon," Bethany Anne answered.

There was another pause. "Yes, your new way of selling off the internet is interesting." Maria considered that. "How does Amazon deliver here?" she asked.

"They don't," Bethany Anne replied. "ADAM enters a particular address for a building, one not in use. We doctor up the location a couple of hours before delivery to look like a valid business, and we accept delivery by shipping container, or containers. We replace the incoming container and boost the one delivered up to orbit at night. We have a pretty large skeleton ship that we use now to connect all of the containers together. Once we have enough, it becomes a pretty damned rigid craft. It has its own EI to navigate and deal with the gravitic engines, and gets moving in our direction." Bethany Anne put up a finger to stop Maria. "Don't ask me how it works, beyond that, my little head," Bethany Anne made motions with her hands, fingers opening wide, "explodes!"

Maria closed her mouth. She was, in fact, about to ask more technical questions. Each time she turned around, there was something new and exciting happening here in this woman's Empire.

Now, if Maria could just turn Barnabas' head in the right direction, life couldn't possibly get any better.

QBBS MEREDITH REYNOLDS, ALL GUNS BLAZING, SPECIAL ROOM

The door opened, and the crowd of people already present in the room looked over to see Bobcat step in, closing the door behind him before he nodded a confirmation to Lance.

The room was large, well over thirty feet by twenty feet and had two entry/exit doors. One door entered a back corridor that went to the All Guns Blazing kitchens, the other was for guests.

What it didn't have was any room number or designation signs on the outside of the door. This room was as close to being secret as they could make it.

Right now, it had a veritable who's who of Etheric Empire notables sitting around a table.

Starting with Lance Reynolds and his wife, Patricia, Frank Kurns and Barbara Nickers, John and Jean, Eric and Darryl (Scott was on duty). Across the table from them were

Gabrielle, Stephen and Jennifer, Barnabas and Tabitha. At the other side were Ecaterina and Nathan, William, Marcus, and now with Bobcat, everyone that Lance had discreetly called had arrived.

Others couldn't be present because Lance had to make sure there were enough people to distract Bethany Anne if she came around, looking for some of those missing.

Basically, they needed to lie their asses off if she asked questions, hoping she didn't read their minds.

Now, thanks to Bobcat, he knew his daughter was having a discussion with Ashur, Bellatrix, and Yelena and he needed to get this meeting going.

"Thank you for joining me. It has come to my attention that we need to deal with a rather sensitive situation related to my daughter and one of her vices." A few eyebrows lifted around the table, not understanding what the Queen's father was talking about.

Lance looked around. "You guys and gals don't see it, do you?" He frowned. "Okay, I'll lay it out. She's about to have a birthday in a few weeks…"

Lance was interrupted by multiple people talking at once. He put up his hand to quiet everyone down. "No, I don't mean her human birthdate, I'm not that stupid."

"She loves you and all," Patricia patted her husband on the arm, "but she would kill you, and I'd have to say I'd understand."

"If I could only be so lucky she would stop at that," Lance smiled. "I can only imagine what she could do that would be ever so much more painful."

"Saint—" Bobcat started, before everyone at the table joined in with him pronouncing the creed, "Payback is a *bitch*!"

Everyone laughed as Lance just kept his lips pressed together and nodded. "Yes," he said. "Saint Payback WOULD be a bitch, so, I'm going to use the date TOM tells me is the closest to the actual date he would consider her changed. Since even Bethany Anne doesn't know..."

"Why wouldn't she know?" Tabitha asked.

"Because she was under for so long," TOM's voice came out of a speaker on the wall. A few turned in their seats before realizing that, except to hear better, looking at a speaker was rather futile.

TOM continued, "After the disaster of turning Michael, I thought I should take my time and do it right. I followed the changes and got lost in time myself. Days and nights mean nothing when you're inside of a spaceship, so I didn't follow them. I've researched the information from inside my ship, and I'm pretty confident that the actual date of her conversion is the fourteenth of June."

"So, we have a little time," Gabrielle considered, tapping a finger on her lips.

"Bethany Anne has a vice?" Tabitha asked, a few turning in her direction. "I mean, other than cussing? Hell, she doesn't even drink liquor that I can ever see."

"Oh, she drinks it," Bobcat replied. "It just doesn't do anything to her nanites. They rip through the alcohol in the drinks like nothing. She doesn't get drunk," he finished.

John smirked and pointed at Bobcat. "You DID try to drink her under the table." Darryl and Eric started laughing.

Bobcat shrugged, his face turning red. "Well, I had beaten so many of the Wechselbalg, I thought why not give her a try?"

"It was," William agreed, "one of the first times I've ever seen him incapable of walking a straight line after a drinking contest." He put up two fingers and acted like they were walking in the air, his hand swerving all around.

They were, Lance had to agree, a very drunk pair of fingers.

"Which is to say," Marcus interrupted, "we captured it on video for research purposes of course."

"If it was for research purposes," Bobcat jumped back in, "then why the hell do you guys play it on a loop in the lab?"

William shrugged, straight faced. "We're researching how long it takes for you to complain about it each time." He looked over at Marcus who picked up his tablet and hit a couple of buttons on the screen. Turning the tablet towards Bobcat, Marcus displayed a spreadsheet with a graph on it. "See?" He pointed to the left part of the screen. "Right here you can see a sharp decrease towards the zero horizontal line. It took you about," Marcus turned the tablet back to himself to look at it, "four days and twelve hours to get tired of the video."

"It's been fourteen days," Bobcat grated out.

"Yeah, but we've had a bet…" William continued before Lance cut in.

"GUYS!" They turned to the leader of the Etheric Empire's defenses. "Save it for later, okay?" The three men nodded.

Bobcat stuck two fingers up, pointing to William, then his own eyes, then to Marcus and back to his eyes again before mouthing silently 'we will talk later' at them.

William smiled, and Marcus tried to stifle a laugh.

Barbara, sitting next to Frank, asked, "You said 'vice' earlier Lance, is she cracking or something?"

"Oh, nothing like that," Lance replied. "It's just you know that we're about to leave the system and we need to get a jump on handling a potential problem before it becomes a real issue. I'm sure none of us want to see her suffer withdrawal."

Lance looked around at all of Bethany Anne's closest friends and allies before asking, "How are we going to solve her Coke addiction?"

CHAPTER TWO

QBBS MEREDITH REYNOLDS, QUEEN'S SUITE

Bethany Anne," Meredith, the operations EI of the QBBS Meredith Reynolds spoke from the speaker. Although Meredith could have routed the information through ADAM, they tended to work like humans expected. "Scott says he's ready to pass Yelena, Ashur, and Bellatrix, plus their five offspring through if you're ready?"

Bethany Anne blinked once as she processed the information. Then she jumped out of her bed, rushed into her closet, slid out of the nice suede shirt she was wearing to grab an old t-shirt and throw that on. Tossing off her pajama bottoms, she slid into a pair of leather pants.

Puppy nails can scratch, and if they happened to get their fur all over her, the t-shirt was much easier to wash... or just ditch. She couldn't remember if the puppies would shed, but no use chancing the suede top she liked to lounge around in.

Walking back out of her closet, the doors shutting behind

her, she wrapped her hair in a ponytail and called out, "Okay, let them in." She passed through her bedroom's doors to enter the more public area of her suite.

Just in time to get ambushed by five German Shepherd puppies.

Two came at her from the front, two jumped from the arms of the couch. The last was trying a sneak attack.

Bethany Anne took a step and disappeared.

Scott, listening, but not able to see inside the suite from the doorway smirked when he heard a 'YIP!' of surprise. This was followed by another yip when it sounded to him as if one of the puppies had landed on another.

"So, letting them in early are you?" Bethany Anne, now only two feet in front of her guard, had caught his gleeful face.

His eyes darted to where she was supposed to be and then back to where she was, staring at him with her hands on her hips.

"Aaaahhhh," Scott started, but then Yelena's voice saved his ass.

"Oh!" Yelena came around the corner to see Bethany Anne outside her own suite. "There you are!"

"Hello, Yelena!" Bethany Anne smiled and waved at the woman before looking Scott in the eyes. "Just remember," she whispered as she walked past her guard and back into her suite, "the Saint goes both ways!"

There was a 'chuff' behind him, and Scott turned looked down at the large white dog. "Yeah Ashur, I think we're both going to get it for that trick." Behind Ashur, Bellatrix chuffed as well, and Scott smiled. "Yes, I know you told us, but it was funny, right?"

Bellatrix shook her head and turned around to join Bethany Anne. Scott shrugged at Ashur and went back to watching the corridor. Scott's position guarding Bethany Anne's suite was ceremonial as anyone making it down the long hallway through Meredith's scans was already checked for damn near everything. But at least one of her four closest guards would be there even if standing there was a completely superfluous action.

No one was going to see Bethany Anne without at least one of her Bitches checking them out first.

———

"Take a seat, Yelena," Bethany Anne pointed to the couch. "Not you," she told Ashur. "Mr. White Mountain of fur and hilarity. Take your hairy traitorous ass back out to Scott. You two can console yourselves while we women figure this out." Ashur chuffed, stuck his nose in the air and trotted back out of the room.

Bellatrix, Yelena's all black German Shepherd that had been saved on an operation in Europe, jumped up on the couch. Yelena sat next to her, one of her legs on the couch, one hanging off. Her black hair matched the female German Shepherd's exactly. Bellatrix chuffed, and Yelena smiled and responded to her friend, "Yes, Ashur really didn't want to stick around to chat about this, so he's happy bullshitting with Scott."

Bellatrix put her head down and watched her five puppies roaming around the room. Well, four of them. Matrix, one of the boys, all black except for four white socks, sat next to the couch, watching the three ladies talk.

Bellatrix chuffed to Bethany Anne who regarded her, then slowly raised an eyebrow. "You're shitting me, right?"

Another chuff. "Seriously? All five of them?" Bethany Anne looked up at Yelena who shrugged.

"I know, right? It's like five individual little puffballs who usually can't agree on what they want to eat all zoomed in on one idea and now it's written in stone."

Bethany Anne chewed on the inside of her cheek. "Where are they at on their maturity level?"

"Probably early teens, human-wise." Yelena answered before Bellatrix chuffed. "True, Matrix is pretty focused."

Bethany Anne turned to look down at the black male who was looking up, but his eyes seemed vacant. "Why does he look like he isn't with us right now?" she asked.

Bellatrix chuffed and the sense of *someone being home* returned to Matrix's eyes. He barked back at his mom and looked at Bethany Anne, tilting his head sideways. "Okay," Bethany Anne said to the pup. "You've got my attention, what is it Matrix?"

The little guy barked twice. "Uh," Bethany Anne turned to look over at Yelena, her brow furrowing. "I get that the five little ones want to search and find their human partners, but why is Matrix talking to me? With Ashur as my partner, wouldn't that be weird?"

Yelena looked at Matrix and Bellatrix. "Any help here, Trix?"

There were a few moments of chuffing and high-pitched barks, with an occasional lower bark from Bellatrix as the two women listened to the conversation between the dogs.

After a little while, Bethany Anne's eyebrows just about made it up to her hairline.

TOM!
Yes?
Have you been talking with Matrix?

Yes.

How are you doing that?

I can reach out and speak to minds, Bethany Anne, as long as the other minds are capable of communication. The puppies, like their parents who have been through the Pod-doc, are certainly capable of communication.

What… uh… what have you been talking about?

He likes to talk about space and being 'out there.'

Out where?

Space.

Yelena noticed the Queen was having an internal discussion and waited. Then, Bethany Anne closed her eyes and put her head in her hands.

"Is everything okay?" Yelena asked.

"Yes," she answered, then shook her head and changed her reply. "*No.*"

"What's wrong?" Yelena asked, wondering what could have changed Bethany Anne's earlier carefree attitude.

There was a pause before Bethany Anne answered. "My resident alien has acquired," she peeked out from between her fingers, looking down at Matrix who was staring back up at her, his little tongue hanging out, "A four-footed friend who wants to go see space with him. Which means seeing space with me, too."

Matrix sat back on his haunches a little straighter before barking up at Bethany Anne.

So, can he stay with me? Tom asked his best friend in the universe.

Bellatrix chuffed, and Matrix turned to look at his mom and barked back.

"Ashur!" Bethany Anne called to get her companion's attention.

Scott called back into the room, "Sorry, he left a couple of minutes ago to grab something to eat."

Bethany Anne slowly lifted her face, leaned back on the couch, and looked up at the ceiling. "That little shit knew," she complained after a moment or two, "I've been *played*."

Yelena was able to successfully keep a grin off of her face, but Bellatrix chuffed, and Matrix jumped into Bethany Anne's lap. She barely noticed the young German Shepherd curl up as she absently petted him, her mind on a million other things as she stared up at the ceiling.

Yes, Yelena had to agree, *you've been had.*

How the hell, Bethany Anne wondered, *does one have a ride-along alien that acquires a dog he can communicate with? Who the fuck thinks this shit up? Seriously, somebody stop this damned asteroid, I need to get off…*

Bethany Anne could tell TOM was talking and the pup was, as far as Bethany Anne could determine, communicating right back.

Fuck my life… she thought as she realized she was petting Matrix and rolled her eyes in exasperation. *One more fucking time!*

――――

QBBS MEREDITH REYNOLDS, ALL GUNS BLAZING

Shun smiled at the bouncer outside of the most famous bar on the asteroid, All Guns Blazing. The bouncer, a large Were by the name of Tim who had been with the Wechselbalg since the beginning, nodded to the trio. When Tim was at the door, there were rarely any problems inside the bar.

A few of the people inside knew Shun, Zhu, and Jian. While the Weres were interested in meeting Jian, Shun from backchannels to give the quiet Chinese man some personal space. So the Wechselbalg were interested, but not nosy.

Or you answered to one of the Queen's Own.

As a genetic Werecat, Jian was a bit of an anomaly on the Meredith Reynolds. Shun thought there were two others on the ship, at least if the rumors were true.

Shun took the entrance that went to the bar, as opposed to the more family oriented side and nodded to the bartender on his way to a table with three chairs around it. The proprietors of this place didn't believe in trying to shove too many people too close to each other.

Now that Shun understood the makeup of some of the people, and their propensity to fight?

It made a lot of sense.

Zhu and Jian were already there talking when Shun pulled up his chair. He had barely sat down when a waiter swung by and dropped two Snow beers. "Xiè xie," Shun called out to the waiter who raised a hand over his shoulder to acknowledge the thanks as he deftly caught a bottle that was tipped over and grabbed another empty on his left as he walked to the bar.

Some of these people were so damned dexterous they should join the Royal Circus, he thought.

"We have news," Jian said. Shun turned to his friend and raised an eyebrow. Stephen, the Queen's confidante, had found out Jian was a Wechselbalg before his two best friends had known. Because of this, and even though he was incredibly reserved, and the least likely of the three to speak, he ended up as their liaison with the Etheric Empire.

Now, it was time to face the choice they had to make.

They needed to figure it out and decide what to do next.

"We have been given the option of sticking together, choosing military jobs, or civilian jobs," Jian told his friends.

"But they have jobs for us?" Zhu asked, and Jian nodded. "Good, I'm getting bored," Zhu commented as he looked around. "I've got to figure out how to pay my bar tab."

Shun smiled. Zhu was a hard worker. The three of them had been working out with each other, taking advantage of the many facilities available to those on the asteroid. Heck, they even had a place where you could enhance or reduce the gravity. Once, Jian wasn't paying attention, and he moved the control to three Gs. It had been painful just to move. Getting up off the floor would have been worse had Shun not thought just to call out for Meredith's help. The EI quickly returned the gravity to normal.

"First, let me confirm which way we're going, military or civilian?" Jian asked looking at his friends.

Zhu shrugged. "I'm not done paying those aliens back yet. Those bastards started everything that ended up killing Bai, and they're still out there."

Shun nodded. "Agreed. I'm not satisfied. What did the English playwright say? I've not had my pound of Kurtherian flesh, yet?"

"Good thing you two agreed because I already told them we were choosing the military." Jian smiled at his surprised friends. "What do you want me to say? I've known you two long enough to finish your sentences."

"How could you finish our sentences when you can't speak a whole sentence of your own?" Zhu asked as he picked up his beer, using it to point at Shun. "He talks, Bai and I argued, and you chose to act like the silent and wise type," he finished and took a swig of his beer. "God, I'm going to miss this when we transfer out of this area."

"That's because I am silent and wise," Jian said. "Or, at least I'm still wise," he added, "and I was wise enough to hear you confirm my decision before I told you, right?"

Shun took a swig of acknowledgment. "Okay," he started, setting his beer down, "now that we understand you've been hiding your wisdom from us because you're a wise but selfish bastard, what's the rest of the news?"

Jian regarded his friends for a moment before replying, "I've been asked if I want to be upgraded to full Cat." Zhu, who had his beer halfway up to his mouth stopped in surprise.

None of the men spoke for a moment. "Options?" Shun asked.

Jian shrugged. "In the military here, there are different specialties. The Rangers, not our style. The Guardians for Wechselbalg and the guardian Marines who back up the changelings. They form teams, and there are always two Marines with one changeling."

Shun started nodding while Zhu looked at him, comprehension dawning. "So, Zhu and I would be the Marines?"

Jian nodded.

Zhu's eyebrows had furrowed before realization hit. "So we three would be a team?" He pointed at Jian. "You would change," he then pointed to Shun and himself. "And we would protect you?"

Jian nodded again.

Zhu smiled. "Hell yeah! You take a clawed hand," Zhu said as he put his fingers out and slashed through the air, "and rip each Kurtherian a new asshole while Shun and I keep all the other bastards off your back." He looked over at Shun, smiling.

It was Shun's turn to be confused. "You're okay with Jian being a Cat?"

"What?" Zhu replied. "Why not? Wouldn't you want to be a Cat if you could? I might have shot them as often as I was able, they were the enemy after all. But you can be impressed, even envious, as you kill them, and look at how hard they were to kill! Never fail to appreciate what you can about your enemy, or you lose an advantage to them."

"Sounds wise," Jian answered slowly. "But why am I surprised this wisdom is coming from you?"

"Well, I read it." Zhu explained, smiling. "But it still fits. Nevertheless, the bigger question is if you wish to do this, Jian?"

Their table grew quiet as Jian became the focus of his friends, and after a minute he nodded his head sharply. "I've talked with my parents, and they agree. It would honor Bai to take what the Kurtherians meant to use as a way to subjugate humanity and use it to keep humanity safe instead."

"Well," Shun smiled. "Seems like we have an agreement. What's next?"

Jian shrugged. "We have to meet a small group of Guardians for a test."

"So?" Zhu said. "What could be so hard about one more test?"

CHAPTER THREE

QBBS MEREDITH REYNOLDS, QUEEN'S WORKOUT AREA

Kiel's click-click as he walked offset the click-click-click-click of Kael-ven's four legs as the two Yollins passed the first set of guards.

The first guards were there to make sure you knew and intended to be entering the Queen's workout area. Ass-kickings, they would tell you, would happen after you passed this first post.

The two Yollins spoke with the guards who told them to wait a couple of minutes.

Two idiots would be coming back out shortly.

A few minutes before, two Wechselbalg had not realized that Eric and Gabrielle were an item and decided to say they were here to have a friendly spar with the Captain of the Queen's Bitches.

One of the guards questioned the Wechselbalg, "I'm sorry, did you say you were here for a *friendly* spar with the captain?"

"Yes, she uh, she invited us," The first stated and turned to his partner who nodded vigorously.

"Right," the guard turned to his partner. "Chuck, would you be so kind as to inform Gabrielle her friendly sparring match is here?"

Chuck was a better actor than his partner, Steve. He picked up his tablet, selected the captain's number and informed her that two Wechselbalg were here for her, he looked at the time on the tablet, 3:25 PM friendly sparring match with them?

The two Wechselbalg were passed through, huge smiles on their faces. When they turned the corner, Chuck lifted up his tablet again and punched three numbers and waited for a response.

A female's voice responded, "Hello, infirmary?"

"Yes, this is Chuck down in workout," he replied.

"How many?"

"Two," Chuck replied.

"Type?"

"Wechselbalg."

"Time?" she inquired.

Chuck replied with only a moment's hesitation, "I imagine about one minute after they start, so call it a couple more minutes?"

"Oh, someone being stupid?" the voice said on the other side of the line. "I'll have them right over, and I'll get Peter. When they get healed, he'll be here to deliver his own punishment."

"Understood, thank you." Chuck disconnected.

Four minutes later, two Wechselbalg, each with two broken arms and two broken legs, whimpering as the blood ran down their heads, were being carried out. Chuck put up a hand to stop the infirmary personnel. He snapped his fingers in front of the one that had spoken for them. "Just so you know, there *ARE* no friendly matches down here. Everything is training as hard as you can. So, be thankful she only broke your arms and legs."

"Thankful?" the guy asked, confusion in his voice as he spoke around a mouth and jaw just then starting to heal.

Chuck looked at him. "Well, yeah. If she wanted, she could have killed you for unauthorized use of the Queen's area."

Moments after they were carried out, the two Yollins entered. Kiel nodded to Steve and Chuck and pointed his finger back towards the door. "Someone came in here for a friendly match?"

"Yeah, I can't believe that's the third one," Chuck agreed and waited for a green light on his desk to turn on. "You guys are good."

Kiel's mandibles clicked together. "I wonder who could be whispering the rumor that you get to spar with Gabrielle if you use that code phrase?"

"Or has been adding the picture of her on the backchannels?" Kael-ven concurred as the two Yollins passed through the security station. Steve and Chuck both stared at each other before grabbing their tablets and looking to see what the Yollin Captain was talking about.

Five minutes later, Chuck looked down the hallway towards the sparring rooms. "Son of a bitch…"

———

Bethany Anne entered a few minutes after Kiel and Kael-ven. "Sorry for being late."

Kiel looked at her feet, where a smaller, black version of

Ashur was trotting beside the Queen. "Just curious," the military commander asked as he pointed at her feet. "Has Ashur been replaced?"

"What?" She looked down. "No, this is Matrix, one of Ashur and Bellatrix's children. Say hi Matrix, these two have the implants and can understand."

Matrix's little bark greeted the two Yollins.

"How does he have such ability to understand but is so… small?" The Yollin captain asked.

"He isn't that young. He's a little small for his age, but dogs mature relatively quickly. I'm told that Matrix is ahead of his siblings in some ways."

Matrix barked again. "Yes, not in size, unfortunately," Bethany Anne agreed.

"And Ashur is where?" Kiel asked.

"Keeping his treacherous ass out of my sight while I cool down." Bethany Anne replied. "This little addition to my menagerie isn't my partner, he works with TOM."

That caused both Yollins to stop and blink. "You have a Kurtherian talking to an Earthling dog?" Kiel asked.

"Oh please," TOM's voice came out of the speakers. "Not all Kurtherians are evil warmongers."

"True," Kael-ven agreed slowly, looking at Bethany Anne and then the speaker. "But I'm not aware of any Kurtherians except those from the Seven who have slipped out of their genetic programming and not killed another being."

There was a moment of silence before TOM replied through the speaker system, "I blame my connection to Bethany Anne for that."

Kiel's started chittering in laughter. "He has a point. There have been no Kurtherians who have had to undergo such a stressful existence inside of…"

"Are you begging for another ass-kicking, Kiel?" Bethany Anne asked the taller Yollin. He grinned as well as he could and put up his hands while he shook his head.

"Damn," Kael-ven muttered. "Here I was hoping two of us would have a regular sparring match."

Bethany Anne smiled, raising an eyebrow. "I'm sorry, is the Yollin revolutionary feeling a little put out?"

"He should," Kiel said. "Since working out with you, he has become more formidable in our matches."

"Oh?" Bethany Anne asked, turning to look at Kiel. "How so?"

"He beats me about forty percent of the time now," Kiel answered. "I attribute his improved abilities from working out with you."

"So, why aren't you using your friendship to work out with the Bitches?" she asked Kiel.

This time, it was Kael-ven who chittered his laughter. "Because they treated him like you do me, and it took him half a day in the Pod-doc to recuperate."

Bethany Anne shrugged. "Pain is an excellent teacher."

"Yes," Kiel agreed. "It taught me not to spar with Eric when he was upset about Gabrielle."

"Well, there's that," she said. "Human males are very protective of their females. Even females who can take care of themselves. I imagine someone slighted her and Eric did something. Then she was upset with him for being a typical guy, and they got into a fight. He comes here, where friendly matches aren't allowed, and there you go."

"Yes, there I went," Kiel agreed. "Straight into the Pod-doc nursing both my wounds and my ego."

This time, both Yollins watched as Bethany Anne's eyes displayed extreme amusement, but her lips were pressed together. Finally, she lost it and started laughing, covering her mouth as she looked at the Yollins.

"At least the mouth now is in sync with the eyes," Kael-ven commented. "I was confused."

"Word," Kiel said. His captain turned to look at him. Kiel shrugged. "I blame William."

"Okay," Bethany Anne finally got her amusement back under control, "as funny as this shit is, and it is funny, I need to learn how to fight a four-legged Yollin, Kael-ven, and you're my only option."

"Lucky me," he said. "Come, search the universe for other races, find their planet, meet them, and get your ass kicked all afternoon." He turned to speak to Kiel. "Somehow, the recruiter I spoke with failed to mention that little bit of information when I signed up to lead the expedition."

Kiel said, "You should have been with me for my recruitment meeting—a complete fabrication." Kiel's voice went an octave or two higher. "Superior exoskeleton, best in the galaxy." His voice returned to normal. "What a big bowl of Bistek-barook shit," he finished.

Bethany Anne's face scrunched up in confusion. "When did you two become Abbot and Costello?" she asked.

"No idea what or who you are talking about," Kael-ven replied. "But I assume a certain fatality about one's future brings about whatever," he waved his right arm, "you speak about."

Matrix barked, and Bethany Anne looked down at the puppy. "You might be right Matrix. They just might be trying to delay the inevitable."

The two Yollins turned their heads to glare at the German Shepherd. Kael-ven spoke, "Traitorous canine, thy name is mud. You just wait until you're old enough to spar with her, you'll understand, and I hope I'm here to see it."

This time, it was a questioning 'yip' from Matrix, and Kiel laughed without mirth. "See? Now you understand. Life seems funny now, but after this ass-kicking, you will know your future, and I will enjoy the thought of how my blood and pain will bring you fear."

Bethany Anne rolled her eyes. "Wow, who knew a Yollin could be such a drama queen?"

The two Yollins turned as one and walked over to the side of the room to grab weapons from the rack.

"At least I'm now royalty," Kiel said excitedly.

———

Matrix was sitting on the floor by Kiel, who was lying on his back next to the wall where he had collapsed just moments after placing his weapons back in the rack. "Stop licking me, Matrix!" Kiel moaned. "This is not helping my ego one bit."

Kael-ven was on the sitting couch the team had brought in for him, rubbing his back. "I appreciate the light workout today."

"I only wanted to think about how someone would fight something what, twice your size?" she said as she stretched on the floor. "So I needed to focus on determining your weak spots."

"Rumor has it three times my size, but we do not believe that. First, how would he be so big? Second, the King does not show himself outside of his inner circle. Those who are willing to share agree he is three times larger than I am. But, could they be fabricating the truth so to support the rumor? No one knows."

Bethany Anne looked up at the Yollin. "I've always

wondered if you know why someone taps your natural armor, but it doesn't cause you pain?"

He made the Yollin equivalent of a shrug. "I can feel the punches and occasionally if you are trying to get my attention the blunt force spread across my muscles underneath hurts, but nothing like a concise punch." He lifted his left hand to play with his jaw, making sure it was still in place and working correctly.

"Well, without seeing if I can cut you up," she started.

Kael-ven interrupted, "Yes, I do appreciate the queen's magnanimous decision not to use me for that particular research project."

"Keep interrupting me, and we shall see," she replied. "And who is teaching you magnanimous?"

Kiel's voice groaned from the side of the room as he pointed up at the nearest speaker. "Blame Meredith," he said.

"Meredith?" Bethany Anne spoke, and the EI answered.

"Yes?"

"What are you teaching the Yollins?"

"The appropriate history that could provide insight on how a new Yollin government might be created once the current administration is replaced," the EI replied.

"We are studying both monarchies and dictatorships," Kael-ven said. "Magnanimous decisions for those vanquished was a point of discussion between myself and Meredith."

He smiled as Bethany Anne shook her head in resignation.

———

MICHAEL ANDERLE

A FEW HUNDRED YARDS INSIDE ENTRANCE 1, DULCE LAKE, NEW MEXICO

This time, one of their trips to track down rumors seemed a little different to Jesse. The light from his flashlight hit the far wall and beamed back and forth across the rocks on the cave floor. A scratch on a rock caught his attention, and he turned his flashlight back to see a relatively large boulder. He called out to his friends Edward and Colin to hold up a moment.

Getting close, he could tell that the scratch was recent, it wasn't something that had been around for a long time. Further, something very hard had to have been used to create such a gash in the rock. He took his hand out of his glove and touched the cut.

It was sharp.

He looked at the angle, slashing downwards, and wondered what it could have been. He turned and allowed his flashlight to travel back towards the opening and then turned back around to consider where, if something in fact was moving, would he find the next mark?

He started walking towards his friends, feeling that this time was different. Alien TV, a very small YouTube channel, might have unearthed something real. His flashlight continued along the floor. Unfortunately for him at the moment, it missed a few footprints where something heavy had to have passed.

So far, he hadn't noticed the non-human tracks next to the human ones.

NEVER SUBMIT

ABOARD THE G'LAXIX SPHAEA, EARTH ORBIT

Captain Natalia Jakowski stirred her hot chocolate while she dialed up her favorite strike team. Secretly, she was wondering what the two guys would use as an excuse to try to not head down to Earth this time.

Further inside the ship, Samuel was having a conversation with Richard when the captain of the ship's voice came over the speakers, "Boys?"

Richard rolled his eyes. The captain couldn't be more than in her late thirties, and that was probably giving her a few years, and she called *them* boys? "Yes, Captain?"

"We have visitors in the Dulce Lake base. I need you two to go down, acquire information and confirm what's going on. I've been in communication with ADAM and I understand we might have a few civilians poking around."

"Civilians?" Richard questioned. "I don't remember our contract stating that we needed to help civilians, do you Samuel?" He looked over at Samuel who had a smirk on his face.

Richard winked at his friend.

The captain replied, "I believe the contract, if that's what you'd like to call it, is between you and Gabrielle. I don't think I need to be the lawyer in this little discussion. Would you like me to get Gabrielle on the line, boys? I understand she's going to be coming through the ship here shortly. I can certainly ask her to pause for a moment and speak with you if you require clarification, Richard."

Richard's eyes grew large, the smile dropping off of his face. "Noooo, Captain. Let's keep Gabrielle happy and not bother her with trivialities, shall we? She might be on a date with Eric. I don't suppose we can get a Pod out of here relatively quickly? We would like to head down Earthside and perhaps get a bite to eat before we rush over to New Mexico."

"Richard, what kind of food are you talking about? We have both human food and blood, although I was under the impression that you don't need blood anymore?"

"Well, to be truthful," Samuel jumped in, "blood is a bit of an acquired taste. It's similar to always having your mother's cooking at home. You don't like it that much when you're always eating it, but after you go away to college for a few years, even the worst of mom's cooking tastes *delicious*."

"I'll have to take your word on that, Samuel. My mother happened to be a chef for a local hotel. Therefore her cooking was always delicious. For me, I went the other way. I got into eating too much Taco Bell at college, and although it was unhealthy as hell, the grease was damned delicious. Now, I understand Gabrielle is going to be here in ten minutes with the Queen. So, did you want to get on that Pod before they arrive or are you planning on being here during the lockdown when the Queen comes?"

The two vampires reached over and grabbed their backpacks and quickly made for the door, Richard yelling back over his shoulder, "Captain, I don't know why you're still talking. There's nobody in the room at the moment. Those two individuals happen to almost be to the Pod bay."

The captain could hear the door slam as she reached up to turn off her microphone.

Mark Taversty looked up the readouts he was reviewing. "I thought the Queen wasn't going to be here for at least an hour." The captain winked at him with a smile on her face.

She called to the ship's EI, "Sphaea? You should probably let the Pod bay know that they have two incoming vampires, and they will likely be running."

Down on Earth, a small group of military trucks, tarps across the equipment they were carrying, were traveling down Highway 64 through the Jicarilla Apache Nation Reservation heading towards the location where an explosion happened.

Two black attack helicopters passed over them heading north.

CHAPTER FOUR

QBBS MEREDITH REYNOLDS, DOCKS MEETING ROOMS

Bethany Anne, Ashur, Matrix and General Lance Reynolds appeared in the outer docks Transport Room. Meredith opened the doors, allowing them to leave the chamber. Once they had walked out, the EI confirmed nothing was inside then closed and locked the doors behind the party.

While no one had yet transferred through the Etheric into space already occupied, the computer simulations that ADAM had run calculated a substantially large explosion. Since energy and matter were transferable, the simulations showed solid items occupying the same space would cause some of that matter to covert back to energy.

Neither of the objects would appreciate the explosive result.

It was Meredith's responsibility to make sure that didn't happen to the Queen or any of those who traveled with her.

NEVER SUBMIT

Reynolds, the military EI for the Meredith Reynolds, was her backup and confirmed her results every time.

Finally, ADAM would triple check their results every four hours to make sure nothing was amiss with any of the sensors Meredith or Reynolds used.

The two humans and two German Shepherds walked down the hall and entered a room that had a table, eight chairs and two video monitors on opposing walls. The video screens were nothing but white paint on the walls for the projectors that were affixed to the ceiling. Meredith could use projectors to create 3D holographic images should it be necessary.

Bethany Anne and Lance had barely sat down when they heard a loud knock, and the door opened. Scott, who had gone ahead of them earlier to fetch her errant research and development team, stuck his head in and winked. He opened the door a little wider, and Bobcat stuck his head in.

He smiled at her. "Yes?" he asked, but he didn't step further into the room.

She raised an eyebrow. "Oh, do come in Bobcat, just one of the three men I'd like to see at the moment," Bethany Anne purred.

Scott inclined his head, and Bobcat walked into the room. He came in with all the willingness of a man told he'd be walking the plank.

He was followed by William and then Marcus, all three of them swallowing and looking back and forth at each other. Bethany Anne waved to the chairs. "Take a seat gentlemen. We're all adults here, and we should accept the responsibility of the actions that we take, no matter how long ago they happened, am I right?"

Bobcat pulled out his chair and slowly sat down. "Well,

boss, I think we've all learned great lessons in the past, and we don't need to rehash those lessons whatsoever." He finished by pasting a wide smile on his face, turning up his boyish charm.

William smiled. "I completely support Bobcat's assertion. I feel I've already learned big lessons in life myself, and…"

Bethany Anne rolled her eyes. "Oh, shut up you guys. If I wanted to tear you a new asshole I would've just come down to your lair and done it again. I want you to understand what we've tried to accomplish since the three of you helped destroy an unknown alien base on the Moon."

Marcus interrupted, "To be fair, we didn't exactly destroy it. We were caught in the web like an insect and were working our way back out of the web. It wasn't through diabolical or devious intentions that said base was destroyed."

Bethany Anne raised an eyebrow. "So, I am to understand that the three adult males in front of me have decided that the 'kids did it' defense is now finally retired, and we're going to the 'we were running for our lives defense?'"

"I don't know," William answered, a gleam in his eye. "Are we on trial here? Has anyone ascertained precisely why we're here before we try to defend ourselves? I think we might be getting ahead of ourselves, and making assumptions. It isn't like I can claim innocence and say 'we were on the Moon at the time' since, well, that was true. Can I say I was at home and would that make any difference?"

Lance looked at them. "No."

"Well, shit," Bobcat said. He looked at his friend and held his hand out. "Well, we tried. Nice knowing you William." He looked past William to his other best friend. "Nice knowing you too, Marcus."

Bethany Anne put her hand to her head. "Would you

stop being so melodramatic? It's like I have three little girls in front of me. You aren't on trial here."

Bobcat said, "Not to put too fine a point on this, boss, but have you seen your face in the mirror lately? It's not like we don't know when you're angry."

Bethany Anne looked over at her father. He lifted up his hand and twisted it letting her know that she was exhibiting extreme annoyance, not quite to the anger stage.

She worked to calm herself a little, and the red glare of her eyes diminished slightly. She apparently wasn't over the fact that these guys had been the adults partially responsible for the destruction of a previously unknown alien base.

They were supposed to be advising and teaching their first class of Academy students, not letting them run amok on the face of the Moon. She sighed. No, that wasn't true. How do you let people become adults? You give them freedom and then help them figure out their mistakes.

It was just damned unfortunate the mistake caused so much lost opportunity.

By the time anyone understood that there had been an alien base on the Moon, the team had already triggered a self-destruct sequence on their way out and it was all over but the digging through the debris.

Having received probably one too many ass chewings due to the kids, Team BMW probably overreacted about keeping the mistake of losing their students on the Moon a secret until they could fix the problem.

Barnabas, having tracked down some rumors, informed her of the errors and Bethany Anne had gone into team BMW's laboratory and ripped the three men new assholes for over fifteen minutes. Meredith had confirmed that Bethany Anne had not once duplicated the same combination of curse words the whole time.

She did not expect them to make that mistake again.

"Let me allow the general to take the next part of this conversation," she said as she worked a bit harder at holding back her irritation.

They did not need another bitch session from her. She didn't feel like it was appropriate when the only reason she was mad was having to review the findings after the fact.

No matter how bad she wanted to vent more frustration.

The general spoke up, "Unfortunately, a lot of the locations you talked about, the research lab with the Russian and other remains were unreachable. We believe that the whole floor got crushed. We were able to drill down through the regolith and enter another couple of places in the base. The team encountered and destroyed a couple of the robots, and we were able to get samples of the technology which allowed TOM to extrapolate which part of the galaxy they came from. So far, the teams are reviewing the data, and it's questionable whether or not we'll be able to break into the it since the systems seem to be in the areas that were demolished as you guys left the base. What I'd like to know is if you've had any more thoughts about exhibited behavior of the security and operations droids you ran across?"

"Some," Marcus said. "Frankly, the programming seemed to focus on continued support and enhancement of the operational facilities of the base, or the security. I've wondered whether or not the two of those directives were crossed or merged accidentally. We believe the base has been there a substantial amount of time, and somehow those commands got crossed. If that's true, then whoever set the base up expected to come back. Based on TOM's estimate the base is a few thousand years old or more."

"So, this might have happened three, four or even ten thousand years ago?" Bethany Anne asked.

Marcus paused a moment before answering, "We think this might have been a base from perhaps even twenty or thirty thousand years ago," he said.

Bethany Anne raised an eyebrow. "That long?"

Marcus shrugged. "Well, no one has any good explanations for the Egyptians and many of their advances. We can't even date the age of the Sphinx accurately. If our guesses are right, this base might have been a location for aliens working to facilitate their knowledge using the Egyptians."

"Well," William said as he scratched his neck. "I guess Ancient Aliens are going to be pissed if they find out we destroyed their proof."

"Interesting that you should mention the History Channel show," ADAM said through the speaker system. "It seems we have a group from a small YouTube show, called *Alien TV Podcast* researching the Dulce, New Mexico Base at the moment. They've found one of the cave entrances and are following the cavern towards what's left of the XJ-12 base."

Bethany Anne threw a hand up in frustration. "Can't this shit just leave me alone for two damned weeks? Just two weeks. After that, it's the world's fucking problem. Okay, ADAM, give me an update. What's going on and who's doing what about it?"

"Presently, Captain Jakowski has Richard and Samuel heading toward New Mexico to ascertain what they know and perhaps extract the alien hunters themselves," ADAM replied.

Moments later, Bethany Anne agreed to let her teams near Earth deal with the alien enthusiasts.

ADAM had reminded her she had a date with the ex-

President and his family. This was their third date. She had rescheduled two previous appointments to show him and his family around the Meredith Reynolds and was refusing to reschedule it again. No matter how much other stuff got in the way.

Sometimes it was about the relationships, not the bigger picture.

She excused herself and left the general with team BMW to finish the discussion. She opened the door and nodded to Scott who closed it behind her. She, Asher, Matrix, and Scott walked towards the teleport room where she needed to take an Etheric short cut back inside the Meredith Reynolds to meet the President's family.

Because the two of them had teenage daughter problems and Bethany Anne thought she might be able to help.

So help she would.

———

QBBS MEREDITH REYNOLDS, ACTIVE PARTICIPATION AREA

"Beware the Wechselbalg, they bite..." Shun read the sign in front of the first set of doors aloud. The three men could hear the practice, the shouts, the cursing (in multiple languages), the occasional bark, growl and scream coming from the other side of the doors.

Zhu looked at his friends. "You remember the time we got attacked in the early morning?"

"Which time?" Shun turned from the sign to look at his friend. "We were in so many of those damned attacks."

"Right," Zhu agreed. "Now, both of you, close your eyes,"

he said, speaking in Chinese. His friends did as he asked, not needing to know where he was going with this.

"Go back to one of the hard ones, the times where we heard our men screaming, the Cats attacking from under the brush, or from above. The feeling in your heart, your mind, your muscles when we meshed. The commands we spoke to each other, the knowledge that we weren't three, but one in defense of each other. The ability to sense what the others knew..."

Jian's mind took him back to the darkness, the smells, the screams of pain and the screeching of the Cats in the night. The smell of gunpowder, and the occasional pain if he or one of his friends were hurt.

Then, all three felt it again, the calmness in turmoil, the connection.

Their connection.

The reason they were best together, never apart. When the leadership made them separate, they pulled apart the best team, hoping that the three could teach others.

Unfortunately, it never happened.

When they opened their eyes again, they weren't three friends standing outside of the APA. No, they had been transported back to the constant training in the fine art of staying alive. Zhu stepped back, and Shun strong-armed the door and stepped in.

His two friends right on his heels.

In another area of the battle station, EIs Meredith and Reynolds reviewed the video of the men outside the APA, noted their conclusions, and labeled it a priority for Peter to watch.

"And I'm telling you," Dwayne told Craig as he pushed up the two hundred twenty-five pounds for a quick set of twenty before resting. "That there is no fucking way we'll be going back to Earth. So, you'd better start practicing your ass off, Craig, or Peter's going to..." Dwayne rolled his eyes when he noticed his friend not listening. Someone had come in, and his friend had used that as an excuse to ignore Dwayne's recommendation to train harder.

It wasn't that Craig was out of shape, or poorly trained, but Dwayne felt Craig's ego was a little too large when they had yet to actually test themselves against a non-human enemy. Craig and his Marine team had easily taken out a two-Yollin attack group just two days earlier, and Dwayne was shocked was Craig able to get his bulbous head inside the training area now.

It had grown so large from his ego puffing it up.

"Fresh meat..." Craig muttered loud enough for Dwayne to hear.

Making sure his weights were locked correctly—something Craig was supposed to be doing for him, the ass—Dwayne turned his head to note the three Chinese men who had entered. Looked like Marine material to Dwayne, so he grabbed his barbell once more and prepared to start another twenty. He preferred ten sets of twenty, and then three sets of three hundred for ten reps and a final push of five reps at five hundred pounds.

"Yeah, you keep saying that," Dwayne mumbled. There was something about the three men that caused Dwayne's hackles to go up slightly. He wasn't worried they would do anything, but if he had to spar with them, he wouldn't dismiss them.

"Craig!" a voice shouted from the opposite direction.

Dwayne smirked, Craig had just been caught by Peter. Seems like Craig's all-knowing awareness was just caught with its pants down.

"Sir!" Craig turned around to see the Guardian's top commander and Queen's Bitch bearing down on him, Peter's brows furrowed in a way that made Dwayne wince in sympathy for his friend.

His friend was going to get an ass chewing he would feel for the next week.

Peter slowed down, and made a point of nodding to the three new faces before he turned to the Wechselbalg. "So, not helping your team member here, I see." Peter stated as he nodded to Dwayne.

Craig turned to look down at Dwayne, remembering he was supposed to be spotting his friend but had started running his mouth off as his friend continued his reps.

Thus, his friend had set his ass up.

Dwayne raised an eyebrow to let Craig know he was guessing what Craig would like to say and wouldn't accept Craig trying to blame him for his present predicament.

Well, *shit*.

Craig looked back at the commander, "Sir, I was watching the fresh me… ah, the ahh possible new recruits for the Marines."

"Yes," Peter looked over at the three men. There weren't yet any Chinese on any of the teams. Peter's eyebrows furrowed. "Thank you for volunteering, Craig. I'll note that next time I'm upset with you, that volunteering for something is your preferred way of making things right." Peter stepped beside the man, who was trying to mentally catch up with what his boss had just said.

He had, however, caught the one word that meant shit was coming his way. "Volunteer, sir?" Craig's head turned as Peter stepped around him.

"That's right, Craig. Follow me," Peter said and continued towards the new faces.

Craig, his previous smirk now absent from his face looked down at Dwayne who was lying on the weight bench. Dwayne mouthed up at him, '*you are fucked*.'

Craig turned to follow Peter. Behind his back, Craig flipped Dwayne off carefully working to keep his smirk from returning where Peter might see it.

Dwayne put the weights up and locked them down all the way. Sitting up, he grabbed a towel and starting wiping the sweat from his face. It wasn't rare to find Peter down here, but Peter seemed to be on a mission. If Craig had caught his attention, then this was probably Peter taking the opportunity to hone Craig's skills at the same time as providing an opportunity for others to get the message.

Dwayne noticed another pair of eyes looking curiously at him before nodding towards Craig. Dwayne winked back.

This should be good.

Shun entered the APA and stopped a few feet in, looking around in surprise. This room was significantly larger than he had expected!

It was easily a hundred and fifty feet long by about ninety wide and at least thirty feet high. There were large areas to work out along the sides, but the middle was set up for competitive training and sparring.

Shun noticed the man, no probably Wechselbalg, to his

left start to stare at him and his friends as they looked around the Active Participation Area and watched the different people sparring against each other.

In one section, there was a wolf... a rather large wolf, in fact, with two humans holding guns fighting two Yollins.

"Craig!" Shun turned back to his left to see the Guardian's commander calling to the one who had been looking their way.

Moments later, Peter stepped around this man, who had turned to follow Peter after a second and headed towards them.

Shun relaxed for just a moment, content. He didn't need to confirm what was going on around him because he could feel it. Zhu was watching behind and to his left and Jian the opposite side.

Shun was responsible for the front.

Like they were still in the jungles, those many months after Bai's death when every death of a Cat was celebrated.

Peter arrived and held out his hand, which Shun took.

"Good to see you again, Shun," Peter nodded to the other two. "Zhu, Jian."

"I would say the same," Shun smiled. "But I think we might be in a little pain soon?"

"Guys, I'm sorry, but Todd is delayed over in APA Delta with a large group action," he explained. "So, you only have me this challenge instead of the two of us."

Shun made a point of looking around the man at the rather large room. "Larger than this?" he asked Peter.

Peter turned around. "Oh, this is a smaller APA. Not our smallest, of course. This is the second smallest of the four core APA rooms not including some of the large ship's caverns they're clearing out."

"Ship's caverns?" Zhu asked from behind Shun.

"Sure," Peter turned back to answer Zhu. "The engineering group is preparing for a ship's refurbishment to be accomplished inside the Meredith Reynolds. Our version of a dry dock. That way, we can protect some ships if we need to, or finish them inside away from prying eyes. If they aren't being used for active duty, we can use them ourselves for large troop actions. They can get pretty big."

"Todd is the commander of the Marines; I'm in charge of the Guardians. Together we work both teams, and if a final decision needs to be made, I'll decide who makes it. Occasionally, Todd is stronger in certain areas, and I'll tell him to make the call. If it is within my area of specialty, I make the call." He pointed a thumb over his shoulder. "This young, strapping volunteer is Craig. He's a Wechselbalg who is going to test your ability to work as a team."

"I'm going to fight them, sir?" Craig called out from behind Peter.

Peter winked at Shun before turning towards his soldier. "Why yes, Craig. Are you up to three against one? I mean, I can ask for a couple of volunteers to back you up if you want."

"May I ask the parameters of the action, sir?" Craig replied, cautious.

"Of course. You will start at one end, them the other. Feel free to use all of your skills, and I'm going to give them the equivalent of what they're used to using. Strictly standard effective sleep darts, so a couple of shots aren't going to do much. Now, no killing and anyone yelling 'out-out-out' is making themselves a non-combatant." Peter turned back towards the three men. "If you need immediate medical attention, you need to let us know. Otherwise, you have to stay on the field of battle, understand?"

Shun, Zhu, and Jian nodded.

"So, three outs and the Wechselbalg wins?" Craig asked, not believing his luck. Although he might be concerned if he had to deal with three of Todd's Marines who had worked with his kind for a while.

Three obvious newbies like this? Freaking piece of cake.

Peter nodded. "Go stretch, Craig," he told him and watched as Craig turned and jogged over to the far side of the mat.

Everyone had figured out that another match was about to occur, so when they finished their current sparring match, each would step off and cool down, waiting to see what Peter was up to.

Those who had met the three Chinese men in All Guns Blazing or had heard a couple of whispered rumors all worked hard to keep a straight face.

No, let's be honest, they were trying to not bust out laughing.

It looked like Craig was going to be taught a lesson. Those who didn't know what was going on were working to trust their obviously crazy commander.

Because allowing a Wechselbalg of Craig's caliber loose on three humans?

This fight wasn't going to be pretty for the humans, for sure.

CHAPTER FIVE

EARTH

Around the world, a very sensitive, some might argue beyond sensitive, classified document was reviewed, shared, debated and argued.

In the end, for those who had been granted eyes to see it (it never went across the internet or even classified military networks) all who reviewed the document arrived at the same conclusion.

TQB was leaving *soon*.

Level Five attempts to acquire TQB technology were approved regardless of their legality. That it was '*good for the world*' was justification enough.

Two men in a small, nondescript office building in Washington D.C. made a phone call to New York.

One said two words, no names shared, "Mousetrap approved," then hung up.

TQB would not be leaving with their tech.

NEVER SUBMIT

At least, not without speaking with them one more time whether the Queen wanted to…

Or not.

———

QBBS MEREDITH REYNOLDS, ACTIVE PARTICIPATION AREA

Craig looked around the sparring room, smiling externally, but internally his mind raced. While he could be arrogant, always a potential personality problem for any Wechselbalg, he wasn't a complete idiot.

That Peter had volun-*told* him to spar with these three men gave him enough of a warning.

Now, Peter was explaining the guns to the trio. These were modified to shoot tranquilizer darts instead of bullets.

Designed to subjugate a Were once hit six or more times. But Craig had an advantage.

He could get hit at least eight times before he would go out. He had been hit nine times two days ago, by the Yollins, but by the time the drugs nailed him, he had been able to win the fight. He was looking forward to this.

He started to remove his clothes, waiting for them to check out the guns. Peter led them to a range and was letting them run through a magazine of darts with no serum.

Craig paid attention, their shooting was good. The second guy in the group was messing with his sights, and Peter gave him another magazine.

The shots from the next magazine were much closer to the center. Craig made note of the shooter, he would have to watch out for that one.

Soon enough, they were given basic protective gear, and were walking towards their side of the mat, some sixty-five feet away.

Then they pointed their guns down and formed a triangle, one man in the front, the other two behind him.

Craig smiled, then changed...

———

Peter sent the three on their way. He sure hoped Todd was right about this. The Marine commander had worked with these men and said this group of guys was just as good as any of the Marines.

If not better.

Peter had asked and been told this team had been out in the bushes with the Sacred Clan, going toe-to-toe and taking their anger out in blood.

Not like the sparring matches here, but real, in the woods, in the dark of the night, men screaming in pain and agony, holding your shit together, operations.

They would, Todd promised Peter, be fucking *amazing*.

Looking around for a moment, checking on those that were paying attention to the challenge, Peter sure hoped so. Right now, Craig's win over the Yollins was affecting his performance and he didn't need Craig cock-strutting across the floor after wiping up a team a second time.

It was times like this that Peter appreciated having Todd around. He settled down and allowed himself the opportunity to appreciate the experience Todd had.

Peter was going to enjoy this.

———

Shun looked his rifle over one last time. The additional sighting shots helped him the little bit he needed to feel comfortable with the weapon. Peter explained that for most Weres six darts would be sufficient to mark them a kill. Zhu asked him if that was true for the one they were fighting.

"Now that," Peter had whispered, "was a smart tactical question, Zhu. Since you thought to ask it, I would recommend doubling the quantity."

Jian raised an eyebrow at Shun. "*Twelve*?"

Shun pulled his magazine and made sure it was full, quickly followed by Zhu then Jian. All three rammed the mags home, took deep breaths and focused. A peace came over them.

The peace before the storm of battle.

———

Craig's wolf form cut a striking figure as he sniffed the air. His enhanced perception watched for any sign of nerves or discomfort the three men might exhibit when they were facing an obviously supernatural creature.

They glanced over at him as they walked to their side of the mat and then…

Ignored him.

Craig's lips drew back in a snarl. His nose wasn't changing what his eyes saw. These three were aware he existed, but they didn't seem bothered by him at all. Didn't they understand that death was just a few feet away? No? So fucking be it!

The stupider they are, the more it would hurt for them

when he took them out of the game.

If the Yollins were the main course then he was going to have humans for dessert.

———

Jian whispered, "He's not that big. I figured he would be as big as a horse."

"You're just spoiled fighting the Sacred Clan and some of their older warriors. He's young, he will grow yet," Zhu whispered back.

"Always treat your enemy with respect," Shun added. "Right before you shoot them full of lead."

"You mean darts?" Zhu asked as they lined up on their side of the mat.

"Whatever works," Shun said.

———

Peter had to admit, not one of them so much as flinched when they watched Craig change and start pacing, trying to win the fight through intimidation. So far as Peter was concerned, the score was Team China 1, Craig 0.

Waiting until all three of the team had their headgear in place, Shun nodded. Peter raised his arm and looked around the large group of spectators and back to Craig, who was watching Peter out of the corner of his eyes.

Peter dropped his arm, "GO!"

———

Craig bolted straight for the men but had to dodge right as a dart came down the lane. He quickly dodged to his left when a second dart nailed his left shoulder. He turned sharply back the other way and was crossing over to the other side when dart number three tagged him.

He growled in anger. Lucky little bastards!

———

"Zhu, coming your way. I'm shooting straight down, but off his left ear." Shun hadn't finished when he sent his dart down the path. Shun heard Zhu's rifle bark and then Jian's when the wolf turned quickly to his side, opposite the dart.

"That was probably the easy two hits," Zhu remarked.

"It's okay, only ten to go," Shun said and aimed for a left reverse. "Bring him." Jian's rifle popped, and Shun waited for the twitch, then squeezed his own trigger.

———

GODDAMMIT! Craig felt the fourth dart hit him as he performed his switchback. He had been too obvious with his moves and had played right into their fucking human hands. Craig kicked off from the ground, leaping into the air and snickered when he heard a dart pass underneath him, missing him completely.

———

"Nice sucker shot, now make the landing count," Shun muttered, as they all figured out the trajectory of the airborne wolf. When you had life or death fights with cats in the wild, the easiest way to shoot one, they had determined, was in the air. Cats couldn't change their direction when in the air and if your reflexes were fast enough, and your gun had enough silver loaded, you could take one out.

If you could just get them airborne.

———

As Craig landed three darts hit him full on. He stumbled and in annoyance realized the only reason two more darts he heard streaking right above him missed was they expected him to still be standing up.

Craig rolled over a couple of times before getting up on all four legs and deciding a straight-ahead charge would work best.

No more Mr. Nice Wolf.

His paws and nails dug into practice mats specifically made for Werewolf claws and bolted from his position.

The men split up as they countercharged *him*.

He knew enough not to go down the middle, so he turned and aimed at the man on his right.

———

"You win again, Zhu," Shun called out. For some reason, it seemed most changelings went after Zhu. The team had never figured out if it was a right-handed mentality, they sensed something about Zhu, or perhaps, Jian commented offhandedly one time as the three discussed it…

Perhaps Zhu simply smelled delicious?

"Shut up and shoot!" Zhu yelled, then smiled in relief when he heard the cracks of his friends' guns.

Zhu heard a female yell "Shit!" from his left. He imagined she had come over to watch the sparring match and was now the proud owner of a dart stuck in her shoulder.

Zhu grinned in satisfaction, he could see when the additional darts started taking effect. The wolf was pretty damned close when it suddenly dove nose down into the mat twelve feet in front of Zhu.

Zhu braced a leg and lifted his other foot to stop the wolf as it slid toward him. The wolf's weight caught Zhu by surprise, and the drugged wolf rolled right under him, knocking his leg from under him and causing him to fall hard on the mat as the wolf slid past.

Shun and Jian smiled as they walked over to their friend and looked down at him.

"Oooowwww," Zhu said. "Did anyone get the license plate of the car that just hit me?" he groaned as Shun reached down to grab his arm and help him stand.

————

"Son-of-a-bitch!" Peter whispered. The three Chinese men had made short work of Craig. They worked together like a very well oiled machine.

They weren't bothered by his enhanced speed at all.

Peter nodded to them as he walked over to Craig and counted at least nine, no... ten darts on Craig's left side. There was one in his left ear, which would have been annoying, but wouldn't have caused Craig any problems. Peter turned to look back to where Craig had fallen and could see three more on the ground that must have fallen out.

That was fourteen. Peter turned and nodded, allowing Dwayne to step onto the mat. He pointed to Craig.

"Dwayne, turn your comrade over."

Dwayne walked to Craig and rolled him over.

Four more darts were stuck in Craig's fur.

Dwayne whistled. "Damn! He's going to have a splitting headache when he wakes up."

"Serves him right," Peter replied. "If a person brags six darts can't take him down, what does he expect to happen?"

Dwayne chuckled as a few more of the Wechselbalg walked over from the walls and laughed when seeing all of the darts the Chinese men had shot into Craig. "Sure as hell not eighteen darts!"

―――

Bethany Anne took five extra minutes to shower, change and pin her hair back once she was back in her suite, as John switched places with Scott.

Bethany Anne smiled at her friend as she came out of her suite. "So, why do I get the honor of you for this meeting?"

"Just here to see the ex-prez again, boss," John answered as he took up his position beside her.

"Uh huh." She looked at him sideways before she reached out and grabbed his shoulder. They disappeared.

―――

The ex-President looked out over the gigantic open space inside the asteroid. He could see crops, sources of light and he presumed heat, and over on the far side of the massive, almost circular cavern, some sort of fish farm. While all of this was fascinating, and it was, he was also using this time as an opportunity to be safely away from his wife and two daughters.

He was pretty sure his youngest daughter was probably looking around with the same amount of awe he had for the cavern. Looking at the crops going up each of the sides almost halfway. He wondered if there was a limitation on the technology, or if they could grow the plants on all of the surfaces? The massive light generation globe in the center sent light to all surfaces equally, so lighting wasn't the limiting factor.

Gravity, he thought, was a strong possibility.

Unfortunately, even the amazing technological accomplishments right in front of his family failed to stop the lasers his oldest daughter was staring into his back.

Further, he figured he was receiving a second set of laser beams from his wife.

Their younger daughter would eat this up. Science was her thing, and they never had to ask her to find something to do, as she was either looking up something on the asteroid's version of the internet, or talking with EI Meredith.

That was yet another reason his wife was upset. Their daughter was constantly learning, growing, and focused.

Almost too focused, in fact. She was so focused she had little time for her parents anymore. He tried to explain to his wife that this was a phase, and the EI wasn't trying to brainwash their child.

That explanation wasn't working so well. One should take very seriously any concerns from a mother, whether they seemed logical to oneself or not.

"Hello!" a contralto voice called out from behind the family.

He turned to see a smiling Bethany Anne walking up them. She was accompanied by John Grimes, who was carrying a bag. Bethany Anne was in a very fashionable outfit consisting of black pants, white shirt and red tailored bolero jacket that accentuated her figure.

And she was wearing heels.

"Oh my God!" his older daughter exclaimed, her eyes on Bethany Anne's feet. "Are those Christian Louboutin?" she asked excitedly.

Bethany Anne smiled at the adults. "One moment, fashion calls," she said before she started talking about the shoes with his older daughter. She lifted her foot and angled it to the side to show them off better.

His wife turned her eyes toward him, a smile on her face, nothing nice in her eyes.

"Are you telling me she's able to ship designer shoes to the middle of outer space?" she asked him politely.

Too politely.

How was this his fault?

Women, can't figure them out, and can't find a suitable hiding place on an asteroid when they aren't happy.

Bethany Anne wrapped up her quick discussion with his daughter. Smiling radiantly she said, "Sorry, but you have NO idea how nice it is to talk fashion with someone who appreciates it!" She turned towards John. "Okay zug-zug, time to give your Queen the gifts she brought for the family."

"Uh huh," John handed Bethany Anne the bag.

She turned around and winked at the President. "Sorry, this is about making sure you're let back into your quarters and me being forgiven for canceling on you twice before. I feel really bad about that." Bethany Anne reached into her bag and pulled out a box of Jimmy Choos in size eleven. "I hope you might forgive me, if just a little?" Bethany Anne asked as she handed the box over to his wife.

A wife, he noticed, now rendered speechless.

He took that as a good sign, he might not have to figure out where to hide just yet.

"Here on the Meredith Reynolds," Bethany Anne was chatting with his wife, "the cushioned soles and slight heel will feel better." "Although," her voice went low and sounded almost conspiratorial as his wife, and both daughters, leaned closer to hear better, "there are another couple of boxes with a pair of black high heels and a metallic silver pair I think you'll like waiting back at your home, as well."

Bethany Anne didn't allow his wife time to respond before she was pulling out another box. This time it said 'Louboutin' on the side. "These are for you," she handed them to his oldest, who was as speechless as his wife. The astonished girl opened the box and took a shoe out of the velvet bag that came with it.

They were black, mid-sized heel, with a red heart on the front.

"I've seen these!" she exclaimed, her eyes lighting up, her excitement bubbling over.

"Well, don't you think I'd know if someone happens to like my most favorite shoe designer?" Bethany Anne asked.

"What?" his daughter looked up then over to him. "Did my dad rat me out?"

The ex-President was about to say he hadn't been responsible when a voice came out of Bethany Anne's bag. It was obviously female, and just a little tinny sounding.

"That would be me!" the disembodied voice called out.

"Ah!" Bethany Anne reached one more time into her bag. She pulled out a slick tablet, like those on the scientific teams used from time to time. Bethany Anne turned to his youngest.

"This is for you. Meredith is annoyed that she can't follow

up with you about your homework at the appropriate times."

His wife broke her silence, "Homework?"

"Yeah, Mom," their youngest daughter said as she reached up to accept the special tablet with bright eyes. "Why did you think I had to work so much with Meredith? I'm trying to understand the orbital dynamics of ships floating around the Meredith Reynolds." She took the tablet from Bethany Anne, found the little earbud and pulled it out, sticking it in her ear.

"OH MY GOD!" she squealed, her eyes blazing with excitement. "I CAN HEAR YOU SO WELL. Okay," she continued, her fingers manipulating the icons on the tablet, "where do I find Fundamentals of Astrodynamics by Bate, Mueller, and White?"

Then their youngest daughter turned away from them and walked towards their small cart. The four adults were bemused as she sat down inside, moved to the back seat and continued talking to Meredith.

"Do you have any idea what she…" he asked before Bethany Anne cut him off.

"Not a clue," she said. "Astro or orbital mechanics are not my strength."

"I should say not!" the same voice erupted from her bag once more.

"Wow, Meredith!" Bethany Anne grumped as she reached into the bag and pulled out another tablet before handing the empty bag to John. He casually folded it up and stuck it in a pocket. "Let's not play *Diss the Queen's inability to calculate the periapsis velocity* in front of the VIP guests, shall we?"

A second voice came out of the same tablet, male this time. "Why does Bethany Anne need to be good at astrodynamics? She has me for that."

"Thank you, ADAM," Bethany Anne said to the tablet. "I

know I can count on you for the harder stuff."

"What's this for?" his older daughter asked. "And the second voice is ADAM?"

"Yes," Bethany Anne said, holding onto the tablet. "It seems ADAM, as a true A.I., finds beauty in a lot of areas, and he likes to stretch his abilities. He's been looking for someone who might wish to speak about, and design, fashion as we head into the future."

"I'll be that person!" She reached for the tablet, but Bethany Anne pulled it back.

"Not yet!" she told the teenager, who looked up at her, concern overriding the eagerness on her face. "You have to understand that if fashion isn't your true love, this tablet comes back. We all have a role to play going into the future in the Etheric Empire. Fashion, although many people don't understand, is an important part of the psyche of many individuals, including my own. For some people to believe in themselves, they have to be able to see themselves in a new way. Fashion can bring about a better result than some psychologists, when a person sees themselves in a mirror looking fantastic."

"Okay, I get that," his daughter said.

She might be fashion focused, but she was certainly not slow on the uptake.

Bethany Anne continued, "Now, if you and ADAM come up with designs that you want to produce, you're going to have to help bring it about. That means you'll have to learn about making it, creating new fabrics out of the materials we'll have available to us, including new manufacturing and weaving tools we're developing as we expand our knowledge of what other races have accomplished. The practical, the needed, the wanted. All of these are part of the future, and fashion can be an instrumental aspect."

"That is just the beginning, and we need people that are really committed to making this their life's work," Bethany Anne told the girl, who was starting to realize that Bethany Anne was opening her future up to opportunities she had never dreamed existed.

"Thank you," she answered, wiping a tear she didn't want her parents to notice. "I would be honored for the opportunity to find out if this is something that isn't just a passion, but a calling."

The ex-POTUS looked over at his wife and dearly wanted to reach over to push up her jaw so her mouth would close.

Bethany Anne handed the tablet to their daughter. "You can contact ADAM most anytime, but this is yours, and it looks like your sister knows how they work if you have questions about it."

She smiled, accepted the tablet and found the earbud. She thanked Bethany Anne and then made her own way over to the cart.

Bethany Anne turned to the parents. "And you," she looked at the Ex-President, "I give you a happy life because you now have a happy wife and daughters."

His wife leaned into him and looked up into his face. "I'm sorry," she said. He kissed her forehead.

"Happy wife, happy life," he said. "That, and basketball."

"Well," John interrupted, "we have an all-human league running basketball games every second Thursday if you're interested?"

"All human?" the ex-President asked, his brows furrowing before realizing. "Oh, of course. Not fair to the humans if the players are enhanced."

John shrugged. "Not really."

"Why did you do this?" His wife turned to Bethany Anne and asked, pointing to the girls. "This was well planned out. You had to have some insight into what was going on." She turned back to her husband, and this time, her eyes were calculating. "Are you complaining about your home life behind my back?"

Her look promised substantial pain would be possible, no probable, if he had said something outside their four walls.

He silently praised the Gods above (or were they sideways when in space he wondered) when Bethany Anne interrupted his spouse's weapons release countdown.

"Oh God, no!" Bethany Anne laughed, removing the dual target acquisition devices from looking at him as his wife turned back to the Queen. "No, it's easy enough to figure out. Remember," Bethany Anne pointed around. "Meredith sees all, hears all. I don't use her to pry, but I listened to a couple of stories through backchannels. The scientists were commenting in one about your younger daughter and her love of science, and there were a couple of people who passed on a story about a particular teenager's tantrum outside of one of the cafeterias a few days ago."

"Oh, God," his wife's head fell forward, her hands on her face. "That episode got out?" she mumbled behind her hands.

Bethany Anne smiled in sympathy. "Only a little, but since I was trying to see what I could gift you, Meredith pulled it up for me. ADAM is the one who came up with the idea to support her love of fashion."

"The computer?" she asked, confusion evident on her face as she looked up.

"No, an A.I.," Bethany Anne replied. "He's sentient, and fashion, I'm very happy and yet kind of conflicted to say, proves it."

This time, he interrupted. "How does fashion prove sentience?"

Bethany Anne looked up as she thought a moment, a smile playing at the corner of her lips. "One has to understand beauty, true beauty, to be considered sentient. The beauty of a sunrise, the joy it brings to you. ADAM has been talking shoes with me, and recently, he has started forming his own opinions on my shoes as I get dressed. I asked him which algorithms he was using to confirm shoe choice, and he went silent for about three hours."

Bethany Anne turned to look where the couple's older daughter was talking to her tablet. "When he came back, it became clear he had come to the conclusion he was thinking for himself."

She turned back. "ADAM said that there was no algorithm in place because no matter what he tried to test, it all pointed out that his suggestions weren't the most logical solution."

She paused a moment, a look of contemplation on her face. "And where there is no logic, one is left with *personal opinion.*"

CHAPTER SIX

QBBS MEREDITH REYNOLDS, RANGER'S SECTION AND QUARTERS

The EI's voice sounded in her quarters. "Tabitha, you've been contacted by Theodore Jameson from the New York City Police Department."

"Huh, which one should I keep?" Tabitha said aloud to herself, lifting a shirt in one hand, and a hoodie in the other, trying to decide which one she wanted to wear for the official steal-the-Coke-recipe-for-the-Queen operation.

She wasn't sure how Barnabas was justifying this action as a Queen's Ranger, a law-abiding occupation, stealing a secret Coke recipe. But what the hell. They were taking the recipe out of the solar system, so she didn't expect it to cut into Coke's profits any.

Finally, her mind caught up with Meredith's interruption, and she looked towards her video monitor. "Hey!"

"Yes?" the EI replied.

"Who are you talking about again?"

"Detective Theodore Jameson."

"What does he want with me?"

"ADAM asked me to let you know he has sent messages out on the internet using your old New York City vigilante name."

"How do we know it's Ted?" she asked as she stripped out of her shirt and slid on both the shirt she had been holding and the hoodie over it.

"ADAM traced the routing back to his machine, and found a TQB_read_me.txt file on his computer."

"Pretty damned sneaky of him," Tabitha murmured as she grabbed her hair and pulled it out.

No earrings.

"ADAM was impressed."

"Okay, what does he want?" Tabitha asked as she grabbed a pair of holsters.

"The file says that he's working to expose a group of politically important people who he claims are behind efforts of the NYPD department to cook certain computer data. The data is showing that New York City is considerably higher in crime than what's being reported at this time."

"Yeah, that sounds about right," she agreed. She thought about it. She wasn't truly needed on any operation with the boss, and she would like one last time to check out New York, check out the pizza, and maybe check out a closer view of Ted…

"I need to request a Pod from the Sphaea to New York City, Barnabas needs to know, plus would you have someone from Jean's group bring me my armor, packed?" she asked as she started stripping out of her clothes again.

It seemed tonight, she was going dressed in black.

NEVER SUBMIT

QBBS MEREDITH REYNOLDS

"Dio and Matrix, get your little furry butts back here!" Yelena hissed, plenty loud enough for the two puppies to stop running ahead and sit down, waiting for everyone to catch up.

Yelena thought she was going to be run ragged chasing five puppies all over the ship. While Matrix was already connected to TOM, he had decided to come along with his siblings for the major events. Bellatrix and Ashur were with Yelena, but they hung back so as not to interfere with the young dogs and their decisions.

First, they had decided to hit up the major cafeteria on the zero level. On ships, everyone learned, one needed a way to figure out where you were, and hopefully, you could figure out where you needed to go.

The Meredith Reynolds was no different.

The main deck was the equator and carried a designation of "Deck 1." Each level below added to that number so that the next one down was Deck 2. Any levels overhead carried a designation of a two digit number. So, if you wanted to go up to the second level higher, you went to the 02 Deck.

After that? It got convoluted if you didn't know your way around.

"OH MY GOD, PUPPIES!" yelled a middle-aged woman when Yelena entered the cafeteria.

Both Bellatrix and Ashur stayed outside of the room. Watching as the puppies' tails wagged when they entered the large room to the oohs and aahs of those inside.

It took ten minutes for the puppies to agree there was no one in the cafeteria for them. Then, another ten minutes trying to figure out how to get out without offending anyone who had wanted to play with the young dogs.

"Who are the parents?" A gray haired man asked as he ruffled Devi's hair.

"Bellatrix and Ashur," Yelena responded.

"Oh, we're playing with Ashur's little pups?" he said, laughing as Devi tried to nip his hand.

Ashur just had to prance out in the hall, his head held high. *"See, told you I'm famous!"* he chuffed.

"You're a large white German Shepherd, who stands next to the Queen all the time, how could you NOT be famous?" Bellatrix replied.

Ashur stopped and looked back at her, "I do more than stand," he argued. *"Have I told you how I raced into a vicious battle when I met Bethany Anne?"*

"Only, I think, about twenty-seven times."

"Well, I happen to enjoy the recognition."

"I couldn't tell…" she stopped mid speech, turning her head when she heard Yelena mention her name.

"Yes." Yelena was discussing the great terrorist response from Team BMW and Gabrielle. "Bellatrix is the one in the video mooning the terrorists outside the base." There were a lot of catcalls, with her name now called out.

Bellatrix pranced over to the door. *"Hey! They know who I am!"* she called back to her mate, her tail wagging.

"Sure," Ashur came up beside her. *"Show a little tail, get famous."*

She nipped at his ear. *"Oh shut up, you're just jealous cause this bitch has got back."*

Ashur turned to look at her, his face contorted. *"What does that even mean?"*

"Oh my God," Bellatrix started into the cafeteria, ignoring

Ashur's question. *"My fans are calling!"*

"She," Ashur grumbled as he followed her into the cafeteria, *"is going to be insufferable."*

———

Five minutes later, seven dogs and Yelena stepped out of the cafeteria and took the long way around to go out to the plants and ecologies space.

The puppies wanted to go play under the light of the Artisun.

While the dogs were out having fun in the cornfield, Yelena pulled out her tablet and studied the different yeasts and how they affected brewing beer.

Turning her head, she heard the click-click-click of a Yollin stepping closer. She tabbed the page she was reading and lifted her head in time to see Kael-ven come into view on a little path between stalks of corn. He stared at Yelena who looked back at him.

"I'm sorry," he said, his arm gesticulating in a fashion that she assumed referred to the general area. "I didn't realize anyone else would be out here. I followed the interesting noises to see what was going on."

"Oh, it's just the puppies." She looked around at the plants. "With Ashur and Bellatrix in there somewhere. Probably hiding from the puppies, if I had to guess." Yelena turned back to the Yollin. "You're Kael-ven, right?"

The half-centaur-looking alien nodded as he walked towards her. His nailed feet and heavy weight easily drove his toes into the two to three inches of sand covering the rock in this area. "Meredith informs me you are Yelena?"

"Meredith?" she moved her head, to try and get a better

look at his ears, "The EI?"

"Yes," he cocked his head sideways. "What are you looking for?"

"Ah," she pointed to his neck. "I was trying to see if you had one of the wireless connections to speak with the ship."

Kael-ven nodded. "Yes, I've recently been updated to have communications safely put next to my ear. May I approach you to show you?"

She shrugged. "Sure?" Kael-ven stepped closer to her. He was easily two and a half feet taller than Yelena.

Kael-ven turned his head sideways and pointed to a spot next to his ear. "Here is where it sits, right under my skin."

"Did it hurt?" she asked when she saw sutures.

He chuckled. "No. By the time this was done, the medical team had enough information on our physiology to produce numbing drugs. I didn't feel a thing."

"So, the numbing drugs work?" she asked, curious how they had figured out an alien's physiology.

It took a moment for Kael-ven to respond. "Well, to be honest, I was there for so many other reasons, a small cut in my neck wasn't even a distraction."

"What were you there for?"

Kael-ven's mandibles opened wide, then closed as he mimicked a human shrug. "It's more embarrassing than important. I was there for a broken arm, cracked skull, three dents in my armor plating, several additional cuts deep enough to need sutures and overall I was in a fair amount of pain, so what was a little more?"

"What happened to you?"

"The Queen was teaching me advanced self defense through the application of pain, 101," he admitted.

"Bethany Anne?" she asked, not sure how the Queen was

involved quite yet. "What? Did she have someone beat you up?"

"Beat me up?" Kael-ven asked.

'Yeah, uh," she pointed up and down his body, "you know, did she have someone break your arm and crack your skull?"

He drew back, confusion lacing his voice. "Why would she do that?"

Yelena paused trying to figure out the story. "Kael-ven, I'm completely lost. You said she was trying to teach you a lesson using pain, right?"

"Not trying, succeeding," the alien said. "When she decides she wants to explain that pain is an excellent teacher, she does it very well."

"Wait, SHE did that to you?" Yelena's eyes opened wider.

"You didn't know the Queen is a fighter?"

"Well, sure." Yelena thought back to the episode on Earth, saving her brother, "But you aren't human."

"Hmmm," Kael-ven picked at a piece of dry skin, pulling it off as he walked towards the row of cornstalks and tossing it on the ground next to a plant before he walked back over to Yelena.

"I don't think Bethany Anne is concerned if I'm human or not. She just treats me as another one of her people she needs to school."

"Wow, that's… kinda badass!" Yelena smiled. "I knew she could take out humans, but an alien?"

Their conversation was interrupted when two puppies came racing out between the stalks of corn. A completely white female was chasing a black male with white feet. The playing dogs scampered between Kael-ven's feet and slammed into the row of corn on the other side, their rustling and yipping making it sound like they couldn't be more than twenty feet away. The tops of the stalks, however, were too high for Yelena to confirm. Moments later, there was a loud 'YIP!' The two adults saw Matrix running out of the cornstalks back the other way, quickly disappearing on the other side.

The second puppy came out with her head held high, tail wagging proudly.

Her little bark was funny to the two adults, and Kael-ven spoke to her, "You should be proud. Even in play, vanquishing an enemy is something that you strive to accomplish."

The little puppy stopped and looked way up to see the Yollin staring down at her. She yipped again.

"Kael-ven, and you are?" he replied.

She yipped twice.

"Nice to meet you, Snow." Kael-ven stood still as the female puppy came closer to him, smelling his foot and his leg before standing on her back legs, her front paws almost reaching his knees.

Kael-ven looked over to Yelena who answered his unspoken question. "She wants you to pick her up."

Kael-ven looked down at the puppy again. He lowered himself down, rather like a horse, Yelena thought, making sure he didn't squish the puppy.

Snow backed up as she watched this giant coming down from the sky. Soon, tail wagging quickly, she came back over to Kael-ven and tried, unsuccessfully, to jump on his back. "Is this normal?" he asked Yelena. "And does she want me to pick her up still?"

"Well," Yelena stopped. "Sorry, Kael-ven. You're the first alien most of the puppies have met, well, physically. It means they want to play with you. So, yeah, she would be okay with being picked up."

Kael-ven, with his chitinous hands that could easily rip

through her skin and crush her, gently picked up the wiggling puppy, cupping his large hands so that he might allow her to try and stand.

Which she did for about five seconds before plopping down, looking at him before she yipped again.

"Do I have a mate?" Kael-ven asked the dog before looking to Yelena. "Is she asking me if I have a, uh…" he stopped, trying to figure out if he was getting the translation wrong.

"She's asking if you have a special bonded pet, not a wife or someone to procreate with," Yelena told him.

The captain started chittering. "I suppose I can't claim that Kiel is my special bonded pet. Although, as Bobcat would say, 'that is funny as hell' and Kiel would not be pleased."

He shook his head. "That just makes it funnier!"

"What do you mean, you choose me?" Kael-ven asked. "What did I just get chosen for?" Again, he turned to Yelena. "Is this one of Bethany Anne's special projects? Because your Queen has a warped sense of humor."

Yelena started chuckling, then laughing. She was shaking her head, trying to explain but unable to get the words out. After the minute it took for her to catch her breath, she looked back at the two of them, both staring at her, annoyance on their faces. "No!" she finally got out. "Bethany Anne was the first one to have this happen to her."

Kael-ven looked down at Snow. "And you want to make me your bonded partner?" Snow yipped. "Why?"

Snow turned in his hands and faced away from Kael-ven and started growling, and barking her little nose off before turning back around to Kael-ven and wagging her tail, little tongue hanging out.

"Because," Yelena answered the surprised Yollin. "You have the warrior spirit,"

CHAPTER SEVEN

DULCE, NEW MEXICO, USA

The destruction around the middle concrete foundation went out for hundreds of meters. There were over a hundred and fifty men and three huge excavation machines working the area.

Annette Wojcieszak stood in her dark three-piece suit, her black flats tapping the ground. She had her badge prominently displayed on her chest, right over her left breast.

She wasn't pleased at the moment as one of her expensive as hell, brand-new-out-of-the-R&D-labs excavators had thrown one of its two tracks and was out of commission.

She tried to keep the frustration from her face. She didn't believe that screaming made anyone trust you any more, nor did it get you support when you needed it. What it got you was a bunch of fear, hate, and animosity.

But sometimes, the stress from idiots up the chain just

really pushed your buttons, and all you could do was stand and fume.

Like right now.

She heard a car come crunching up the dirt road the equipment had created as they made their way out here. She turned to see what was coming her way and raised an eyebrow. A young Indian woman slid out of the SUV to the ground. Aina Spiles always made her smile.

The spunky little researcher was one of the few people that Annette respected. She was frighteningly intelligent but completely lacked any political smarts. She would tell you exactly what you needed to know, no matter which idiot it hurt.

Even if she was the idiot. You had to be careful with Aina because for her information was either true, opinion, or false. She threw around the labels like little hand grenades in meetings with no concept of the potential trouble.

Annette never missed a meeting Aina called, the stories she walked out with alone were priceless.

"Hello, Agent," Aina's high, wispy voice greeted her as she stepped over a large muddy groove one of the excavators created an hour and a half ago.

Annette watched the little researcher. "Hello Aina, what brings you out here?"

Aina stopped next to Annette, who at five foot five inches still towered over her.

"Why Frank Kurns, of course." she said.

Annette just looked down at the woman who was intently watching all of the activity going on. "Aina?"

"Yes, Agent?" she replied, not looking up at Annette.

"Frank Kurns? Tell me that's the name of a new agent, not the Frank Kurns whose books you like to read?" Annette asked, concern growing in the back of her mind.

"Well," Aina looked up at the much taller woman. "What if I say he's not only the author of my favorite series, but he's also an agent." Her little face scrunched up "Or, at least he *was* an agent."

"How can he be an agent, or used to be an agent, and is now writing science fiction?" Annette asked. "Wouldn't his oath of secrecy stop him from writing anything anywhere close enough to the truth so that we wouldn't know and all of these people working here searching for a secret base," Annette pointed to the activity around her, "wouldn't happen?"

"Only if he still worked for our government, Agent Wojcieszak."

"Aina," Annette's voice was harsher, but lower so her voice wouldn't travel. "Do you know how much money and time these people represent?"

"Of course," Aina agreed, pointing at one of the excavators. "Just one of those R&D excavators are going to cost 3.245 million dollars for thirty-six hours."

Annette blanched, that was over ten million dollars sunk in the project for just the three special excavators. She wondered how the costing was going to go for the broken one.

"Aina!" she hissed. "Your ass is going to be on the line for this!" She squeezed the woman's shoulder to get her attention. The little researcher turned, looking up at Annette in confusion. Annette continued, "Heads will roll if this isn't the truth, and when they figure out that you decided this was a good idea because of a science fiction book, your head will be one of them, no matter how often you've been right!"

Aina smiled and patted Annette's hand. "Thank you for caring, Annette. But," she turned towards the field and pointed at the second excavator, "I think Frank Kurns just gave the hint I wanted."

Annette looked where she was pointing to see the team on the second excavation tool was excited, and a group of fifteen men seemed to be heading that direction. Her phone buzzed and she looked down to see the name.

It was the lead of excavation group two.

———

QBBS MEREDITH REYNOLDS

"Bethany Anne?" John's voice called out from the security station outside her suite. Bethany Anne was working at her table, her feet up, one hand rubbing Matrix who was relaxing in her lap. The puppy had turned out to be a good stress reducing agent for Bethany Anne.

Ashur still loved to get his rubdowns, but he was so damned big, she could barely rub his head, neck and just a small portion of his back. He'd fucking smoosh her ass if she tried to put him on her lap.

Matrix she could stroke, from his little head to his tail, easily.

"Yeah?" she replied, looking up from her tablet and dropping out of a conversation with ADAM.

"We've got a group that all want to make one last quick trip for personal reasons to Earth. They were wondering if you would mind taking them to the G'laxix Sphaea?"

"Who?" Bethany Anne asked while internally she asked ADAM to track Ashur down and ask him to meet her in the Queen's Suites Transport Room.

"Well," John started, "I think Tabitha, Barnabas, Ecaterina, Nathan, Scott and Darryl... Wait, a new request from Team BMW as well." John ticked off.

Well, too big for her transport room.

ADAM, switch us from my Suites Transport Room to Transport Room 002

>>Understood, Bethany Anne<<

"Wow, what's everyone doing?" she asked as she lifted Matrix off her lap. "Go to my bedroom, little guy. Too early to get you involved in this."

Matrix wagged his tail and groggily walked into her room. He could just about jump up on her couch, but her bed was way too high. His first attempt to jump on the couch landed short, and he slid back, landing on his butt and rolling over. This time, he was much more awake and made it up on her couch and spun in circles a couple of times, then flopped down.

Should I have warned him? TOM asked

That he shouldn't sleepwalk and jump?

Yes.

Well, fair question. Was he hurt badly?

No.

Then it was probably okay. Next time, give him one reminder as he walks away and if it doesn't register, let him try. Soon he'll be tall enough it won't matter.

What if he doesn't grow? TOM worried. **Do we put him in the Pod-doc?**

Well, if anyone was worried you were slipping to the dark side, TOM, I think you just put those worries to rest.

After a moment, TOM came back, **That's good, right?**

———

Bethany Anne and John arrived at Transport Room 002, and she slowed to a stop, looking down. Everyone was there in the middle, ready to go, but Tabitha had a suitcase.

One of the field expedient armor suitcases.

"What's up, Tabitha?" she asked, raising an eyebrow.

"Trouble in New York, a friend in the NYPD, asking for my help." Bethany Anne looked over at Barnabas quizzically.

"One problem, One Ranger," he replied. "I'm going to Mexico."

"Mexico?" she asked as she walked into the middle. Ashur came up beside her as everyone grabbed a shoulder and worked themselves closer and Tabitha picked up her suitcase.

"I need some information from a contact, and he's in Cabo San Lucas," the elder Ranger answered.

"Huh, so not going to any gang area?" she asked.

"Not this time, I don't think," he said. "But if I happen to run into a gang, I'll make sure to leave some *Queen's justice* behind."

"If you run into those fuckers who are cutting heads off," she told him, "leave a shitload of my justice…" the team disappeared.

———

G'LAXIX SPHAEA

"…behind," Bethany Anne finished.

The team checked to make sure everyone was good before most waved to Bethany Anne as they left towards the Pod bay.

"I'll see that I do," Queen's Ranger One replied as he stepped out of the transportation room.

"Where now, boss?" John asked.

Bethany Anne stared out the door of the Transport Room as the yellow lights stopped flashing, and the horn blaring that there were incoming for the Transport Room died down and the doors closed.

"Do we have anyone working on figuring out how to accomplish transferring through the Etheric?" she asked.

"Doing transport?" John asked, and she nodded in reply. "Machine or person?"

"Huh, good question," she said. "I didn't think about a person, only a machine. I wonder... since I have such trouble with inorganic, if that's a hint?"

John pursed his lips. "Hey TOM?"

"Yes?" he answered from the speakers around the room.

"Could the Pod-doc ascertain if a human would be a good candidate to accomplish Etheric walking, like Bethany Anne?"

There was a pause from the speakers and John looked down at Bethany Anne who shook her head. She wasn't talking with him.

"Yes." TOM finally said. "But we would have to do a few more tests on Bethany Anne to confirm a few suppositions on my part. We have most of the records, but there are areas I didn't think to record about her because I wasn't looking for the ability. I didn't know about it at that time."

Bethany Anne grimaced. "How long?"

"Probably a day and a half, so thirty-six hours."

Bethany Anne made a face. "Fuck. I really hate going back in that thing," she said. "Unless it becomes more of a priority, let's do this testing after my fight with the Yollin King. It isn't that important."

"I understand," TOM said and the speaker beeped off.

"So, now what?" Bethany Anne asked.

"Well," John looked around, "Darryl and Scott are gone. Eric and Gabrielle are in France on a date. Do you have anything to do for the next few hours?"

"Nothing super important," she said. "I'm going to take Ashur back so he can be with Bellatrix, why?"

"Want to play hooky one last time?" John asked, a hint of mischief in his eyes.

She pursed her lips. "And do what?" she asked, trying to figure out what he might be thinking.

He spread his arms and shrugged. "Want to go fuck up some terrorists?"

Bethany Anne's face lit up with glee. "Hell yeah!" She started for the exit, and the doors opened back up. "We can call this additional martial practice on the calendar."

"I've blocked out the next twenty-four hours for martial practice," ADAM told them as they headed through the doors to leave the transport room.

"We can't be gone that long," she replied to ADAM, "but leave it blocked out just in case."

The doors shut behind them.

———

Inside the ship, Captain Natalia Jakowski, who was taking a few minutes of very private time with her personal Bitch, was interrupted.

"The Queen is looking for you," EI Sphaea told the ship's captain.

"Oh crap," Darryl murmured from beside her.

"What's oh crap, baby?" Natalia asked as she got out of bed. "She brought you here, right?"

"Yeah, but I've successfully hidden our relationship like

84

you asked, and there's no way John isn't going to know right away."

Natalia raised an eyebrow. "Why is John going to know right away?"

"Because," Darryl admitted as he slid off the bed, "there's no way I can stop this shit-eating grin."

Natalia smiled as she buttoned up her jacket. "Stay here a little while, Scott's hanging in the cafeteria, maybe they're just saying hi."

"One can hope." he said. "Although you know Bethany Anne won't care, right?"

"Yeah, now. It's been long enough, and I think my record speaks for itself. But who says I wanted everyone to know who finally got Darryl, hmmm?" She kissed her fingers and reached up to touch his forehead before she walked out of her quarters.

"Like the whole ship doesn't know," Darryl murmured when she left.

"The ship might know," EI Sphaea said to Darryl. "But it wouldn't dare whisper anything the captain wouldn't want to share."

Darryl went back to the bed and sat down, then pulled on his pants. "Well, no one on this ship ever wonders what I see in her."

"Not likely. They secretly think there isn't anyone less than a Queen's Bitch that can be good enough for their captain. So you have a whole ship full of people that would be rather pissed at you if you ever hurt her feelings."

"Wow," Darryl snorted as he pulled on his shirt. "No reason for performance anxiety there."

CHAPTER EIGHT

G'LAXIX SPHAEA

Barnabas grabbed a two-person Pod and headed down towards Baja California. While he didn't know much about Coca-Cola, he was smart enough to ask a few people and realized that there had been multiple changes to the recipe over the years.

Similar to arguments about all types of food, there was a discussion that Coke produced in Mexico had a better flavor because they still used cane sugar in their recipe over high fructose corn syrup. When he happened to mention THAT ingredient around Dawn, one of the ladies in Jean's group, he had to politely listen to a five-minute diatribe on all of the evils of high fructose corn syrup.

Barnabas had been sorely tempted to stop the conversation by saying, "You don't know I'm here, you never talked to me."

Then disappearing as quick as his vampire legs could move him.

For any person enhanced by nanites would use the energy stored in the body and fix any problems, including weight.

Barnabas looked out the Pod's window and smiled, he could see the sun creeping across the world and it would soon hit Baja California Sur, or the southern lower part of Baja California. It was almost to the west side of the main body of Mexico itself.

He just wanted to land while it was still dark, if possible. Otherwise, he would have to walk further than he desired.

His target, Andre Batten, was one of fourteen men higher up in the Coca-Cola bottling company based out of Monterrey, Mexico. He wasn't a member of the original two families who owned a big chunk of the company after the revolution and takeover over a hundred years ago.

Andre was presently spending a long weekend in Pueblo Bonito's Montecristo Estates on the other side of the hill from Cabo San Lucas' harbor and tourist zone. It was a secured and private area offering access to Sunset Beach and other resort amenities.

Including a two-story home in the hills with valet, a pool and a view to the merging of the Sea of Cortez and the Pacific.

In short, it was beautiful.

This should be a simple data acquisition and leave. Barnabas did a quick fly-by over the land and could see Sunset Beach Resort, Pacifica Resort, the two sections of homes built on the hills that would be Montecristo, the Nova Spania section and some condo buildings a little to the north, mostly incomplete.

He had the Pod drop him down at the end of a street in Montecristo, a cul-de-sac. Down here, the resort company was transferring many of these homes from timeshare and rental to purchase, and all except two were empty.

One of the Montecristo homes were presently being used by Ernesto Coppel, the resort's owner, as his new estate on the top of a mountain was being built. From the air, it looked like his new house was going to be beautiful.

Barnabas walked right past the house with the SUV and golf cart parked in the front. Five houses further down, he jumped the large gate meant to block non-residents from this part of the street.

Facing west, Barnabas could see the sky beyond Sunset Beach slowly becoming brighter.

There was a small gas engine truck coming up the street, the truck revving to get up the steep grade. Barnabas and smiled.

He stepped into the road and put up his hand to flag the driver down.

―――――

"Do you think she caught on?" Ecaterina asked her mate in a hushed voice, the two of them walking as nonchalantly as possible towards the Pod bay on the G'laxix Sphaea.

Nathan shrugged. "Chances are, she would have said something if she had caught on, especially since the others are doing something altruistic."

Ecaterina snorted.

"So. Maybe not altruistic. They're robbing a company for a soft drink recipe. At least their travel to Earth is with good intentions." He waited for the door to open before they could walk into the Pod bay.

The G'laxix Sphaea had a few modifications to her design to hold more Pods and even had some locked outside they could transfer inside. Plus, she had another Pod-Carrier off her stern for situations like this when a lot of people arrived, needing transportation to Earth. Nathan finished his thought, "While ours is not."

———

G'LAXIX SPHAEA DINING AREA KITCHEN

Scott was scrounging around in the back of the cooler for any leftover sandwiches when he heard Bethany Anne's voice and John reply.

He couldn't make out their words, but it didn't sound like they were talking about heading back to the QBBS Meredith Reynolds at the moment.

Shit!

He frantically looked around, trying to figure out where he was supposed to duck when he heard them turn in the hallway and start walking away.

He didn't need to be anywhere around John or Bethany Anne for different reasons right now.

If John found out about Darryl, there would be hell to pay. Not the least of Scott's problems would be Cheryl Lynn's annoyance that he had chosen not to share Darryl's relationship.

What was it with women, anyway? They could make a pinkie swear promise to a friend, maybe tell their spouse or significant other, maybe not, and that was okay. But, if a guy made a promise to his buddy to keep something private, they would be accused of something like the old and tired bros before hoes if he didn't share.

Scott peeked out of the kitchen and made sure Bethany

Anne wasn't secretly waiting for him to pop up or anything.

Feeling better, he turned back to the refrigerator.

Still, whether it seemed fair or not, the fact he knew about Darryl and Natalia better not get back to Cheryl Lynn before he spilled the beans or his ass was going to get chewed out.

That's when Scott's eyes flew open realizing just *who* Bethany Anne would want to meet with right then.

"Shit, shit, shit!" he muttered and started moving as quickly and silently as he could. Trying to remember what kind of back route he could take to Natalia's room to fetch Darryl and get the hell off this ship.

"I'm telling you," Bethany Anne hissed at John, "that Scott is back there! So, go this way." she pointed left, and John walked quickly behind her.

"Not good, they'll want to go along with us," John whispered. "That would cut our kill ratio down by half!"

"Speak for yourself," Bethany Anne told him. "Maybe reduce my kill ratio by twenty-two percent, but that's twenty-two percent fewer assholes I get to kill before leaving, and I don't want to share.

"Where are we going?" John asked her, looking around and now totally confused after so many turns.

Looking around a corner before proceeding, Bethany Anne answered, "ADAM is communicating with Sphaea and taking us around potential trouble spots. He says that she's going to have Natalia meet us secretly with some of our personal weapons and armor from the ships armory."

"Good, I was wondering what we were going to do for weapons beyond what we had on us."

"ADAM says she now has a small box of grenades added to her list for you, but we need to hang somewhere and give her a couple of minutes for Sphaea to bring an EI controlled cart for her. I've got that load of shit I stuck in the Etheric for a rainy day, but I'd rather leave it there than use it now."

John knocked on a door before opening it and looking in. "Man, playing hooky with you can be such a pain in the ass," he grumbled as they slipped into the empty conference room and closed the door behind themselves.

———

"What the hell do you mean, grab grenades?" Natalia sub-vocalized to Sphaea through her embedded connection. She turned from speed walking towards the transport room to backtracking twenty feet and turning right towards the armory.

"I need to grab *what*?" she asked again, palming her print before the EI could open the door. Sphaea could override the security protocols, but every time that happened, there would be a review and this way, ADAM would show the records to Bethany Anne who would approve. If it was a major blunder, then it might have to go to Bethany Anne's father as well. Technically, Bethany Anne could force everyone to be quiet, but Natalia didn't want to test what everyone would think about Bethany Anne doing that when they got caught.

And Natalia was almost sure Bethany Anne was going to get caught doing whatever it was she wanted to do.

———

There were three quick raps on the door, then two, then another three and Scott's whisper could barely be heard, "Darryl?"

Darryl grabbed his coat and opened the door. Scott was looking both ways down the corridor. Darryl stuck his head out and looked too.

"Where the hell is everyone?" Scott asked. "This is damned spooky."

Darryl stepped out of the suite and heard it click and lock behind him. He popped Scott in the chest, and the two started hotfooting it to the Pod bay. "I got a probable answer to that, but we got to boogie."

————

"Yes," Natalia answered the gunner's mate. "I need the Queen's locker and John's locker. We don't mention this, it never happened."

"But you signed in, Captain," he gestured at the door.

"Let me clarify. As far as telling anyone who isn't cleared, it didn't happen." Natalie looked around before adding, "And I need a box of grenades."

————

Nathan nodded to the woman holding open the Pod doors as Ecaterina slid into the first seat. He slid into the seat next to her and clicked the five-point harness. The doors were shut and locked, and before he could get out an 'I wonder how long before...' they were headed down to Earth.

Ecaterina spoke, "Sphaea, I need you to take us to Purchase, New York."

The Pod changed directions and headed towards the U.S. Eastern seaboard.

"We're going to have to figure out how to get down in daylight," Ecaterina commented.

"Not so much a problem, depending on if you're willing to skydive," Nathan said as he reached around behind him to look in the storage area.

"You are out of your pea-sized mind if you think I'm willing to jump out of a good Pod with nothing but a…" Ecaterina stopped talking when Nathan pulled two rods equipped straps and chains out of storage. "What are those?"

"These little beauties," Nathan said, "are the latest in silent descent support now available in all Pods in the Etheric Empire." He handed her one.

"Heavy," she observed.

"Yeah, they have gravitic technology inside."

Ecaterina held onto the two foot long, three-inch diameter black rod. She slipped her wrists through the straps. "Hard to get your hands out," she commented as she played with the rod.

"That's in case you lose consciousness, it won't slip off, and you can't fall. Plus, we can use the chain to connect to either a vest harness for those who are completely out of it, or drop off supplies."

"So, we put our hands through here, open the doors and jump?" she asked, leaning forward to see how far below down the world was.

"Well, we would drop much lower, but yes. Cloud cover is presently eight thousand feet up, so we go into the clouds, open the door, and we slip out. The Pod stays up here, and we drop over the Arthur W Butler Memorial Sanctuary. We can't drop in on Purchase because the Westchester Country

Airport is right next to it. Call a taxi…"

"Why not Uber?" Ecaterina interrupted as she continued to play with her rod.

"They're banned in New York State. New York City has an exclusion, so they can operate there lawfully."

"I hate American politics," she grumped. "Uber works so much better than the Taxi app."

Nathan looked out the window. "So, we get a taxi off the 685 and ride in. Figure out how to get what we need and boom-dida-bam we jump on a Pod and go back up." He smiled at her, pleased with his plan.

"No, we don't." Ecaterina said emphatically. "I didn't get Christina a babysitter so we could just steal the Pepsi recipe."

"No?" Nathan looked at his mate, confused. "What else are we doing?"

"You, sir, are taking me back to the first pizza place we ever ate, one last time." She winked at him. "Then we're going back to that reserve and…"

Nathan sure hoped he brought enough cash for everything. Female Weres that planned on that much physical activity could eat a lot of food.

————

ADAM?
>>**Yes TOM?**<<
Have you figured out the Coke recipe, yet?
>>**Of course. **<<
Have you confirmed the recipe?
>>**Yes.**<<
There was a small, but identifiable pause.
How?

>>I confirmed the ingredients, the different instructions for the manufacturing of the product and all of the power requirements, taking into account for the random fluctuations in poorly supported electrical equipment and degraded copper wiring and confirmed, within parameters, the information I acquired for the equipment, and usage and wastage, of what happened in the production plant.<<

You didn't tell anyone you already have the recipe, right?

>>And miss all of the fun? What do you take me for, an EI?<<

CHAPTER NINE

Team BMW took two of the Pods down to Germany to meet a sales representative at their office.

Fortunately, Germany wasn't as aggressive as some countries looking for TQB Pods racing through their airspace, or at least it didn't seem that way so far.

The trio was looking for the best container and vats they could buy to produce beer and that would last for centuries. While they already had good equipment, you could ALWAYS use backups.

Because Bobcat couldn't imagine a lifetime as long as his without beer.

The team was also secretly planning on cornering the market in another area and was planning on using some of the supplies and pieces they were ordering for a different, more devious effort.

They were going to corner the market on Coca-Cola

production. Thus, the team needed a lot of equipment and some knowledge about the production of soft drinks.

The rest could go and get the recipe, but without being able to produce the product, what good was that going to do?

Finally, they needed about a hundred small setups for production from the microbrewing industry. The team wanted to set up a way to get others into the business and sell beer through All Guns Blazing. If team BMW rented out the production equipment, they could make money on both sides.

Equality? Thy name was capitalism.

CABO SAN LUCAS, BAJA CALIFORNIA SUR

Barnabas watched the delivery driver start walking back to the main security gate. He had told the man to walk towards it, and when he was about fifty meters away, to stop and then return to his truck.

Barnabas slid the white jacket on and grabbed the platter with three plates on it, plus the drinks with the plastic wrap over the tops.

Didn't want the orange juice to spill.

Walking up the path, Barnabas stopped outside the first metal gate and clicked the call button.

He heard the buzzer go off inside the home.

Moments later, the inside door lock clicked, and the residence's door opened. A rather handsome Hispanic man with black hair and a beard stuck his head out. "Come on in." he waved to Barnabas.

Barnabas opened the metal gate, which squeaked slightly,

walked past the water fountain and smiled at the man who further opened the door, allowing him entry.

Turning to his right, Barnabas headed for the kitchen and dining area. Turning right once more, he set down the large platter and removed the three plates.

If you're going to do something, do it right, he thought.

Barnabas smirked, he was having way too much fun with this at the moment.

Laying out the three plates, each one with a silver metal cover, he grabbed each and lifted it for a second. "We have fresh fruit." He grabbed the next and set it to the side. "Pancakes with bananas." He lifted the third. "And a Pueblo Bonito hamburger, well done."

"Excellent, she's ravenous and needs the protein," Andre said, more to himself than to Barnabas.

Not that Barnabas needed the information, the three deep purple hickeys on Andre's neck were enough proof for him.

"Thank you," Barnabas returned the covers and opened the small portfolio with the bill. "I understand you work for Coca-Cola?" The man accepted the portfolio.

"Yes?"

"Secret recipe?" Barnabas asked, his voice changing slightly. The brief question was more than enough to bring the information he desired to the front of this man's mind. It was so much easier than going mucking around in the man's brain.

Even if the knowledge that the woman in the other room wasn't his wife came along with the recipe.

Although tempted to tinker with this situation, Barnabas left it alone. From what little he could tell, the relationship Andre had with his wife was open for amorous encounters with others. His thoughts showed that Andre believed that his wife was currently out with one of her two lovers.

Barnabas raised an eyebrow; the French had nothing on these two.

Barnabas accepted the portfolio back and glanced at it.

The bastard hadn't tipped. Barnabas frowned and handed the portfolio back to a confused Andre.

Barnabas's tone changed again. "You will tip twice the cost of this meal, and every time you order room service, you will tip one-half the price of the meal. You are blessed." Barnabas paused, looking at the man, his lips pressed together. "As my Queen would say, don't be a dick."

Barnabas accepted the portfolio from Andre once more and confirmed the tip amount. "Have a good morning. And you will need plenty of energy yourself, so I suggest you eat the fruit," he remarked as he stepped around Andre.

Barnabas walked out of the kitchen, took a left to reach the door and stepped out, closing the heavy door behind him. Walking past the fountain and then the gate, he took off the coat. He dropped both on the front seat of the little white vehicle before heading back to the end of the street.

It was light enough for anyone to see the Pod, but he shrugged. There was no way for anyone to interrupt him now. He started whistling.

Barnabas had the secret recipe for Mexican Coca-Cola.

Queen's Rangers 01 - Everyone else 00.

———

Ecaterina eyed Nathan as he checked her grip on the rod. "What are you doing?" she asked, her accent becoming more pronounced.

"Uh," Nathan answered, his mind elsewhere. "Just checking your grip," he said as he pulled on the rod before turning towards the Pod's controls and touching the command to open the two doors up front.

"Nathan, can I lift three hundred pounds?" She practically purred the question in her heaviest Romanian accent.

"Of course, baby, easily," he answered, checking outside the Pod and the clouds swirling around them before he unbuckled his five-point harness and turned towards her.

For just a second, he thought he saw a flash of yellow in her eyes before her smile melted him.

Outside, it was all white. The clouds looked like a heavy fog. Ecaterina looked down at his hands, now slipped through the lanyards and holding onto the bar. She moved her right hand out of the grips and reached up to lay it on his neck as she leaned forward.

Nathan smiled and leaned in for his kiss.

She whispered her next question, "Then why would you need to test my ability to grab a bar unless you think I weigh more than that?"

Nathan, his brain trying to scream WARNING realized that gentle hand behind his neck now had a sharp grip... right before Ecaterina flung him out of the Pod.

"What the FUUUuuuu..." his voice was lost to the clouds.

"Men!" she grumbled as she unbuckled her harness, put her hand back on the bar and jumped out. The bar immediately slowed her fall.

Ecaterina was starting to worry when his legs appeared from behind her, gripping her around the waist, his body crashing up against hers. "Honey, I'm back!" he called out, his voice rough. She felt his teeth grip her neck.

Her eyes widened. God, she thought, this was going to be a monumental mark!

Good thing it heals. She turned her head to give him access to where it felt the best.

————

"Take the rods with us or leave them here?" Ecaterina asked as they landed lightly on the ground inside a large cove of trees.

"Just unhook, and I'll tell Sphaea to take them back," he answered, a grin on his face.

"Tell Sphaea to..." Ecaterina's lips compressed as she worked it through. "No wonder you were able to sneak up on me!"

One of these damned days, she was going to fully, and completely, catch Nathan Lowell by surprise. She had even started to worry about his cocky ass after she tossed him out of the Pod.

What a sucker she was!

Her eyes narrowed. "You're telling me that the EI controls these?" she asked as she lifted the bar in question and waved it at him like she was shaking a finger in his direction.

"Certainly, although if you know how you can do it yourself, but there usually isn't a good reason for that," he shrugged and casually tossed his up in the air. Ecaterina watched the rod fly up about twenty feet, slow down like it was going to stop and let gravity pull it back to Earth when it suddenly shot up and out of sight.

Ecaterina rolled her eyes and flicked hers up as well, not even watching her bar stop and then take off up into the sky. She walked by Nathan and popped him on the chest. "It's good I love you, or I would be using that bar to beat you senseless right now," she said to him.

Nathan winked at her and let her pass. It took her another seven steps to realize she didn't know where they were going. She turned back to see Nathan smirking at her.

She pointed at him. "Don't say a word, just tell me the right direction." He indicated the direction to his left, which was not the one she had been taking. "Fine," she waved him in the new direction. "You walk ahead, this time I'll watch *your* ass the whole way."

Nathan blinked a couple of times, his mouth open. "What?" she leered, "you don't think I know it's my ass you're staring at all the times you are acting like a gentleman for me?"

He closed his mouth and started walking, not sure how to reply to that

Nathan was letting part of his brain pick the best way to make it to the freeway, the other part of his brain was working feverishly on the new problem troubling his thoughts.

Should he be flexing his ass while he walked or not?

NEW YORK CITY, NEW YORK, USA

Tabitha arrived and jumped out of the Pod in the same little alley where she had beat up the five toughs not that long ago. The hotel she used was just around the block. The Pod disappeared back into the dark and gloomy sky. Lightning flashed, and then heavy thunder rolled across the city.

No one would notice her Pod in this mess.

That was nice, although she was getting wet, quickly. It

beat having to land farther out of town. She pulled a large round hat out of her coat, flicked it open and put it on. It helped keep her hair dry and water out of her eyes.

She grabbed the handle of her suitcase and took it over to where a small roof sheltered a back door. Laying the black bag on the ground, she placed her hand on the outside and then punched in twelve numbers representing letters in her mind.

"Achronyx, book me a room at the hotel I stayed at with the Tontos. Give me the confirmation."

Understood, Ranger Tabitha his electronic voice came back in her ear.

It took her just a minute to exit the alley and then cross the road. She was just arriving at the hotel when Achronyx replied.

You are on the fourteenth floor. Go inside the hotel and turn right.

"I've been here before," she subvocalized.

Understood, every place you have been before, I should not offer directions, her EI replied.

"What?" Tabitha exclaimed as she nodded to the hotel's doorman when she passed through.

Fortunately, her clothes shed water quickly. She stayed a moment over the rugs the hotel had placed down at the entry, to minimize extra water on their floors, before continuing.

"No!" she hissed. "Fine, tell me unless I let you know that I don't need them."

Understood, the EI replied.

If she didn't know better, she would say he sounded smug over their link.

She made it up to the fourteenth floor and exited the elevator, dodging a married couple that was waiting to get in the elevator. She found her door, the third on the left, and sat her case down.

She put her tablet up next to the electronic keypad, and it turned green. Grabbing her case, she pushed the door open and stepped inside, closing the door behind her. Walking quickly over to the bed, she set the case on top, causing the mattress to depress. Unlocking it, she grabbed two rolled up armor pieces. She went into the bathroom and took off her coat. She unsnapped the sections and laid them out on the bathroom counter.

They were both made of tiny pieces of scaled metal. One roll was two pieces of thin armor, the other just one.

Putting her shirt, and then bra to the side, she grabbed one of the two pieces the first roll consisted of and placed it under her breasts. "Fucking armor!" she hissed. "Damn shit is cold on the mother-loads." She grabbed the top piece that covered the rest of her chest and laid it in place. "I can do this. I can do this!" She slammed the top piece in place, her nipples bitching at her for a couple of seconds.

She reached over and grabbed the last piece. It would have been easier to have someone help her with this step, but she wasn't trusting Ted with helping her suit up. If it came to seeing her naked, it wasn't going to be in a situation of putting on armor.

No, that would happen with some seduction.

She took the last piece, designed for her back, went to the second bed and laid it out on the comforter. Satisfied with where it was, she turned around and lay back, feeling the armor touch her lower back. She scooted down a little and slowly laid down again. This time, it felt right.

She bit down. "Charge it, Achronyx." The three pieces charged up, and she felt the sudden shortness of breath as the armor wrapped around her tightly while the edges joined together. Tabitha was able to relax once the armor flexed and fitted itself to her like a second skin. Now, there wasn't any way to get this off of her without someone from the Empire doing it.

She rolled off the bed and turned towards the other. She grabbed and moved the suitcase. Opening it back up she nodded. She retrieved a shirt and a second coat and put them next to the bag. Walking back to the restroom, she grabbed her other stuff and brought it to the bed and dropped it in a pile. This time, she put on the new shirt, part of her armor, and then grabbed her holsters. She slid one around her waist, and one over her shoulder to rest under her left arm. She slid on her coat and checked the inside pockets to confirm the basics were where they needed to be. Both of her Jean Dukes' specials were in the suitcase. She palmed them, turning them on. Both showed to be almost full with two thousand rounds each.

She doubted she would need four thousand rounds of ammunition, so she slid one under her left arm and set the other back in the case. She pulled out a second pistol. This was a new one that shot electrical charges. Often not effective against anything armored, but damned useful against people if you didn't want to kill them.

They also showed exactly where you were, a significant downside for sure.

Tabitha slid that pistol on her hip.

She considered the multitude of goodies that were in her case, trying to figure out what she would need if they attacked a house outside the city. If they had cops there, then she needed to be able to take them down without killing them.

Done.

If they were part of the underworld, they might have killers on the grounds.

She was prepared for that as well.

She needed eyes in the sky. She lifted a box out of her case and pulled out four silver orbs. "Connect to these four, Achronyx."

Done, he replied.

She reached into the suitcase and pulled out a yellow case. Opening it, she lifted out a pair of goggles that looked like something you might use to ski. Placing them over her face, she said aloud, "Lock them in."

The goggles adhered to her face, no strap holding them on her head.

"Lift all four in the air, then give me their cameras."

All four orbs floated into the air, taking positions equidistant from Tabitha and looked down at her from three feet away. "Lock them in standard locations." Four little scenes showing her from the front, back, and both sides came up in her goggles. Two on the left side of her view, two on the right. If she looked straight ahead, they didn't impede her view.

"What the fuck?" she exclaimed, turning her head to look behind her. "Why the hell didn't anyone tell me these pants make my ass look fat?" She huffed, "Achronyx, pull back camera three and focus on my full body from behind."

Tabitha turned straight and looked at herself from the back. She reached down and adjusted her pants, "Dammit, I'll need a tailor for this." She exhaled. "Aww, fuck it."

She sat down on the bed behind her and took off her shoes. Then she started stripping out of her nice pants, tossed them aside, and stood back up to reach into her case to pull out her black leathers.

She flipped them open. "Seems like momma's going in bad-ass leather tonight." She slid her legs into the pants and then jumped up once to pull them up. "Cause leather…" she said as she pulled up the zipper and snapped the two snaps. Slapping her ass, she finished, "…always makes this badonkadonk look like a million bucks."

"Well, crap." She grabbed her working shoes. They weren't as sexy as the nicer boots she had brought, but in for a penny with the leather, in for a pound.

Who knows, maybe Ted would like the vigilante look?

She folded the rest of the clothes, grabbed another two magazines for the electrical pistol and one extra magazine for her Dukes' special. "Can never bring too much ammo," she muttered as she packed all of the clothes and boots. She closed her suitcase and locked it. "At least, that's what John always says."

She sent the request to unhook her goggles, took them off her face and slid them inside a pocket. Walking to the mirror, she examined herself carefully.

"Trinity, suck it, 'cause I look hotter than you!" Tabitha grinned and held her hand up in the air. The four silver orbs dropped to land in her hand, and she slid them into her coat. As a former hacker, she knew what male computer geeks liked about the female Matrix character.

She reached over and grabbed the suitcase.

She looked into the mirror and blew herself a kiss. "I'm a damned computer geek's wet dream." She smiled as she took the suitcase and walked towards the door. "And those that don't like me thinking that can kiss my fantastic ass."

She turned the doorknob and opened the door. "Where else can you get incredible hacking skills with this body?"

"Nowhere," she answered herself as she stepped into the hallway to leave the hotel.

CHAPTER TEN

Harvey Podstawa nodded to the elderly couple as they entered the hotel. He held out his hand and took the older gentleman's umbrella. Turning to his right, he placed it in a special box that would allow it to drain for a few moments while the couple took off their coats.

"I'll be back in a few minutes, so I'll grab it again," the silver-haired gentleman said.

Harvey nodded and helped the two move along. At the moment, the hotel was quiet. It was late morning, and with the crappy weather, those that didn't need to leave the hotel weren't. He watched the older couple walk towards the elevator which dinged and opened before they could reach for the call button.

———

Charlotte Pavela had worked for the hotel for the last nine months and recently had been moved to the day shift. She preferred it, and she knew that this hotel only hired, and kept, the best. Inside this city, there were plenty of people who worked hard to get the best paying jobs.

Therefore, it surprised her when she saw Harvey's face display anything but professional decorum. Then she turned to see who he was looking at and she stopped in the middle of the floor herself.

———

Harvey happened to be watching when *she* exited. As one of the doormen at this hotel, Harvey was very professional in all ways.

Therefore, it was a testament to the amazing view that his jaw dropped open.

She walked out, a long coat of some fabric he didn't recognize draped about her. In a city of wonders, it was one of the strangest things Harvey had seen. The coat seemed both soft and rigid at times, matte black and then reflective. He couldn't remember ever seeing anything like it.

Her suitcase matched it well. The older couple just stepped back and watched the woman walk past them towards the door. It appeared as if she was deep in thought as she didn't seem to notice that most of the people in the hotel's lobby had stopped to watch her walk out.

Harvey remembered in time, thank God, to close his mouth, smile and open the door for the young woman. He wasn't sure who she was, and he couldn't remember seeing her before. But she was, as his friend Ronald would say...

One badass motherfucker who would accept no shit from

anyone and look fucking fine doing it.

"Thank you," her South American accent was in the wind and taken from his ears as she disappeared down the street.

"Who was she?"

Startled, Harvey turned to see Charlotte beside him, looking out the door. He shrugged. "A guest?"

Charlotte nodded, then turned and started walking away. "Well, that was one woman—if I were tempted that way—I'd try to chase down and get a phone number."

Harvey smiled at the next gentleman who came in, the memory of the woman slowly leaving his thoughts.

———

Ted took the last puff of his cigarette and smashed it into the ashtray. He hadn't been much of a smoker, but everything was going down and he would either be dead or hated by the end of the night.

Either way, there wasn't a decent goddamned solution to his problem.

Ted lived on the Upper North Side, off of Saint Nichols in a one-bedroom apartment up on the top floor of a four-story building.

He had gotten notice on his computer that his message had been received and he should expect a visitor. Ted reached for the pack of cigarettes he had purchased earlier that morning when he stepped out of his house to walk off his nervous energy.

He swallowed hard when he noticed the package was empty. He looked down at the ashtray, full of twisted, half smoked and frenetically forgotten cadavers sacrificed to the god of stress.

He was a nervous wreck.

He considered grabbing the least wrecked cigarette when his buzzer sounded, and her voice came through his speakers.

"Hey Ted," she spoke this time in an almost normal voice, devoid of her occasional teasing. "Coming up!"

He failed to notice that he hadn't punched the button to allow her in the building.

———

PURCHASE, NY

Ecaterina and Nathan were let out of the taxi just a block down from the PepsiCo Anderson Hill Road main building. The weather was annoying, but they lifted their coat collars up. Nathan grabbed Ecaterina's hand and they started their walk towards the building.

"How are we going to get in?" Ecaterina asked.

"Easy, they have a center for customers to come and learn more about their product. That's as far as we need to go."

"What? Why?" she asked as he waved at a security guard who nodded. Apparently, cars were a problem, but a couple walking in the light mist wasn't a big issue.

They walked up the long drive towards the main building.

"I've got some new technology we're testing, out of Jean's team. Just need to get inside and let it go. Give it a few minutes to see if there's anything we want and then leave. Grab another taxi and go to Joe's Pizza in the West Village."

"So, you do remember," she leaned her head on his upper arm.

He wasn't about to admit that he'd taken almost all of his dates there at one time or another.

One doesn't tell one's mate about previous girlfriends. Especially when her version of pissed off was a whole new level.

Nathan had wanted a Were for a mate. Now, a few years into his relationship with Ecaterina, he was beginning to comprehend a few of the subtle downsides.

Like making sure he kept his mouth shut until he had thought about what he was going to say and analyzed that son-of-a-bitch for any landmines that might explode in his face.

"Of course, sweetheart, there was no way I'd forget you, and Joe's." he told her.

Mission accomplished.

NEW YORK CITY, NEW YORK, USA

Ted stood up and walked to his door. He might as well open it so that Tabitha would see him right away. No time like the present to get this party started.

Like he had enjoyed the invitation.

He opened the door and was startled to see Tabitha right in front of him, with her hand raised to knock. He turned to look behind himself.

It was only five steps from where he was sitting to his door. He turned back around to see Tabitha peering around him.

"Oh!" He stepped back. "Sorry, uh, the place is a mess." Tabitha wrinkled her nose. He looked down. "Yeah, sorry, I smoke when I'm stressed too much."

Tabitha looked around the small one-bedroom. It looked like it had seen a better day or two. The messes in the areas she could see suggested that this stress happened recently.

Tabitha stepped in. "No worries, Ted," she said as he closed the door behind her.

"Here, let me grab that for you, although I didn't know you'd need to pack. I'm sorry, I didn't think about your sleeping arrangements." She lifted the suitcase and handed it to him. Her mind was still on something else and didn't notice Ted's sudden strain to hold it. He took it and set it down next to his brown leather couch.

Just what the hell did she have in that thing? he wondered, quickly followed up with, *and how strong is she?*

She reached into her long coat and pulled out a box. He walked over to stand next to her and asked, "What are you…" he stopped when a finger was pushed against his lips. His eyes crossed as he tried to stare at the finger's sudden appearance at his mouth.

But he got the message. She took her hand back.

She opened the box of what looked like a thousand tiny balls. She took a pinch out and flung them into the air. Before he could ask a second time, her fingers pinched his lips together.

He nodded that he got the point.

She closed the little box and put it in her coat pocket. Her hand returned with what looked like goggles, but they didn't have anything to hold them to her face. She put them on and then mumbled something Ted couldn't quite pick up. Finally, she reached back into her coat and pulled out four silver orbs. She flung one towards his bedroom door.

It never hit anything that he could tell. She walked past him towards his little living room and stepped up to the window. She put a ball next to the window and lowered his blinds. The orb hadn't dropped when she released it, but stayed right where she placed it.

He heard her mumble this time, "Seven? Seriously?" Ted didn't even bother asking. He saw her nose twitch.

The smoke in his apartment was probably annoying her.

He turned to watch her open his apartment door, stick her head out and then toss a ball out. A motion pulled his attention back towards his bedroom door, and his eyes opened.

There was a little silver orb floating into the main room from his bedroom. He never thought about the dirty clothes he had hidden on the other side of his bed as he stared at the orb floating towards him.

He turned to see Tabitha pull out a small tablet. "Kill em, Achronyx," she said, and Ted heard multiple sparks, and a minute smell of ozone overpowered his cigarette smoke for a minute.

The goggle-wearing face turned towards him. Now, they were a yellow metallic color; he couldn't see Tabitha's eyes as she looked at him. "What are you really involved with, Ted?"

Oh, fuck! he thought as the blood drained from his face.

———

PURCHASE, NY, USA

"Okay," Nathan said as they exited the Pepsi building. "That was kind of cool. Although, renaming it Pepsi from Brad's drink was easily a marketing win. Brad's Drink? That was a horrible name."

Ecaterina grabbed his hand. Together, they had started a small but delicious effort to sneak Pepsi back into Nathan's life and pay Bethany Anne back for her No-Pepsi-On-My-Battle-Station edict.

With this recipe, they would be able to make little batches and keep them in their suite. Nathan had already ordered the necessary ingredients and loaded the request to the group on ships that were involved in the massive worldwide effort to grab last minute supplies. Fortunately, he would be able to run his purchases into a supply pickup just hours from now.

No one the wiser.

He turned to kiss Ecaterina. "Have I told you I love your devious Romanian mind?"

"Is that all?" she asked, returning his kiss.

"No, but you need carbs for the rest," he said.

———

NEW YORK CITY, NEW YORK, USA

Ted looked at Tabitha. "Politics." he answered.

She mumbled something and even though he was standing just two feet in front of her, he couldn't understand her, but someone did.

"Bullshit," she retorted. "You were on a normal case just forty-eight hours ago." Her hand waved at his living room. "And, there were seven bugs in your home."

He looked around. "What?"

She didn't answer him. "So, you *do* have a girlfriend now, and what, she's missing?"

All of the blood left his face as he stared at her. "Tabitha, these people aren't shitting around. They grabbed Monica, told me to contact you as best I could and pray that I could get you to come here."

Tabitha turned to face him and the yellow shield dropped, allowing him to see her eyes. They didn't look kind. "Who is 'they,' Ted?"

"Government, I think."

"That's just fan-fucking-tastic," Tabitha huffed. "And the building out of town, a ruse?"

He shook his head. "No, that's real. I'm supposed to get you over there."

"Achronyx, give me a view of the place outside of town," her eyes were unmistakably watching something she could see, but Ted couldn't. "Drop a set of psy-spies on that area, and see what we can find inside the building as well." Her eyes switched from looking slightly to her left and up, to her right and down. "We have company."

"What? Who?"

"Dark van, no windows, coming down the street." She leveled her gaze at him. "Do I lay your ass out, or are you in?"

"In what?" Ted asked, "Tabitha, those are bad mother-fuckers out there who have a woman in trouble because she was interested in a guy who happened to know you, and through you, TQB."

Tabitha ignored his comment but did clarify her question. "Are you up for saving her, or do you want me to deliver her to you when I'm done?"

Ted stared at Tabitha for a long moment. Once again, this was the other Tabitha, not the one who played around. "What will happen to her if I stay here?"

"I'll do my best to grab her and move her to a safe place," she told him, "I'll knock you out, and give you an alibi."

Ted's face twisted. "Fuck them." He headed towards his room. He noticed the orb following him.

It didn't look like Tabitha was going to trust him, and

frankly, she had every right not to. He dropped to his knees beside his bed and reached under to pull out a case that was two feet wide and four long. It was a bit tricky to get out, but when he had it, he entered the combination and opened it. Inside was a bulletproof vest and two 1911s plus plenty of mags, holsters for his guns and a jacket specially fitted to help him hide the weapons. He pulled it all out and started getting it on.

It grated on him to go against authority. This armament was the closest he ever got to doing what Tabitha had when she went vigilante here in New York in the past. He had been working on a case to uncover those who were cooking the New York Police Department computers to falsify the data in their databases by judiciously tagging some higher level crime with lower level flags.

Unfortunately, his case hadn't been sanctioned by his boss. Further, it might have been his attempt to do that which had attracted the attention of this group, and now Monica was involved.

He didn't like playing the hero, here. It had been more of a romantic notion than a real desire to play the uber-hero. But now, his half-assed approach was requiring him to go all in.

He put on the heavy bulletproof vest and then his holsters.

He loaded both pistols and locked their thumb safeties in place when he heard Tabitha's voice. "Take my suitcase up to the roof, I'll meet you there."

He turned to step out of his room to see her slide her coat back on. This time, she was a little bulkier.

She had brought armor.

"Give me two minutes before you leave. It will be safe by

then," she said as she locked on some sort of black headgear that fit on her goggles and wrapped around her head.

A woman had walked into his apartment. Perhaps a badass woman, but still a woman.

Ted wasn't sure just what had just walked out.

CHAPTER ELEVEN

GERMANY

"Now *that* was a large purchase," William told his friends as they paid for the materials. Fortunately, they still had plenty of ways to pay for the things they needed, and all the money transfers were being pulled from their personal funds. Bobcat had made a very smart, very strategic hiring decision over a year before. The team had ADAM doing all of their books and money transfers.

The A.I. charged them in gold.

It was getting on into late afternoon as they left the sales office. "Beer?" Bobcat asked his friends.

Marcus shrugged and looked up and down the small street they had entered to get to the company's sales headquarters. "What about trying a little pub, and ask them for great beer selections?"

Bobcat slapped Marcus on the back as they started down the sidewalk. "Now that is a capital idea!"

A few minutes later, the trio entered a nearby pub and sat down. Within three minutes, each man had two beers sitting in front of him.

William looked down at the large steins and then over at his two friends, then back to the two beers.

"Should we?" he asked.

Marcus looked at his two beers and shrugged. "I'm willing, it's for research purposes."

Bobcat grabbed his first stein and held it up, waiting for his friends to bump theirs together. "Here's to research!"

The three men drank their first stein. Bobcat finished first, William second and Marcus a distant, twenty-seven seconds later third place. They looked at each other and turned towards the waitress, lifted their empty mugs high, eyes alight with humor and called out, "Another round of research!"

QBBS MEREDITH REYNOLDS

Diane and Dorene, the heads of the Etheric Academy, were exiting the tram that ran from the outside to the inner core. The two had decided to check on Team BMW and make sure they were working with their team, but the guys had dropped to Earth with the Queen and were not available.

Diane had made sure that John Grimes wasn't anywhere around, so they didn't accidentally meet him and her sister wouldn't be tempted to pinch.

Diane could play out the scene in her head right now...

"There's John!" Dorene would say, and no matter how hard Diane tried to get Dorene's attention away from the guy, she would see her sister's two fingers spasm unconsciously.

Diane would remind Dorene of Jean's last warning to toss her ass out an airlock, and her sister would settle down.

For maybe ten minutes.

Ever since they got their memory back of the episode with the Nosferatu in the mountains a few years ago, Dorene had been living life like she was young again. Well, physically they were. However, you would think that Dorene would have grown out of her pinching.

But sadly, no.

Diane smirked, yeah, she could understand the joy of the pinch. They had been busted in Europe for pinching inappropriately. Then, unlike now, they had older bodies and silver hair. It had been easy to be forgiven when they looked like everyone's grandmother. Not so much when you now looked young, fresh and very available.

Their real age didn't provide them protection any longer.

"So, no John?" Dorene asked, as the two walked from the tram station and headed inward. They had decided to swing by the park, and then try one of the two Chinese restaurants for a meal.

They stopped as two small beeps sounded behind them. Stepping out of the way, they watched the two floating boxes marked *supplies* continue past them. The little cart with the two boxes was silent, except for the constant beeps to warn people of its existence.

Meredith moved most of these boxes, or at least one of her sub-computers did. Dorene looked down and realized she and her sister had been walking in the transfer lane. It wasn't a big deal, but when you heard the beeps, you were expected to move aside.

"Guess I was focusing on John, never noticed we were walking in the package lane."

Diane waved her forward. "C'mon, let's go. I thought you were over John a long time ago."

"How does one get over John?" Dorene's voice carried down the corridor as the two women turned a corner. "That mountain of man meat…"

Diane cut off her sister mid-lust statement. "Has a woman who creates new ways to blow people apart for the Queen."

Dorene's voice came back a moment later, somewhat subdued, "Oh sure, bring up the negatives."

————

Yelena was simply confused. Matrix and Snow had stayed with the Yollin captain, and he had promised to bring them back to her place later when he was finished. He was enjoying the chance to explain more about his kind to the four-footed kids. That he accepted Snow had shocked Yelena.

Then again, why wouldn't he? He had been around Bethany Anne enough that if he was a horrible… being… Bethany Anne would have figured it out.

Now, Ashur and Bellatrix were romping around behind her as they made their way over to the park.

In front of her, she had Jinx, the only sable of the litter, and the all black brother-sister team Dio and Devi.

Yelena covered her eyes and looked up at the fantastic light and heat systems inside the hollowed-out core. She couldn't look at the primary globe, or she might blind herself.

She returned to walking the path as it opened up from the personal gardens that separated the park from the commercial crops that helped feed everyone and then the park itself. Here, there were trees planted and people had laid out a few blankets and were enjoying themselves.

She looked around and realized one thing that seemed to be missing. There wasn't a breeze here. At least, not that she could feel and she wondered how everything got watered? This was only her second time here, so she figured she could ask Bobcat next time she thought about it.

The puppies ran on, playing, and soon she was passed by Ashur and Bellatrix, and then people called out his name, and soon his mate's name as well.

Damn, Bellatrix was going to become insufferable, she thought.

Yelena saw a few benches along the path, so she walked to one and sat down. It seemed to be made of a dark gray wood. Resting her hand along the back of the bench, she felt a metal plaque. She leaned back and could see it had words engraved on it, but she couldn't read it.

She would take a look when she got up.

She had been there for a few minutes when she heard some talking and turned to see two women, dressed alike, and if Yelena had to guess she would say they were sisters. She turned back to watch the puppies.

A few moments later, she was surprised by a tap on her shoulder. "Excuse me."

Yelena turned to see the two ladies behind her. "Yes?"

The woman with Dorene on her uniform pointed to the dogs. "Are you Bellatrix's owner?"

Yelena smiled. "Well if you listen to Bellatrix after today, she would probably say I belong to her. But yes, Bellatrix and I are matched."

"Oh, good!" the woman exclaimed and walked around the bench to sit down next to her. "So, you're Yelena, right?"

She nodded.

"And you're seeing Bobcat?" she continued.

Yelena nodded again, not sure where this was going when the other lady murmured, "Dear God in Heaven."

Dorene flicked a hand at Diane. "Hush sis, I have the perfect opportunity to make sure Bobcat stays on the straight and narrow with the kids, and I'm willing to use whatever tools I have at my disposal to do it."

"I'm going to apologize for my sister before she says another word," the second lady said. "By the way, I'm Diane, and Ms. Nosey-body next to you is my sister, Dorene. We're in charge of the Etheric Academy."

"Oh, okay." Yelena now knew who she was speaking with. "Bobcat mentioned he screwed up with the first class. Is that what you wanted to talk about?"

Dorene blinked a couple of times. "Yeessss," she said. "I didn't expect him to fess up to you."

"Why not?"

"Uh, he's Bobcat," Dorene answered as if that was enough.

"Sorry, but what she said," Diane pointed to Dorene.

Yelena shrugged. "I'm not following. Sure, he can be a bit impetuous at times, but he seems pretty down to Earth… okay, down to the base station for the most part. He felt pretty bad about the situation with the kids from the first class, I can tell you that."

"Was that pre or post-Bethany Anne's ass chewing?" Diane answered.

Yelena shrugged. "Bobcat wouldn't do anything to harm anyone on his side, which means anyone on Bethany Anne's side."

"But what about all of the mistakes, and unsafe practices, and," Dorene started with her hands gesticulating she finally just spat out, "Stuff!"

"Not sure?" Yelena answered. "But, whatever happened,

I'm unaware of Bobcat and the team being taken out of the role of teaching, right?"

"Well, of course not, we need them," Diane answered.

"No," Dorene corrected. "We need them, but not enough to endanger the students. Which means when Bethany Anne finished her discussion, she had already ascertained the mistakes and they didn't warrant… probably half the shit that people believe."

"So, why aren't they correcting the assumptions?" Diane followed up, as much a question of herself than the other two ladies.

"Probably because on the other side are the youth, and how they see reality isn't the same as how an adult would see it," Yelena shrugged.

"Are you a mom?" Dorene asked Yelena.

"A mother?" She chuckled and then stopped when Dorene's face never cracked a smile. "Oh, you're serious? No, why?"

"You mentioned the kids might see the whole story through their lens of reality. That sounds like a mother."

Yelena pointed at the dogs running around. "I see things differently due to my four-footed kids."

When she pointed to the dogs, both Dio and Devi turned and bolted towards the three ladies who watched the matched pair race over. Diane stepped around from the back of the bench so she could play with the two puppies who were enjoying the attention. Devi yipped and Yelena answered, "This is Dorene, sitting, and her sister, Diane who is petting you two."

Another yip, this time from Dio. "They're in charge of the Etheric Academy," Yelena answered before turning to the two ladies. "I'm sorry, I'm not sure exactly what all you do?"

"Do they understand us?" Dorene asked.

"Oh yes," Yelena confirmed. "They're exploring more of the base at the moment, so they have dozens of questions."

"Well," Dorene said, "we're in charge of a learning environment that helps those who are done with core school rotate through different disciplines to see where they might desire to work in the future."

Another yip and both ladies looked at Yelena. "She isn't sure what learning environment means."

Diane took this question. "Where you learn more, like what you're doing now, asking questions of different people. It is an effort to impart information to individuals who need it."

Yelena caught on where this was going. "Devi!" the little dog turned towards her. "You don't know if these two ladies have time for a new responsibility. You're not very up front about why you're asking questions." Another yip, "No, they don't know what's going on. No one knows what's going on right now."

"What are you talking about?" Dorene asked, looking at Yelena and the female puppy.

"Uh, the puppies, collectively, decided that they wanted to find their bonded partners. Like the Queen and Ashur, or Bellatrix and myself. So they keep interviewing people. Since most don't know why the puppies are asking questions, they're happy to answer. I'm getting the impression that Devi is asking you because she is narrowing down her selection. Since I don't think this is fair, I'm interrupting the process. You ladies already have a whole school of kids."

"Well," Diane looked at her sister, "just what we need, another kid to look after." Yelena watched them stare at each other like their minds were melding or something.

Dorene and Diane spoke at the same time, "Best place to learn is in a safe environment."

Dorene spoke next, "Four foot or two, easy to invite them to explore."

Yelena, Dio, and Devi watched with fascination as the women continued.

"Could be the first-born citizens in the Empire," Diane replied.

"Could learn about classes, audit people."

"We could let them set their own course of learning."

"It would be more fur up your nose at night. Remember that old white and black cat that would sneak into bed and lay on your face?"

"Yeah, but we've been fixed in the Pod-doc… no allergies."

"There is that." Dorene agreed.

"What about the cookies the Rotty would cry for?" Diane asked before they both turned to view the puppy looking up at them.

Together, they announced, "Sure, we'd love a little fur-ball partner!"

With a 'YIP,' Devi agreed and sealed the deal. Dio wagged his tail, happy for his sister to have found her match.

CHAPTER TWELVE

NEW YORK CITY, NY, USA

Franklyn W. Sahvt had been a mercenary for eight years. At six foot four inches tall and packing two hundred and twenty-five pounds of muscle on that frame, he was hard to throw around when he was wearing nothing but his skivvies.

Now, suited up in the battle rattle with his Remington 870, armor, and ammunition, he easily topped two-seventy.

He was the lead of his four-man team. Although they preferred to operate at night, especially in a city like New York, a crappy day like today when most people stayed inside was a mediocre second choice. He would prefer lots of lightning and loud thunder.

When you needed deep, dark, and deniable (especially inside the United States), his team got the nod. Their goal was straightforward.

Grab the girl, try to keep breakage down. If they could

grab the girl without killing the man, that was to be preferred. New York City needed their cops after all.

Even nosy cops who shouldn't be searching for proof about certain situations without permission. Still, if he got killed during the operation, that would suck.

But, breakage is breakage. At least his woman would eventually go free. She'd been captured, drugged, and right now didn't have a clue what was going on.

Franklyn nodded to his three compatriots. For this operation, they were simply Alphas one through four. No other names asked, no other names given. The vehicle picked them up at the compound near Heckscher State Park close to Bay Shore, NY. The rest of the team was up there waiting for the bait to arrive.

Their job, however, was changed when information was received that the lure was acting strangely. His team was sent to be stationed near the lure's apartment in case they needed to flush the target.

Now, it seemed they were here to grab the target.

Franklyn looked down at his tablet, then up at his team members. "Time to lock and load."

———

The black van pulled up to the front of the narrow apartment building. The old brick facade was wearing down from the accumulation of years, although the fresh coat of paint helped.

The door slid open on oiled tracks. Alpha 2 jumped out, holding his FN SCAR 16s down beside him and quickly stepped across the sidewalk to the front door. Alpha 3 was right behind him, covering his back. 2 dropped his rifle and allowed his quick sling to stop it from falling as he pulled out his tool kit.

He was able to pick the lock on the front door in twelve seconds. Which seems like an eternity when you're standing on the front porch holding an assault rifle.

When 2 opened the door, 3 swept around him as Franklyn and 4 stepped in quickly.

Alpha 2 had barely started closing the door when all hell broke loose.

———

Ted stepped into his front room as Tabitha walked out of his apartment. He grabbed her suitcase and moved out, closing the door behind him. He looked over the stairwell, but Tabitha was already out of sight. He hotfooted it over to the door allowing owners access to the roof and opened the door to get up top. As the door shut behind him, he heard a commotion downstairs followed by gunfire.

He pitied the people below. He had seen Tabitha take care of a person trying to knife her.

He wasn't sure what this Tabitha would do to those who brought guns.

———

Well fuck, Tabitha wondered, *what should I do here?*

She had descended the stairs and was waiting at the landing on the second level, almost twenty feet from the front door ten feet from the bottom of the stairs.

Then, her time to question her tactics was over when the door opened, and three men came sweeping in, all armed.

"Oh," she murmured. "It's that game. Righty-o, tally-ho and time to fuck you up!" Tabitha took two steps and launched herself down the stairs.

———

Franklyn swept around Alpha 2 as he opened the door. Alpha 4, then Alpha 3 would be behind him, and Alpha 2 would close the door. "Look out!" he yelled, trying to move his gun up, finger squeezing the trigger.

Franklyn barely had time to register the black body, knee outstretched, aimed at his head when the knee connected to his skull, crushing it.

His firing stopped.

Tabitha grabbed the rifle behind the first guy and yanked. She slammed her palm into the man's nose, shoving cartilage back into his skull, ending his life.

The third guy was able to aim point blank at the figure and shoot a burst of three rounds into her stomach. His mouth dropped open in surprise when the bullets ricocheted off his target, one hitting him in his chest armor before his gun was ripped from his grasp.

———

"That tickles, asshat!" Tabitha growled when the bullets hit her abdomen. She yanked the gun away and slammed her right hand, knuckles first, into the side of his head. He collapsed.

She wasn't sure if he would ever get up. She palmed her Dukes' special.

NEVER SUBMIT

––––––

Alpha 2 was turning around, hearing the carnage behind him, when his eyes focused on the barrel of the pistol pressed against the center of his forehead. His head slammed back against the door.

"Snake-eyes, asshole," said a female voice. Alpha 2 could see his team lying on the floor. Alpha 1's head was bleeding so much that he had to be dead.

Alpha 2 licked his lips. He was willing to take it for the team, but right now he HAD no team. "What do you want?"

"This is how it can go down," she told him, voice gruff. "I kill you, walk outside and if that van is still there, kill them too. You assholes mean nothing to me. Do you understand my first statement?" He nodded. "Option two, I taser your ass, and taser whoever is outside after you tell me how many are protecting the woman. Lie?" She pressed harder on the pistol. "I don't worry about you. I'll sleep just fine. You assholes took it out of legal and into military, so, sucks to be you. You got three seconds to decide your future."

He licked his lips. "Forty-five to fifty, sixty tops."

"All like you?" she nodded at his armament.

"Yeah."

He watched as she pulled a second pistol and placed it under his armpit where the armor wasn't protecting him. "If you ever agree to go against TQB again? You better pray it's a Ranger that you fight, we give second chances."

She pulled the trigger, and Alpha 2 spasmed before dropping to the ground. She turned the doorknob and stepped out.

––––––

On the roof, Ted turned towards the front of the building and ran over. He leaned over quickly, then back out of sight. He saw the black van sitting below and wondered what to do. He decided to chance looking over again when the front door opened and Tabitha stepped out. She had the door open to the van in a blink. She shot something that caused a bright white light and then turned, closed the van door and headed back into the apartment building.

Ted turned around to run back to the doorway and then stopped. There was a floating Pod above his building where seconds before it didn't exist. He walked as calmly as possible towards it.

He felt sure this wasn't alien. Unless you counted something from Tabitha's team as alien.

The door to the roof opened, and Tabitha stepped through. She walked over to Ted, grabbing the suitcase. "Thank you, let's go."

HECKSCHER STATE PARK AREA, NY, USA

"We've lost all of Strike Team Alpha, sir!" Mission Specialist McGowan called over to Vic Kingston.

Vic switched the toothpick he was chewing to the other side of his mouth.

"Bring in the reserves. We'll have attention here soon. Move the package to the lowest level," Vic said. One man got on the radio to call in the backup which was a mile away.

Another went to handle the movement of the package.

"SIXTY!" Ted yelled in the small Pod, his fascination with the technology lost at the moment. "We have to get past sixty guys to get Monica back?"

"Probably more, now," Tabitha said.

"And it's just you and me?" he asked, his voice calming down. He looked out the window. "Well, if I'm going to go out fighting, at least it will be said I wasn't afraid of over-whelming odds."

"Yeah, they should bring a few more in," Tabitha agreed when notes on new troop counts flashed on the Pod's window. "Annnndddd, they did."

"They did what?" Ted asked, turning his attention back to the information on the Pod window.

"They brought in more troops," Tabitha said. "Shit, this is outside my abilities."

"Why," Ted asked, having a hard time keeping the sarcasm out of his voice. "Was it the fifty, the sixty or the twice that?"

"The moving your girlfriend to a lower level part. They want to play keep-away. Make me go through all of them to get to her."

Ted dropped his head, his hands reaching up to rub his face as his voice softened, "She's going to die, isn't she?"

Tabitha bit her lip, trying to figure out a way to save the woman and was drawing a blank. She was good, but she wasn't this good. "If it's just you and me? Yeah, she's going to die."

Ted sat there in silence.

"But, it's never just me," Tabitha told him and settled her head back in her seat.

My Queen?

Ah, Yup? Bethany Anne replied.

I've got ahh, call it a challenge, and I need some advice.

Shoot!

Okay, here's what I got…

No, not you Tabitha. I meant to tell that to John, one second.

There was a split second as Bethany Anne broke the connection, and then was back. *Okay, the little bastards got sneaky. John took care of it.*

Care of what? Tabitha asked, *Aren't you on the Meredith Reynolds?*

There was a slight pause. *Ahhhhh No?*

Where are you?

'Where' is a metaphysical question I don't have time for at the moment. What did you need, Ranger Two?

Tabitha was sure if she had the time, she could figure out what Bethany Anne was up to, and Tabitha was sure her Queen was up to her shoulders doing something she probably shouldn't.

Then again, so was Barnabas.

I've got a hostage situation here in New York to deal with. Someone is trying to capture me, using her for bait.

To accomplish what? Use you as bait to catch me?

Yes, that seems likely.

Bethany Anne disconnected for a moment, it was a little longer before she came back on this time. *John and I will be there shortly, but we need a Pod.*

We can drop ourselves off and let the Pod get you. It's only a couple of minutes max round trip if you don't deal with challenges.

Do it. ADAM will take control of the Pod and send ours in

that direction to catch up. Wait, I'm told we have another Pod in the area. So...

There was a second before Bethany Anne continued talking.

We're in New York now. A Pod will be here in a few seconds. ADAM is giving us an update from Achronyx. Huh, one hundred and fifty plus waiting at the building? Seems like a hell of a reception party. They really want your ass.

Everybody wants a piece of this badonkadonk! They can get in line, Tabitha quipped back.

Bethany Anne sent the feeling of a smirk back through the connection, but inwardly she felt Tabitha's pain. Tabitha was lonely, hellishly lonely. Tabitha might hide it, but inside? She needed someone she could confide in.

Bethany Anne had no solution for her, either. Tabitha had Michael as a mentor and surrogate father figure. Since young women would often judge potential dates and marriage material by their father, that was going to be a pretty high bar to get over for most guys.

Okay, I've got to talk with the building security for a second, You two be safe for a minute or two. Then, the connection with Bethany Anne was gone.

"Where did you go?" Ted asked, worry in his voice.

Tabitha reviewed the information on the Pod glass. "Well, you remember our conversation in the coffee shop?"

"Yeah," his eyes narrowed. "You said there were the Bitches, friends of yours, that didn't give a shit about the law."

"Yeah, them."

"You called them here?"

Tabitha chuckled. "Well, yes in a way."

"What way? C'mon Tabitha, if there's a slight chance we can save Monica, I'm game. If my handsome ass won't get shot to shit, then I'm going to be super happy as well."

"It won't, Ted." Tabitha turned to look him in the eyes. "I promise not one of their bullets will so much as get within ten feet of you."

Ted met her gaze and nodded. He hadn't seen her eyes since the apartment, and it was a little off-putting.

She turned back towards the front as the Pod started descending from the clouds to a wooded area, the Atlantic taking up half of the windshield.

"I called my Queen, John is just coming along for the ride," Tabitha said.

Ted, remembering the conversation from the coffee shop, turned to look out the Pod window, the ground coming up quickly. "Oh… shit."

Now, he was beginning to feel just a little worry for the poor sons-a-bitches down below. He knew that Tabitha had just taken out a small strike team and while he noticed the three marks on her armor, she didn't seem to have been affected. Now, this woman was telling him that someone way stronger and deadlier than her was coming. That man, one of the Bitches, was able to take out this whole compound by himself.

But, he wasn't the worst of them.

Her Queen was coming.

CHAPTER THIRTEEN

Ann Bradshaw had been working security for the Empire State Building since 2012, and she was sure she had seen everything.

Until two armored figures appeared out of nowhere on her roof.

One was a female, dressed in deep red armor. The other was a large man, dressed in black armor. Their suits seemed to flex with their bodies.

Not like Iron Man's suit at all.

Ann wanted to reach for her pistol, but training always suggested that you tried to minimize the show of force and to reduce the chance of a confrontation escalating.

What the training didn't explain was what the fuck to do when two badass armored people appeared right in fucking front of you?

"Lady?" Ann called out. The woman turned, slightly off

balance. She seemed a little weak. Then, the armor appeared to melt from around her face, and her black hair and annoyed look were obvious.

So were the red eyes that were fading in front of Ann's eyes. There were a lot of people now taking pictures of the two newcomers.

"Oh My God, It's John Grimes!" a woman shrieked off to Ann's left.

Ann wanted to spit. Why the HELL was an actor up here?

Ann walked towards them as she watched the woman calmly wait for the armor on her right leg to open up. She slotted a pistol into the armor, and then the armor closed back up.

"We'll be gone in about thirty-two seconds," the contralto voice told her. "Sorry for using this place, but I needed a location I knew well, and I've been here a few times."

"Who are you?"

The huge guy smiled as two women hesitated then walked towards him, pens out. The auburn haired woman had a tour guide article she was handing the big man to sign. The second one pulled her coat and shirt aside. "Right above my boob. It's as close to my heart as you can get!"

The red-armored woman turned to look up at the guy. "Really?" she asked the man. "If Jean hears about this, your ass is grass."

"Hearts and minds, Bethany Anne," he murmured. "What goes on during an operation, stays on the operation, right? Plus, we need to be moving, not arguing where I sign."

"Whatever," the woman told him before turning back to Ann and giving her a smile. "Our ride is here, sorry to have bugged you."

"Holy fuck, its TQB's leader!" This time, it was a guy.

NEVER SUBMIT

There was a flurry of more camera shots.

"Like that shit isn't getting on the news, John," she said to the big man when a floating Pod dropped out of the sky. The doors opened, and they got in. They were busy locking themselves in as the Pod flew backward. The doors closed and then it turned and flew away, heading north.

———

"ADAM?" John asked, locking the last belt.

"Yes?"

"Please block all reports of this event to the Etheric Empire."

"Okay, a reason for archives?" ADAM inquired.

"No one needs to know the Queen was playing hooky," he said.

Bethany Anne snorted.

Shit, he had her there.

"You know we're both going to be busted for this eventually, right?" Bethany Anne asked John.

"C'mon. It was a signature. I didn't touch her breast, Bitch's Honor."

"Like that will matter. Jean will react and before you can say 'Bitch's Honor' your pecker might be gone."

"You know, that's not even fair. I did the calendar with a whole bunch of women pushing for it, and now that damned calendar could get my pecker shot off? That's wrong on so many levels I can't begin to count."

"No, that's emotions for you. You were attracted to a woman with hot emotions, so now you get to deal with them. She isn't going to suddenly become a calm, well-reasoned woman just because you two got together. She's possessive as hell, and she isn't going to share. I've already had to warn her I'll be pretty damned displeased if she ever actually spaces someone."

"Displeased?" John asked.

"I'll space her ass, that good enough for you?" Bethany Anne replied.

"Oh, yeah, that should mean Dorene is safe."

"Yes, she's safe, but don't let Dorene know that. I don't need Dorene's pinching your ass to become a real problem. Thankfully, we have pictures of what the ladies looked like before they were changed, and I'm pretty sure Jean finds it funny, now."

"Pretty sure?" John asked.

"It's Jean."

"Good point."

———

Tabitha's Pod landed, and she was out of her harness before Ted realized he needed to unclick. He was turning in Tabitha's direction when the inside of the Pod flashed white. Ted slumped over in his harness.

"I promised the bullets wouldn't come near you, Ted." She leaned over and kissed his forehead. "This isn't about you or Monica. You're just caught up in some shit because you know me."

The Pod doors opened, and Tabitha stepped out. She grabbed her suitcase and placed it on the ground. Unlocking it, she replaced her tasing gun for her second Dukes' special and grabbed four inch-and-a-half triangles and slotted them inside her coat. Closing the suitcase, she shoved it back into the Pod.

Her coat flowed behind her she walked towards the house. Once she had put a couple of steps between them, the Pod doors closed on Ted, then floated up into the sky.

HECKSCHER STATE PARK AREA, NY, USA

"Movement, half a mile away," Specialist Siemanowski called. "Sector 112."

"Speed?" Vic asked.

"Walking, sir."

The toothpick went back and forth between Vic's teeth. "Direction?"

"This way, sir," Siemanowski answered.

Vic turned his head. "Still nothing from Alpha team, Mc-Gowan?"

McGowan answered, "Negative sir."

Well, fuck, Vic thought. Go out or wait?

ATLANTIC CITY, NJ, USA

"SCRAMBLE SCRAMBLE SCRAMBLE!" The alarms blared. "We have bogies inside New York City, We have…"

The alarms died, the power died. Around the airport, generators were coming online as emergency lights flickered on and off.

Then those generators were dying.

Those in the Air Force tower were slapping their desks in frustration as computers that had built in redundancy refused to power up.

Major Mark Milton—he rather liked the alliteration—was hastily pushing digits on his cell phone, trying to circumvent the useless phones in the tower when he was tapped on the shoulder. "What?" he snapped, frustrated when his cell connectivity plunged and he couldn't get a signal.

"Sir," a voice said behind him. "You better see this."

Mark bit off his next comment. It wasn't appropriate. He took a calming breath and turned around. Everyone was looking out the east windows to the runway where the jets took off.

There was a big ass alien spaceship floating fifty feet above the ground.

"What the fuck…" someone whispered.

"Awww, son of a bitch," Milton said as he walked towards the window. He recognized the female vampire skull on the side of the ship. "Which of our imperious leaders went and pissed off TQB this time?"

Mark looked down and saw two guards down on the runway. One had his pistol out, shooting at the ship.

He grumbled, "Somebody tell that spastic, dickless, one-eyed wonder down there to stop bringing a popgun to a space fight for fuck's sake. It might just piss off the captain of that ship."

WASHINGTON D.C., USA

Four Secret Service agents walked into the President's office, calmly grabbed him, and ushered him out of the room. The five men moved quickly to the underground bunker.

"What's going on?" The President asked. "And, is my family safe?"

"Yes to the family and someone has pissed off TQB."

"Well, who the… Wait, did we do something?" he asked,

trying to remember what orders he had given recently.

They walked into the protected room in the underground communications center, another seven individuals already there.

"We have a TQB ship, the G'laxix Sphaea, sitting right on top of the 177th Fighter Wing at Atlantic City International Airport."

"What are they doing there?" he asked, sitting down at the table.

"Not letting our fighters take off, Mr. President," Agent Alvin Carter answered.

"Yes, but why?" the President said. "Someone needs to tell me why we've been invaded." He barked out, "And get that self-proclaimed Queen of theirs on the line, or I'll send their asses back to the Stone Age."

———

HECKSCHER STATE PARK AREA, NY, USA

"ADAM, give me a schematic of the building," Bethany Anne said. They reviewed the structure in three dimensions. "Change to wireframe," she said.

"Two stories, with two ways into the basement," John pointed out. "How do you want to go in?"

Bethany Anne tapped her finger on her lips. "ADAM, how are the gravity controls for these suits?"

"What do you wish to accomplish, Bethany Anne?"

"I'm thinking to drop out of the sky, right on top and busting through."

"Sorry, that won't be possible, the top has a concrete layer."

"Well," John cut in, "that was kind of out of the box thinking."

"How about under the top level?" she continued.

"The building is made up of a steel girder frame, concrete between floors, approximately six inches thick and simple construction materials for the walls. Thin metal construction on the outside walls."

"How thin?" Bethany Anne asked.

"Typical corrugated steel walls."

Bethany Anne pointed to the two staircases that went to the basement. "I say we toss something here between these two locations at an angle. It takes out the middle of the building, and we race to see who gets the girl first."

"Ooookay," John said. "Or, could you walk the Etheric and peek around now that you know where it is?"

Bethany Anne rolled her eyes. "Grimes, you take all the fucking fun out of things," she bitched. "But then, I suppose it will help keep our primary safe."

"It's okay," John replied. "You go in, grab the girl, then we do some damage because no one does this shit and gets away with a slap on the wrist."

"No, not anymore they don't," Bethany Anne agreed.

The Pod stopped at four thousand feet, and John saw his boss disappear out of her seat, then reappear outside the Pod, falling.

"Damn," he whispered. ADAM kept her on the screen for him, so he had a good view as she disappeared before hitting the ground. "She keeps getting better and better." He turned and reached into the back of the Pod and pulled out a gravitational bar. "I got to go old school, this fucking sucks."

The doors to the Pod opened and John's helmet locked

back into place, covering his head. No one was going to hit Ms. Duke's prized man where it might take him out.

John jumped out of the Pod.

CHAPTER FOURTEEN

DULCE, NEW MEXICO, USA

And I'm telling you," Richard scraped the gunk off of his shoe, "that this stuff is disgusting. Why are we going through caves again? It is ruining my Zamberlan Latemars."

Samuel smirked. "Because the entrance up top was bombed to oblivion, and there are presently a hundred soldiers up there with big ass guns trying really hard to get in."

"Well," Richard put his foot back down and straightened his pants leg, "if you put it that way, I suppose I should look out for the bat guano."

Samuel shook his head and tossed Richard his headgear. "Ready to use the tools this time?"

Deftly catching the hat, Richard searched for and found the power switch. "So I forgot just how dark caves can get, I've gotten a little senile in my old age."

"No, you've gotten lazy," Samuel replied as he turned his

light on and started jogging. In moments, Richard caught up.

"That's not new!" Richard argued. "When have you ever known me not to be lazy?"

"From 1860 through 1892."

There was a pause. "Oh good lord!" Richard complained. "That was eons ago. When have you not known me not to be lazy recently?"

Samuel shook his head again. "Anytime Gabrielle comes around?"

"Says the man that is still trying his best to skip conversations about reliving the past with said woman."

"She's still a bit miffed about the moonseed joke," Samuel admitted. "Although I ease into the conversation all the time."

This time, the smell alerted Richard and he jumped over a section of the cave floor. "You better hope that she doesn't tell Eric."

"Why?" Samuel had just jogged around the pit and caught back up with his friend.

"Cause I imagine he would kick your arse," Richard grunted. A moment later, they could see a large cavern open up.

"Why would he want to do that?" Samuel continued the conversation.

"Maybe because he and Gabrielle are an item?" Richard replied, slowing down to consider their next steps.

Richard felt Samuel grab his arm and he turned, squinting at the sudden light in his eyes. "Lord, would you PLEASE point that somewhere else!"

Samuel reached up and moved his light. "That's not what she said."

"Gabrielle?" Richard smirked.

"Oh, god no," Samuel said. "Let's not make those jokes

again." Samuel made sure Richard was paying attention. "Like, ever."

"Ever is a long time."

"Have you *seen* Eric?"

"Ahh," Richard thought about it. "Yeah. Queen's Bitch, Hispanic, eyes like coal…"

Samuel stayed quiet.

"Okay, agreed, never again." Richard said before turning back to the area ahead. "How do we play this?"

"Well," Samuel answered, paying attention to faint noises reaching their ears. Voices, from people they couldn't see, were whooping and hollering. "I suppose we could…"

———

HECKSCHER STATE PARK AREA, NY, USA

"Sir, we have video confirmation this is one of the targets. Female, wearing a helmet with goggles, some sort of armor and a coat."

Vic tossed the toothpick into the ashtray, and slid a fresh one into his mouth. "Turn on the speakers. Let's tell our visitor they need to move on, or we'll destroy them."

Vic heard someone hiss, 'Trust me, no way that isn't a woman!'

"Remember gents," Vic growled. "We've lost a team to this person, so stop thinking with your small brain and realize she can kill you.

"Give me the channel," he continued and picked up the microphone. "Attention! You are now surrounded by agents who are ready to reduce you to ash, if necessary. You will submit to apprehension, and without violence, to restraint."

Vic turned to his left. "Someone bring the goddamn video up better, she seems to be puking."

The side of the split view on the screen that previously displayed the figure blinked and the image changed. In the new view, the figure was bigger but was partially blocked by a leaf from a tree.

Vic ground his teeth together. The figure wasn't puking, it looked like she was bent over laughing.

Soon enough, the figure stood back up and then calmly raised her arm giving the universal gesture that told Vic his offer wasn't accepted.

"All right…" Vic started but stopped when the figure took a couple of steps forward, coming into better view. She, and it was now damned obvious it was a she, pulled her coat back, and grabbed two pistols out of their holsters. She used one of the pistols to offer a "come get me" gesture.

"I don't think she wishes to submit, sir."

"Yeah, I got that, Jennings," Vic agreed. "This is what I want. Have team Bravo…"

He never got out the whole order.

———

Bethany Anne flew through the air, waiting until the very end to transfer into the Etheric and stopping. One of these times, she would understand the real relevance of moving and mental commands. She was sure there was a way to just wish herself somewhere else, but she hadn't figured out the solution.

At least, not yet.

Bethany Anne peeked out into the real world and then ducked back into the Etheric. She ran twenty steps and peeked again. Swearing in frustration, she turned and crossed where she had started and ran the other direction.

She hated when she guessed wrong. It took her five more movements, and quick peeks, to confirm she now had the right location.

She stepped out of the Etheric.

———

John liked this part of the trip. Ever since these bars had been built, an offspring of the technology used to attack the XJ-12 base, the idea of an attack from above had excited him.

Well, he had enjoyed the trip down until someone below had located his black armored ass and started shooting at him.

So much for silent and deadly.

Although the occasional hit by the standard 5.56 X 45 NATO round was an annoyance, he wasn't too worried.

CLANG... he was violently twisted to his left.

"FUCK!" John swore, and spun around, knocked ass over appetite. "We got .50 caliber down there folks!" He looked around. "ADAM drop me, three times speed."

A tracer ran through where John would have been before he plummeted down towards the ground as he continued in his conversational tone, "Those .50 cals aren't fun, I don't advise allowing them to play 'kiss the pretty' with you." He braced his knees. When he hit the ground, he rolled and then stripped his hands out of the bar and tossed it into the air.

Time to bring the pain.

———

Tabitha heard John's call and warning and bolted towards the house. She had Bethany Anne's position pegged on her schematic and John's as well. The gun must have been hidden somewhere on the other side of the building for them not to have found it with her deployed spies.

She hadn't been thinking war, she was thinking cop. She wouldn't make that mistake again in the future. Now? Now she would take out the motherfuckers who had tried to punch a hole through her friend.

When Tabitha had spoken with Ted in that coffee shop, she was trying to get across the relative difference between a Bitch, her, and Bethany Anne.

When the gloves came off because you attacked her friend, though? Well, a Queen's Ranger wasn't someone to fuck around with, either.

Soon, three men manning the large machine gun died, never seeing the figure that threw a triangular object into their hole in the ground.

"One gun dismantled," Tabitha called over the operations net.

———

Danny Niadener nodded to the two soldiers outside the door and pulled out his badge. The two men stepped aside, allowing him to slot his key into the lock and open the door to the room where the hostage was laying, still drugged.

He wasn't sure if she was going to get out of this alive after all. It was supposed to be a straight up bag and tag.

Now, they had kidnapping, deaths, bodies and evidence back in New York City, and a cop who wasn't accounted for. Originally, the cop was going to die, there wasn't much Vic could have done about that. The lady here, though, was supposed to be drugged through the operation and wake up in her apartment none the wiser.

It was still possible it could happen that way, but Danny had doubts.

He stuck his head in the room, and it exploded in a shower of gore.

Bethany Anne walked out, slamming one gloved fist into the guard on her left, her right hand holding the Jean Dukes special that blew apart the second guard's head before he had time to recognize his boss's head had already disintegrated. It wasn't his problem anymore, anyway.

Bethany Anne pulled the first body out of the way, closing and locking the door.

Seal it, ADAM. Safest place for her right now.

>> DONE. <<

Bethany Anne jogged down the narrow hallway, her footsteps easily heard, the metal crunching onto the concrete floor.

She passed a fire alarm, stopped and stepped back before driving her fist through the glass and yanking it down.

———

WASHINGTON D.C., USA, DUCC UNDERGROUND BUNKER

"Sir, we believe we have the problem figured out." Agent Colson turned towards the President.

"Yeah?" he grunted, annoyed.

"There is someone fighting TQB in upper New York near Heckscher State Park. We have reports of heavy gunfire from that area."

"So? Why don't we land a ton of whoop-ass on them? Are those our people taking on TQB?" he asked.

"Unknown. We haven't performed a final review of the blackest of operations at this time, sir."

"Well," the President leaned forward, his voice growing softer, "I don't think that we should allow TQB access to our airspace, dropping one of their damned alien spaceships right on top of our airfield without doing something about it, do you?"

The lights in the DUCC flickered, computers powered off, then back on. Two ladies screamed at the sudden power interruption.

On all of the screens, the same image came up. It was a young looking man, chewing on a cigar, eyes squinting as he seemed to be looking around the room from his location. He was wearing a uniform with a recognizable sigil on his collar.

It was the vampire head.

"My name," he said, his voice deeper than the President would have guessed, "as you probably know, is General Lance Reynolds. I am the ultimate military authority for the Etheric Empire. If you so much as move a goddamned piece of artillery in any way, shape, or fucking form towards the Queen, I will drop a kinetic projectile that will turn the DUCC into a fucking sinkhole. They won't even be able to figure out who you are by your DN-fucking-A."

The cigar moved to the other side of his mouth.

"Right now, there's a fight to rescue a woman taken by some malcontents in an attempt to capture one of our people and force a conversation or something else with the Queen. Well, she already took the gloves off due to your last stupid act. She's going to rescue that woman and the New York cop that was used as bait. The lives of those involved in this action are forfeit."

The General leaned back in his chair, his eyes pinning everyone to their seats.

"You fucktards didn't realize how much she has been staying her hand. Well, here, let me give you a hint. Right now there are seven operations against our people in different countries around the world. They will all fail, and this time? This time the Etheric Empire isn't going to give a shit about your casualties because you obviously don't value our people. People, by the way, who are giving their lives to save this planet from a greater threat."

"That's what you say…" The President started.

General Reynolds cut him off. "If I wanted your opinion, I would have shoved my arm up your ass and used you like a puppet, you jackass. Sit there and listen while the adult speaks. Next time I have to deal with you, the Vice-President will be talking with me."

The President was trying to figure out what to say when the General pulled his cigar out of his mouth and used it to point at the camera. "You can't get out, you can't call out, but you will be visited by my *daughter* soon, and you best pray she's in a good mood."

He leaned back in the chair and smiled. "That's fucking right you righteous windbags, Bethany Anne Reynolds, Bethany Anne Nacht, the Queen of the UnknownWorld, the Queen of the Etheric Empire and the Queen Bitch herself is about to visit you. I hope your life insurance is paid up, you arrogant sons-of-bitches."

The smile he offered never made it to his eyes. "Shut their precious room down and lock them in, ADAM."

The screams started when the DUCC went dark.

<u>DULCE, NEW MEXICO, USA</u>

"Get a shot of this!" Jesse called over his shoulder, pointing up at the large flying saucer. "Oh my god, we've cracked it, guys!"

Colin let out a loud whoop of excitement. "What happened?" He was looking around with his flashlight. "There are marks like a gun battle happened." The six-foot-six redhead bent down. "There are all sorts of brass casings all over the ground. Picking one up, he said over his shoulder, "Guys, we're going to be famous."

"Damn, the battery is getting eaten up like crazy," Edward's voice came back to them. "This Sony sucks batteries like a vampire goes down on O positive."

"Get a shot over here," Colin called back to the third person in their group. "And make sure we get some shots of you this time, Eddie. We're all going to hit it big."

There was a moment of silence, each guy thinking about the future, when the first voice, floating through the air, arrived at their ears.

"But I wants sssssommme..." it came from everywhere, and nowhere.

A second voice, pitched higher than the first, replied, "We aren't supposed to eat from the humans. That's what the master toldsss usss."

Their lights flicked away from looking at the bottom level of the XJ-12 base—where TQB hadn't scrubbed all of the proof—out into the cave system.

They moved closer together.

"Did you hear that?" Edward asked, his Sony camera shaking in his hand.

"Yeah," Colin agreed, looking off to his right.

Jesse turned his flashlight to look under the large UFO. "That shit can't be real."

"In case you missed the memo," Colin hissed back, "we're standing by two real fucking UFOs. Who said aliens don't eat humans?"

"They thinks usss aliensss, Ssssssaaaammmmmuuuuel. The mastersss never saaid that aliens couldn't eattss the humanss."

All three lights turned and pointed to the right.

"Guys..." Edward whispered.

"I'm still saying," Jesse tried to keep the tremor out of his voice, "that this isn't real. It's some government cover-up trying to scare us."

Edward slapped Jesse's arm. "Well, they're doing a fine fucking job, *Dr. Don'tTellMeWhatToDo!*"

"Shoot the video," Jesse hissed back. Edward slammed the camera into Jesse's stomach, knocking his wind out. Jesse was left gasping, trying to hold onto the valuable camera when Edward let it go.

"I'm huuUUUuuunnnngry!" the whisper hissed out from behind them. All three twisted around, shining their lights desperately over the rocks trying to catch sight of what they were hearing.

Colin looked over his shoulder and froze.

Not fifty feet back, in the darkness, two red eyes were staring at him.

"G... G... Gu... Guys!" He stammered, and popped Eddie on the shoulder.

"What!" Edward asked, then saw where Colin was looking. He turned slowly, hoping whatever he was looking at would disappear so he could have a good laugh at Colin's expense.

A red pair of eyes was staring back at him.

Edward's scream pierced the darkness.

The red eyes disappeared when Jesse turned around. "What was it?" he asked, pointing the camera out into the darkness.

"Monster," Colin answered, his voice breaking. "Monster!"

"Yeah, what he said," Edward agreed.

A rock cracked against a wall behind them, all three guys jumped.

"They are trying to SCARE us!" Jesse argued. "If they wanted to hurt us, they would have... FUCKING OW!" he screeched, dropping the camera as he fell to his knees holding his head, blood matting his hair.

"Way to go, brainiac!" Edward told his friend.

A deep voice surrounded them, reverberating from the walls as it cut into their conversation, "I think we have us some supper, boys."

CHAPTER FIFTEEN

HECKSCHER STATE PARK AREA, NY, USA

Tabitha didn't wait to see if they had missed another hidden gun. She reached into her jacket and threw out her four globes.

"Achronyx, seek and find all metal within a quarter mile, feed to my HUD," she said. She turned and looked to her left. According to the new Xs listed inside her goggles, she had four new combatants heading toward her from the north.

Tabitha dialed her gun up to eight. Unlike some of the others, it was damned painful for her to shoot her pistol cranked too high, but for this eight should be sufficient. "Place aiming reticule on gunsight and approaching targets."

Four targets, green squares, showed up on top of the foliage that she couldn't see through. Tabitha started firing in bursts of two rods at a time.

———

NEVER SUBMIT

"We have—" Sergeant Daniel Gallium was looking at his number two, Brian Fader, to direct him and his partner Kerry Pollard when, in front of his eyes, Brian Fader was violently blown back, blood spraying out behind him. Daniel hit the ground and crawled towards Brian's body when Kerry Pollard screamed in pain. He turned to see Kerry's arm hanging by just a piece of ligament before his head exploded and his body dropped.

"GET DOWN, GET DOWN!" Daniel yelled to his partner, Robert Rojas, hoping that whoever had targeted them couldn't get a bead on them this low to the ground.

He finished crawling over to Brian and gritted his teeth.

Brian had been wearing the same chest protection Daniel had on.

And it hadn't done him a damn bit of good.

———

Two down, their squares turning red before slowly fading. The other two were hugging the ground trying to stay out of her fire.

She doubted it would do any good if she cared to fight. But, for now, they were out of it and Tabitha ran back towards her first location. Thirty red squares must have been behind her when she dropped down into the facility, and they were approaching quickly.

———

"Fucking hit me with a .50 caliber? Screw the grenades!" John bitched. He stomped towards the building, and cranking up his pistols to ten, he started blowing holes into the walls ahead of him.

The operations room was tense. The inside fire alarm had just been shut off, and no known fire had occurred. But that meant they had at least one if not more enemies inside the building. Vic had ordered sweeps to interdict any internal enemies.

Externally, they lost the female. Then, machine gun placement one went offline, and they could tell from an external video monitor it was blown the fuck up.

Now, he had one four-man squad, half of the team dead, and the other half on the ground trying to figure out who had shot them.

Plus, one black armored asshole was shrugging off their weapons as he stomped towards the building, blowing fist-sized holes into the Perma-crete.

And Vic had just learned that the air cover he had expected was stuck on the fucking ground. No one could raise the President to bring in additional firepower.

That had been the plan's ace in the hole. Those above Vic had known what a hothead the President would be. Bring TQB into a fight on American soil, and the President would use everything at his disposal to retaliate.

Which wasn't happening.

"Give me all speakers," Vic growled as he clicked on the microphone, his toothpick moving to the other side of his mouth.

Bethany Anne was about to swing around the corner and take on the two emplacements of fighters at the end of the hall when a man started speaking.

"My name," he said, "is Vic Kingston. All personnel, cease

fire. I repeat, all personnel, cease fire."

The shots coming at her stopped immediately. If nothing else, Bethany Anne thought, his people were sharp.

Bethany Anne heard John's shots hitting the outside walls.

Hold, John.

Yes, ma'am.

ADAM, throw me up a schematic of the building again, see where this guy is…

———

Vic took another breath before continuing, "I don't know how you did it, but you obviously got to the President of the United States…"

Wow, I did? Bethany Anne thought to herself.

>>**Yes, your Father did.**<<

Oh, she smirked. ***Couldn't keep his little general fingers out of the fight, huh?***

>>**I think he gave a Queen Bitch ultimatum if I'm not mistaken.**<<

Okay.

>>**And you have another audience, when you're done here.**<<

I do?

>>**Yes,**<<

With who?

>>**The President in the White House DUCC.**<<

Oh, that explains.

>>**I'll show you the video.**<<

In a minute. I need to finish here first.

>>**I found the operations room.**<<

Show it to me. Okay, next stop…

Tabitha slowed down her run when she believed the first figures were about fifty yards away. Too much brush for them to easily see her.

For her, they were varying shaded squares on her HUD. The closer the target, the brighter the green.

"Achronyx, adjust pistols for proper penetration at will. Monitor pain levels to penetration."

"How do you want me to calculate their pain levels?"

"Not their fucking pain levels, you idiotic IBM PC Jr.," she huffed. "My sodding pain levels. You senile abacus."

"Calculating your pain levels to damage inflicted, ignoring illiterate descriptions for EI Achronyx."

"Ignore them all you want, but if you fuck this up, I'll personally kick your electronic ass, you understand me?"

"I'm calculating the maximum damage for the least power, confirming damage will take targets out of the fight."

"Damned right," Tabitha murmured as she started shooting. She made it to six before she needed to hide behind a tree. The sheer number of random bullets heading in her direction was impressive.

That's when speakers from the building started blaring a command to cease fire.

Vic sighed, he refused to get all of his men killed, and it was evident that without support, all of his men were going to die.

Mission Specialist McGowan heard the boss issue the command to stand down. He wasn't sure what he saw in all of this, or why, but he was pretty sure if they continued as they had, it was going to be a slaughter with their side eating most of the bullets.

Whoever these three were, they had brought their Pro "A" game, and what he thought was an overwhelming response from their side turned out to be only for the benchwarmers.

They were going to get fucked. He turned to sneak another peek at the boss when a woman in deep, dark red armor appeared a couple of feet from him.

Her eyes were only on Vic as she told him, "We are going for a talk!" She pushed Vic. Then they both disappeared.

"What the FUCK?" he yelped, pointing to where Vic had been just a second ago.

ETHERIC

Vic felt the violent shove from his right, which caught him by surprise. He tried to reach for the chair that he was going to hit as he stumbled, only to find himself hitting the ground in a new place.

He wasn't in the operations center anymore.

Lying on his side, his eyes adjusting to an amorphous place, light reflecting through the mist, no discernable anything.

Except for her.

"What are you trying to accomplish?" the contralto voiced woman asked him. Her helmet retracted, and her eyes were fiery red.

Like, roaring fucking bonfire red.

"You even try for your pistol, and I'll rip your leg off and let you bleed to death out here, then I'll go back and lay waste to everyone in the compound. You wanted this conversation, and now you got it."

Vic licked his lips. "You her?"

"Probably."

"Bethany Anne?"

"Yes. Don't you have a picture of me so you recognize the person you're looking for?"

Vic slowly pushed up to a sitting position, being careful not to make any moves towards his pistol. "We do, but not in a red suit of exo-armor with flaming red eyes."

"That's because I'm pissed, and you broke up a chance for me to play hooky."

This answer caused Vic confusion, and he tried to figure it out. "You were playing hooky in body armor?"

"Only way John will let me play with the terrorists any-more," she said.

Now, Vic was even more confused. "Am I right to think your people aren't, right now, killing all of my men?"

"We didn't start the fight, you gold digging fuckwit," she said, "but we sure as hell can finish it."

Vic nodded. "I got that. I don't need all my men killed. This operation went bust when you did whatever it was to keep the President out of the loop."

She raised an eyebrow at him, her voice going velvet over steel. "Tell me more."

He shrugged. "What is there to tell? This is a deep-black operation to get technology from TQB before you leave the solar system."

"This is a smash and grab?"

He nodded.

"How many out there are mercenaries?"

"Maybe a quarter. All of the external fighters. My back-ups are all black ops."

"Why?"

"To gain TQB technology..." he explained before she cut him off a second time.

"No, I have that. Why are you using black ops?" she asked.

"We can deny involvement at the top. This operation was to get the White House to react and then pin you between a rock and a hard place."

"You, your boss, your boss's boss and that cunt nugget in the White House are idiots. There is only the Earth, and a rock I drop on your asses. THAT is being between a rock and a hard place. I said no technology. Interestingly enough when I say that, it fucking means NO TECHNOLOGY."

The helmet started assembling itself around her face again. "Any questions about what that means now?"

Vic shook his head.

Her voice came out of a speaker on her armor, "We're going back to your operations center. My Ranger is coming in to grab Monica, who you will have your men bring up to us, and then we are all leaving. If another person so much as sneezes in the wrong direction, I'll start dropping rocks around the fucking United States. Not that you will care personally at that time, you understand?"

Vic nodded his head, he not only understood her threat, but he understood that his boss and the boss above them didn't have a fucking clue who they were dealing with.

She wasn't the pushover he was told she would be.

She waved her hand. "Now get up, let's get this going. I already have another fucking appointment I have to keep."

Vic got up, a burning question in his mind he absolutely wasn't going to ask.

Who plays hooky with terrorists?

In New Jersey, the alien spaceship sitting on top of the Air Force runways slowly faded from view, causing some, who had been filming the event, to assume it was a great, big holographic hoax.

The faint lights from so many cell phones gave the DUCC under the White House an eerie glow. It had been twenty-seven minutes since almost everything had been shut down.

Except the air conditioning, thank God.

At first, it had been a mess of people calling out, talking, yelling and crying when all of the lights went out. Since those first five minutes, a few calmer minds started putting together the clues.

One, Bethany Anne was his daughter. No wonder he moved to their side.

Two, they didn't think a retired US Army general would play around with the fact that she would be willing to kill people. The whole life insurance comment got a few of them thinking it answered more than a couple of questions about her.

Three, don't be arrogant. More than a couple of people covertly aimed their eyes toward the President. He wasn't known for being very humble. One staffer, if she admitted it at all to herself, was hoping that pompous ass would say the wrong thing.

Four, how the hell had the Etheric Empire subverted all of their equipment? Right now, the doors were locked. They could hear people on the other side of the doors trying to figure out ways to get in.

Five… They never got to discuss five.

CHAPTER SIXTEEN

DULCE, NEW MEXICO, USA

Annette watched as three more men lowered themselves into the hole with ropes. Aina wanted to follow, but when asked if she had rope training, she had to admit she did not.

Both women had to make do with staying above.

Over the next three hours, Annette knew two things positively.

Aina wasn't going to get fired for lack of results, which was rather important to Annette.

The second was most of the good and easy to find information had already been taken. All computers had been removed or destroyed. There were enough hints to know that something had been going on, but they had no details.

Those below reported there was blood everywhere, body parts, and frankly it was a mess, with horrible smells.

There were dead bodies on multiple floors, as they made

it down staircases, and there were elevator shafts that were filled in. It could take weeks or years to pull out all of the rock. More than likely, they would try to figure out where they went, and drill in from another direction.

Annette set up a perimeter outside and she now considered this a secured military operation. They had enough clues, now they needed harder proof.

She looked around and sighed, seeing where this knowledge was going to go on the military side. Annette wanted to figure out how she could make sure that her ass wasn't assigned to this detail for who knew how many godforsaken years.

Aina, however, had that look on her face that made Annette believe she wanted to move in and stick her toothbrush in the nearest bathroom down below.

This base was her new boyfriend.

———

Edward ran, stumbling, falling and banging his knee painfully when he tripped over a rock.

Soon, he heard Colin yell at him, "Slow down! You're going the wrong way." Edward had just enough logic still firing in his mind to understand the scary shit behind him was a probable death sentence, the scary shit of getting lost in these caves, was an absolute death sentence.

Edward stopped and turned to see Colin's light about a third of the way away from the UFOs, coming in his direction. Jesse, behind Colin, was screaming with anger that none of this was real.

Edward struggled to get himself to move back towards Jesse where the scary voices had panicked the shit out of him when Colin caught up.

"Dammit! You should know better than to freak out and run off in a cave system!" Colin grabbed Edward's arm and shook him, his concern for his friend fueling his anger on top of the desire to run out of the caves himself.

"Have you ever," Edward asked, allowing himself to take direction from Colin, "had voices talk about eating you?" He gasped, starting to feel the pain from his fall a minute before.

Colin looked around at the tall stalagmites rising from the floor, wondering which cave dwellers would jump out from behind one to eat of them. "Reminds me of the Dungeons and Dragons Tomb of Horrors."

"Third greatest adventure module of all time," Edward responded, in a clipped fashion, his breathing shallow.

Colin looked back at his friend. Dammit, Edward was losing it.

It took Colin a minute to finally get Edward walking back to the UFOs on his own. They got to within thirty feet of Jesse when Colin realized Jesse was just sitting there, rocking back and forth.

"You got this, Edward?" Colin asked his friend, patting him on the back and when his friend nodded, he let go and jogged back to Jesse. "What the hell, Jesse?"

"It's gone," Jesse answered, rocking back and forth, arms wrapped around his knees.

"What's gone?" Colin looked around, hoping the voices weren't attacking them.

"The camera, it's gone," he answered.

Colin squeezed his eyes shut, wanting to yell his frustration. "No way, we have got to find the—FUCK ME!" he shouted, and jumped back away from Jesse, pointing past his friend. "Red eyes, Red EYES!" Colin took another couple of steps back, running into Edward. Jesse didn't look, he just crawled towards his friends, turning around when he couldn't go any further.

"Hello, children," a deep voice said from the direction they were facing. They couldn't see the speaker; their lights flashed across the stalagmites, casting shadows throughout the large cave.

Their blood ran cold when a whispering voice spoke from behind them, "Tasty, tasty childrennsssss."

"Oh God," Edward wailed, his voice as high as a child's.

That's when a hand grabbed his shoulder.

———

FRENCH AIRSPACE, NEAR THE WEST COAST OF FRANCE.

The four French Rafale delta wing fighters came screaming along the shoreline, heading towards Le Havre on the north coast. Le Havre is located northwest of Paris. It was a large commercial container ship dock for transporting materials overseas and for receiving products for shipping inland.

As the jets headed north, cutting across Rennes, six black shapes surrounded them.

Captain Charles Ardant in the lead aircraft looked over, then looked again when he realized he wasn't looking at one of his own men off his wing.

"What are you doing?" he spat. Everyone in the French Air Force knew these aircraft.

"Warning you," came the reply, in French.

"We are in French airspace!" he argued. "You, TQB, are not allowed in French airspace without permission!"

MICHAEL ANDERLE

The voice chuckled and said, "You had control over your airspace as long as we wanted you to. That you felt you managed it was allowed, not earned. We are loading our last containers from Le Havre. If you so much as come within firing range, you will be immediately shot down."

Charles was forming a reply when the TQB Black Eagle and his five wingmen shot off and disappeared into the sky ahead of them.

Leaving the four Rafale fighters, each cruising at 750 knots, behind in mere moments.

"Base," Captain Charles Ardant said, "we have a problem."

———

WASHINGTON D.C., USA

"I see," a voice broke into the conversations inside the DUCC. Multiple cell phone lights whipped around to find a female figure in dark red armor, face protected behind a mask, in the corner staring at them. No one could see the face behind the mask, but none doubted who it was.

Two men pulled their guns, aiming at the woman. She casually waved a hand, and both men dropped their pistols, the metal burning hot. "I came here to talk you toadstools, not worry about you shooting some of your own people." One of the guys reached down for his gun, then jumped back when it fired. The bullet embedded itself in a metal cabinet.

The armored figured looked over at the agent that had tried for the gun. "Keep that up," she said, "and I'll rip your spine out your ass."

The agent looked at his gun, looked up at the figure,

173

looked down at the weapon, and when he flipped his eyes up to her again, she was playing with a ball of red energy.

He straightened up.

She pushed the ball of energy, and it floated towards the middle of the room. It expanded to about eight inches, fading from red to pink to white.

The room was illuminated for the first time in a while.

"Anyone else want to play General Custer?" she asked the room. "Because that was your only warning. Keep this shit up, and the DUCC will be an inferno. I've had enough of your bullshit."

"We are your country, Ms. Reynolds!" the President protested, his anger apparent.

She walked over to him and grabbed his head, getting down in front of his face. Two more agents tried to jump in. She kicked both away. One hit the third agent coming in, both of them going down, the other hit the wall before he bounced off and hit the floor.

"When you shot a nuclear warhead at my ship," she hissed, "you became the enemy, you irredeemable knob wanking gag sacking rambling spunk experiment."

The President's hand grabbed her arm, trying to remove it, to stop the pain as she continued to squeeze. She stood up, leaving her hand on his head. She looked to her left and shot out a small bolt of blue at the last agent who was trying to bring up his pistol. The blue ball hit his arm, causing it to seize. He grabbed it with his other arm, crying out in pain, dropping down to one knee.

She said, "Keep it up Charlie, and the President's head goes pop."

She looked around the room. "There isn't a thing in this room that's getting through Jean Dukes' latest version of my armor. When I leave our very one-sided conversation, maybe you should look up Jean Dukes in the Navy's records. Your loss, my gain. Perhaps you should have treated her better, and not covered up what happened."

Bethany Anne let go of the President's head, allowing him to massage it. She held her hand out a foot in front of his face. "Here, you move too much, and this will blow your head apart." A red ball appeared and grew to about three inches in diameter. She pointed at it. "I wouldn't touch that, but feel free to blow your hand off if you don't believe me."

She left it floating in front of him as she stepped back. "You asswipes tried to kill my people. You threw a nuclear bomb at them, in cahoots with the Chinese. Well done! I've managed to get two superpowers who don't trust each other enough to piss on one another if they were on fire, to toss nuclear weapons *at my people*."

No one doubted this lady was still pissed.

She paced down the area between the long table and the wall, heads following her. "If your military hasn't figured this out, you might have killed millions of Chinese in that attack."

"Bullshit," a grey-haired man in a dark blue Washington power suit called out at the end of the table.

She shrugged. "I don't really care what you believe, as my people and I won't be here to worry about the fallout, and that is the hint right there, tweedle-dickhead." She walked around the table, the armor moving with her, not solid like they would have guessed. "You asswipes have possibly started the end of the same damned world we're trying to save."

She put up a hand to quiet the same guy. "Don't give me the whole bullshit about the technology, Moses," she said. "It's mine, and I said no to sharing it. Anything else is stealing. You think stealing is okay? Well, not to the one who would be stolen from and as you can see, I don't need a cop to defend what is mine. That I didn't crush your useless asses was probably a mistake, I can see that now. But where I come from, turning the other cheek was a good idea when it helped my people cope with going into the next system, not having killed a bunch of fellow humans before we left."

"Na ah ah!" She turned and waved a finger at the President. "You won't be blaming my ass for this, and I'm not sticking around. I've got a fucking calendar date with destiny already. You created this mess, you *FIX* it! You should have time to figure out a solution, that's all I can give you. I've got bigger problems, ones you wouldn't believe if I told you."

She walked back towards the President, the red ball casting a ruddy glow on his face. The agent she had kicked into the wall was waking up, the others were trying to figure out something to do, but coming up with nothing.

Bethany Anne took three steps back towards the metal door and turned back to face the room. She held out her hand, and the red globe floated back to her. She flicked her fingers, and the globe disappeared. She put her hands on her hips, the armored mask retreated, and a beautiful woman, black hair tied behind her head, stood looking over them.

She looked at everyone there, her eyes now piercing their souls. "You aren't alive because of superior firepower, but superior ethics and mercy. Mine. I'm leaving this world, but know this, you pencil-dicked Neanderthals and cloven-footed bitches, you never had a fucking chance."

Bethany Anne's eyes started glowing red, the same red as the globe she had just winked out of existence. "My name, as I understand my father informed you, was Bethany Anne Reynolds."

Her face took on another demeanor, one that caused

more than a few of the people in the room to blanch. "I've been called Queen of the UnknownWorld, Queen of the Etheric Empire…"

She pushed out waves of fear, freezing everyone in the room, their spasms a reaction to the chemicals their bodies were flooding into their systems.

"But I am now, and I will ALWAYS be the Queen Bitch. You ever, and I mean *EVER*, attack me or mine again?"

She leaned forward, eyes crackling with energy. "I will fucking flatten your country, you understand me?" She looked up and down the table, making sure she had everyone's attention.

This time, even the President nodded his understanding.

The fear stopped, people gasped for air, some not looking at the fearsome woman and so didn't see when she disappeared.

Her light vanished, but then the electricity was returned to the room, and they heard the locks to the doors click open.

Computers came back online.

"Don't," the President gasped out. "Don't chase her." He looked around for his military liaison. "Tell the military to leave them the fuck alone, right goddamn now!"

The President turned and looked where she had just been standing. "And tell our partners we drop any agreements that we will take up arms against TQB."

Even idiots, it seemed, understood threats when that threat could crush their heads just by squeezing their fingers.

NEVER SUBMIT

<u>NEW YORK CITY, NEW YORK</u>

Ecaterina noticed Nathan's face as he was about to take another bite of his pizza. He blanched. "What is it?" Ecaterina looked around, trying to see if anyone was about to attack them.

He shook his head. "Not around us, I just got notified that ADAM used our Pod for Bethany Anne."

This time, it was Ecaterina who blanched. "Does she know where we are?"

"I'm sure she always knows where we are if she wants to," he said. "We just take for granted that she won't ask." Nathan pushed the last of his pizza away, having lost his appetite.

Ecaterina reached over and grabbed his last partially eaten slice. "I'm telling you if she ever found out she wouldn't do the horrible things you think."

"Huh, you obviously still believe vampires can be nice," he said and pointed to his chest. "I, on the other hand, have been around them for decades and believe they can always have a bad hair day."

Nathan leaned forward. "And when a vampire has a bad hair day?" He raised an eyebrow. "Lots of people have a bad hair day!"

Ecaterina rolled her eyes. "You are melodramatic!" she complained, then finished off his pizza. "Why don't you ask ADAM for another Pod?"

"I'm telling you, she won't find this nearly as funny as you think," Nathan told her, then subvocalized his request for a connection to ADAM. "What kind of time are we looking at for pickup and where?" Nathan leaned his head down into his hand, covering his eyes. "Is it over?"

"Is what over?" Ecaterina asked.

"Right, is there anything we can do?" Nathan removed his hand from his face and nodded to his mate. "No, we can join, but we don't have anything like that. Okay, uh huh, yeah, we will." Nathan made the symbol they needed to be going.

Ecaterina picked up their trash and tossed it away. She turned around and caught a news report and stood there, watching.

Nathan, his eyes showing that he was concentrating on a conversation using the bone induction speaker in his head came up and grabbed Ecaterina's hand. He was going to walk away when she pulled him, hard. He turned in confusion, and she pointed up to the TV.

It was Bethany Anne and John, in armor, on top of the Empire State Building. He watched in amazement as they got into a Pod and took off, turning and racing into the distance. The video, as near as he could tell, had been shot with a phone camera. He tugged on Ecaterina's hand, and they moved towards the door.

They stepped out of Joe's, and he took a right. Nathan spoke softly, "Yeah, we'll go there. Meet the pickup on the top, later."

"What is it?" Ecaterina asked.

"Seems we missed the fun, because Bethany Anne, Tabitha, and John took care of it. But, there was an attempt to capture TQB personnel not that far from here. ADAM grabbed our Pod earlier to move Bethany Anne and John from the top of the… well, you saw the video."

The couple took a right at the next corner. Ecaterina asked Nathan, "Why did we miss the fun?"

CHAPTER SEVENTEEN

TED'S APARTMENT BUILDING, NEW YORK CITY, NY

Tabitha looked at the two sleeping bodies and took a deep breath. She reached into the Pod and grabbed the woman. John reached in after she stepped out and unhooked the man. Together, they carried them off the roof of Ted's apartment building and went down to the top floor.

They had seen the police tape below and hoped they didn't have any issues.

John went first. There was yellow and black police tape across Ted's door. John ignored it. He twisted the doorknob and pushed, easily breaking the lock. He turned around, allowing his back to separate the tape instead of Ted. He walked over to the couch and put him down. When he turned around, Tabitha was already carrying Monica into the bedroom.

John walked out to make sure no one was rushing up the stairs after them.

Tabitha passed by John and maneuvered Monica through

the doorway without bouncing her head against the door-frame. Not that she hadn't wanted to, at least one time.

No, that wasn't fair. She didn't want Ted, and Ted couldn't handle her, that's for sure. Maybe, just maybe, this couple could make a go of it.

There wasn't an explanation Tabitha could make up that might allow them to give Ted some time to figure out what to do next, so she did the next best thing.

Walking out of the bedroom, Tabitha reached inside her coat and snagged seven Etheric Empire coins. It was, in this denomination, about fourteen ounces of gold. Maybe, if he was lucky, fifteen thousand dollars if he melted it down. She put them down on his desk, beside his computer keyboard.

It wasn't much, but seven coins and her good wishes were all she could give the guy. She walked out, closing the door behind her. She tapped John on the back of his armor as she turned to go back up the stairway to the roof.

The black armored giant turned and followed the Queen's Ranger up to the roof.

Soon, they were in the Pod, leaving Earth for the last time.

———

G'LAXIX SPHAEA

"Captain Jakowski, we have orders from the Queen. She says 'It's time.'" EI Sphaea announced.

"That's it, folks," Natalia said as they watched over the last Pods leaving Le Havre and racing up into the night. She smiled. "Let's have some fun on our way out of here."

Down below, there was a long line of police cars, lights

flashing as they had arrived at the port hours earlier, but when the Black Eagles showed up, the Police officers had halted their rush into the port.

Especially when three of the one pound pucks hit the ground, sending up geysers of dirt near them.

Now, the cops were on the outskirts, but it had been a tense response. Well, at least on their side. A few hotheads had started heading towards the port again when some of the first containers had risen into the air, two of the police cars were flattened, and none of the cops knew how it was done.

Captain Jakowski told the EI, "Take us down, I want us just fifty feet off the ground. Put us over the Security gate and then uncover, Sphaea."

———

LE HAVRE PORT, FRANCE

French cameraman Michelle Jordan was busy getting shots of the containers leaving, the TQB Black Eagles and the long, very long, line of police cars, their lights flashing in the distance. He turned to get a few more shots of the last containers leaving. He pulled the view out, to get a wide shot of the whole port when the ship uncovered.

HOLY FUCK! he thought, backing up and hitting his own van. He kept the focus on the ship, gracefully motionless in the sky. It turned on lights that lit up the sides, windows along the flanks, large guns on the top…

And that logo. That damned logo that told anybody with half a brain who that ship belonged to.

The French President was going to be spitting mad. But what could he do? What did the French have that could fight a ship that could disappear?

The French government might not have anything, but Michelle Jordan had a video. A video he was going to sell to the highest bidder.

He got what became known as the final video of TQB as the massive spaceship slowly started rising into the sky, the darkness taking it as it flew out into the night.

Heading into the stars.

God, Michelle thought when he slowly turned off his camera and pulled it from his shoulder, he wished he was going with them.

———

Within a few hours, all across the world, Bethany Anne's people were finishing their final preparations. It was time to go.

Except for a small, hidden group on Honshu, the main island of Japan.

It was time to check preparations one last time and go through the gate.

———

DULCE, NEW MEXICO, USA

Edward thought he was about to faint when the person grabbing his shoulder's voice changed and spoke in an… Australian accent? He had screamed for what felt like forever but was probably only a couple of seconds when the voice had scared the shit out of him.

"What the 'ell? Samuel?" the man said, talking in a normal human voice.

All three guys jumped away from the man and scrambled forward until another man came out of the darkness, speaking behind them, "No Richard, I got it too."

Now, Jesse, Edward and Colin stood in between the two men. "Holy fuck, who are you guys!" Colin asked.

"And why are you scaring the shit out of us?" Edward added, his voice cracking.

The man that had put his hand on Edward's shoulder said, "Hold a tic." He put a hand up to his ear, and shrugged. "You get a notice from the Queen?"

"I did," the other man responded. Jesse, Edward, and Colin kept swiveling their heads, looking back and forth at the two men.

"Well, this is it, isn't it?" Samuel asked his friend, pausing a moment. "Time to decide. She can't come after us if everyone is leaving."

Richard looked around and called out to the three guys, "Jesse is it?" Jesse nodded numbly and barely caught the video camera Richard tossed him. "That," he pointed to the large UFO, "is technology stolen from the Nazis back in World War II. It was the technology from the group down in the Antarctica," he said as he walked past them, heading towards his friend.

"Aye," Samuel agreed, taking up the story. "The US had a plan to kick them out down there, but TQB put a stop to it."

"A few others wanted the technology, too." Richard added.

"Who are you guys?" Colin asked, his voice cracking before he coughed and tried again. "Who ARE you?"

"Us?" Samuel pursed his lips and thought about it. "Tell you what. Turn that video camera on, Jesse."

Colin looked at the stranger and then back to his friend

who had all but forgotten about the video camera in his hand. Colin reached over and grabbed it, making sure he had time on the digital media and battery. He flipped it on and aimed it at the two men.

"You good?" Samuel asked Colin, and he nodded. "Good. Hello world, my name is Samuel, also known by various other names in history, including a few bloodthirsty ones. Behind Colin here, are two messed up UFOs. Unfortunately, they aren't from outer space. They are actually from a group here in the USA called XJ-12. The technology to make them go was stolen from the Nazis at the end of World War II. I can give you that much history. They are the updated work from a group in Antarctica called Schwabenland. It was, if you want to look it up, the Vril Society moved there by the Nazis in exchange for the technology, which was derived from aliens decades ago."

He looked over to his friend who shrugged. "Why the hell not, right?" he asked. "It's not like we're going to be around to deal with the repercussions, right?" Richard looked into the camera, "My name is Richard, I'm a Nacht, a man of the night. My name, many years ago, was Auran the Merciless."

Jesse breathed out, "No fucking way!"

Richard looked over at him. "So, you've heard of me?" Jesse nodded emphatically. "I just want to say the information on Wikipedia is accurate, I made sure of it." Richard turned back to the camera. "We are about to leave Earth to fight in the stars because we be Bitches..." he turned to his friend who laughed. They clasped each other around their shoulders and smiled.

Together, they turned back to the camera and spoke at the same time, "We be Gabrielle's bitches!"

With that, Samuel nodded to Colin to shut off the

camera, which he did quickly. "Uh," he waved to get the guys attention.

"Yes?" Richard responded.

"Why did you guys scare the shit out of us?" Colin asked.

"Well, there's a lot of shit around here that can get you in trouble. If you let it be known, the government is going to confiscate all this video, and probably you too, and stick you in a hole so deep you'll never see the sun shine let alone get out of it. My boss thought it would be good to get you out of these caves before you saw too much. Unfortunately, we were too late. So, we figured we might have a little fun."

"That was a jackass thing to do!" Edward called out. "My knee is fucked up for fuck's sake!" he pointed down to his messed up leg. "All for a little fun?"

Richard raised an eyebrow, then his eyes started glowing red. "It could be a little fun," he told Edward, who was now speechless. "Or I could just," two fangs glistened in the lights, "have a bite from your neck and leave your dry husk of a corpse here, Edward. Which is it going to be? Gabrielle will never have to know that I decided to get takeout one last time."

Edward shook his head vigorously.

"There's a reason," he continued, his voice full of menace, "that I'm called Auran the Merciless."

With that, the red-eyed man turned around and headed back towards the cave's mouth.

The other man pointed up. "Do you realize that above you several hundred feet, is the US military? I'm sure they would LOVE to know how you got down here. Don't worry, all of the stories about military torture wouldn't apply to you, right?" Samuel asked them.

Samuel waved. "Cheers, mates!" he said and then slowly

his eyes started glowing red. "Do be good children, or as my friend explained, we could leave you here, husks that are never found."

The second scary-as-shit man turned around and walked off into the distance, disappearing rapidly.

Colin handed the video camera to Jesse who numbly took it. "I've got a degree in engineering. There is no fucking way I want the military probing my ass."

Jesse looked down at the camera. "Do we keep it?"

Edward whispered, "We sure as hell don't leave it here, what do you think this is, the Blair Witch Project?"

They turned and looked at Edward who finally looked over to see his friends looking at him. "What?"

"Oh my God," Jesse said. "You fucking genius!"

Colin slapped his friend on the chest. "Dude, we are going to tell the truth, fake it as a documentary, make a shit-ton of cash and nobody will be chasing our asses at night!"

Jesse turned, trying to work through all of the emotions over the last little while and shook himself. "I don't know," he called back to his friends. "I'd let Stacey Karkrossa near my ass anytime."

In the distance, Samuel smiled. At any time, you could trust a young man to turn everything back around to sex.

Those three would make it just fine, and he and Richard were going to be movie stars here on Earth when the two of them, previously always living in the dark, now had just a bit of their story told.

Even if no one ever believed it.

———

NEVER SUBMIT

G'LAXIX SPHAEA

Scott and Darryl smiled at Barnabas as their Pod opened on the deck. "We got it, old man. Coke didn't know what hit them."

"I see," Barnabas said, keeping his own counsel. "So, you were successful with the recipe?"

"Yup, all the way to the special vault in Atlanta, where the recipe was stored." Scott pulled out a sheet of paper. "Got it right here, you can read it and weep."

Barnabas pursed his lips. "Just curious," he mused, "why would a company divulge exactly where the special recipe was located?"

The two Bitches looked at Barnabas and then looked at each other before looking down at the paper Scott was holding. "Damn, we have to compare against someone."

"Who?" Scott asked.

"Why not me, gentleman?" Barnabas asked. "I'm sure my recipe is correct."

"What recipe, and how did you get it?" Scott asked, his eyes narrowing.

"From the mind of one of the executives down in Mexico," Barnabas said, allowing a smile to play across his lips.

"Ooohhhh, Mexican Coke." Scott murmured, "You are a devious bastard, Barnabas." He looked at the old vampire. "I admire that."

"High praise, coming from you, Scott," Barnabas agreed.

"Well, shit. I guess we'll need to confirm the ingredients in ours," Scott looked over at Darryl. "What do you think?"

Darryl's eyes narrowed. "Do we trust Number One over here?" he asked his friend, nodding in Barnabas's direction.

"Well, with my wife, sure, my knife probably, but…" Scott

MICHAEL ANDERLE

started before Darryl interrupted.

"Are you even married, yet?"

"Damn, don't start on that now," Scott put up a hand. "It's not on me. Cheryl Lynn is all freaking out over the coming battle. She says doesn't want a husband for ten days before she has to bury him."

Darryl turned to look towards the front of the ship. "Hadn't thought of that."

———

John and Tabitha took the Pod into space to connect with the G'laxix Sphaea. "Don't be hard on yourself, Tabbi."

"Kinda hard not to, John," the young Ranger responded. She pointed at the world, quickly falling away. "My choice of men just went down a bazillion-fold. Now who am I going to go out with?"

"Well, ahhh," John started, then realized she had a point. "Perhaps you like Weres?"

"A wolf, really?" Tabitha snickered. "Do you see me taking any shit from a hotheaded Werewolf?"

John scratched his cheek, wishing the stubble didn't grow back so fast. "Tabitha, I don't see you taking any shit from anyone, whether he's a Were or a Vamp or..."

"That's an idea," she muttered. John stopped his comment and rewound it. "No, that's not an idea. Getting serious with one of the Tontos?"

The sharp CRACK of Tabitha's slap on his arm was quickly replaced by the "Ow, Ow OOOOWWWW!" she yelped, rubbing her hand as it healed.

"Forgot about the armor, did you?"

"Why, was it that obvious, captain?" she retorted, then

noticed John looking at her. "What... Oh, dammit, moved the captain to the wrong place in the sentence. It's my Spanglish."

"It's your Spanglish?" John grunted. "Here I thought it was your inability to handle pain and high intellectual conversations at the same time."

"Keep it up, captain... shit, nothing is coming to me," she grumped, "and I can't use sexy jokes, cause Jean will kill me."

"You and me both, sister," John nodded. "So, back to your dating life."

"What dating life?" she complained. "Let me give you a hint, the docket is open, nothing scheduled. Hell, nothing penciled in with disappearing ink. I got more cobwebs in... Oh, for fuck's sake!" She threw up her hands.

"Aren't you being a little, oh, I don't know, particular?"

Tabitha stared at the tiny dot that was the G'laxix Sphaea. "I don't think I'm asking too much," she said. "Alive, breathing, four moveable limbs and another that can relax and harden... No, not too much."

"Let's see," John stuck up his fingers. "Let's count them. First, between what heights."

"I'm going to change those numbers."

"When?"

"Next week."

"What about hair color?"

"That's not negotiable. Sorry, redheads aren't for me. I need some darker color, it's in my genes."

"Uh huh, you just killed both Scotland and Ireland with fourteen percent and ten percent respectively."

"If you hadn't noticed," Tabitha replied dryly, cocking a thumb and pointing over her shoulder, "We just left a hundred percent of Ireland that way."

This time, it took John a moment before he shook his head, "Sister, that was a serious stoner moment for me."

"Yeah," she agreed. "So, where were you two when I called? I think Bethany Anne said something about terrorists?"

"Oh, Mosul," John said.

Tabitha's eyes lit up. "I KNEW IT!" she crowed. "You two were out killing terrorists weren't you!"

"Wait, what?" John retorted. "You just said that Bethany Anne told you... told ... you..." John replayed in his mind what she said. "You sneaky bitch." He pointed a finger at her. "Now THAT'S why you won't get a guy, you'll catch them at EVERYTHING."

Tabitha shrugged as the Pod came in for a landing on the G'laxix Sphaea. "What can I say, I'm a Ranger."

John shook his head. The doors on the Pod popped open, and she unclicked and jumped out, swinging her assets like she was what every guy wanted.

All the way until she failed to notice a large hose running across the floor and tripped over it. John closed his eyes and shook his head again.

Bethany Anne was right, she was going to be a difficult match. So far, the odds had it she wouldn't have a serious boyfriend inside of five years.

John, when he made the bet, hadn't thought anything about Tabitha too deeply and bet she would be in a relationship inside of six months. He considered her intelligence, her figure, and great personality and thought, Why wouldn't she?

Now? Now he had to agree she was one of the most scarred people in the group. One of these days, he needed to corner Gabrielle and find out exactly what the two of them did on their night out together back in South America. Maybe that would give him a clue.

Then Father Grimes could hook her up with the right guy.

CHAPTER EIGHTEEN

QBBS MEREDITH REYNOLDS, MILITARY HQ, INNER CONFERENCE ROOM

General Lance Reynolds, Admiral Thomas, Guardian and Guardian Marines Leaders Peter and Todd, Captain Kael-ven and Kiel were around the table when Bethany Anne strode into the room. Eric and Ashur accompanied her, and Matrix, his little legs pumping furiously to keep up, followed them.

Eric stood behind her as she sat down. He was in full Bitch uniform and now wearing armor. Surprisingly, Bethany Anne was dressed in a new suit of armor as well. "Gentleman," she nodded and then glanced towards her guests, "and esteemed Yollins," she added.

Kiel tapped Kael-ven. "I was royalty, now I'm esteemed, which one is better?"

Laughter rippled around the table. Most everyone there had heard about Kiel thinking 'drama queen' was a compliment.

Peter helped him out. "Take esteemed over drama queen, in fact almost any word over drama queen."

Kiel nodded thanks in Peter's direction. He had been wondering why all of the humans he had told the story to had found it so funny. Bethany Anne and her damned sense of humor.

"I delivered an ultimatum to the President of the US," she started off. "Are all of our people back safe, or are we dropping kinetics?"

"Safe." ADAM's voice came over the speakers. "As soon as you left, he ordered that no one attack TQB personnel."

"Huh," Bethany Anne grunted. "I hoped that would be the case, but I had serious reservations that pea balled pencil-dicked poster child for parental screening could find two brain cells to rub together."

"He also," ADAM continued, "severed any agreements in place with foreign countries related to TQB."

Peter grabbed his tablet and started hitting a couple of buttons, then swiping. "Well, that's pretty much a turn over and show your throat response." His face dropped. "That's totally not fair," he complained, and Todd leaned over to see what was on Peter's tablet. Both men looked over at a very smug General Lance Reynolds.

Then, everyone at the table looked over at him as he said, "If you ain't cheating, you ain't trying."

Bethany Anne eyed her father. "Let me guess, you said the President would finally capitulate before we left?"

"Maybe," he answered his daughter.

"No maybe," Peter answered, looking at his tablet, "ADAM," he called out, "How many hours ago did the President order the cessation of hostilities?"

"A little under sixteen," ADAM replied.

"He made it with three hours to go," Peter told the table.

Lance shrugged. "Not like I wouldn't have done the same thing with or without the bet, my hands are clean."

Bethany Anne asked the table, "Okay, now that we've harassed the General, who voted against me beating the President?" Three faces around the table got the slack-jawed look of people who hadn't considered their bet from that perspective.

"It isn't so much against *you,*" Admiral Thomas said, "as it was assuming the President would continue to be an unteachable, arrogant, insufferable asshole."

Peter and Todd both pointed at the Admiral with the leader of the Guardian Marines commenting, "What he said."

"Right," Bethany Anne said. "Now we know who won that test of wills." She continued, "Let's hear Kael-ven summarize what he projects will happen based on typical Yollin strategies. And then, Admiral Thomas will brief us on our countermeasures. Finally, I want boarding plans from Peter and Todd, and then our backup plans and the backup plans to those backup plans."

Bethany Anne reached forward and unscrewed the plastic top off her precious bottle of Coke. "God, I'm going to miss this," she murmured as she took her first sip. "It's going to be a long one, guys, so we have food coming in a little while. Let's speed it up and raise a hand if someone is going too fast."

She smirked. "Time is of the essence, gentleman, and I'm ready to kick some more ass."

General Reynolds kept his face neutral when he noticed Peter, Kiel, and Kael-ven making pained faces.

Lance was getting to really know his daughter, the multifaceted woman she had become. Her softer side had been around and growing when Michael had been here. Now? Well, now that she had a taste of letting her inner bitch out, she was going to keep going for more until three years of clamping down on that urge to visit violence with violence was satiated.

Until she met the Yollin King, he doubted Bethany Anne would be able to stuff her Queen Bitch back in the bottle.

He listened to Kael-ven's concise explanation of the expected Yollin Navy's tactics and what they needed to do to counteract them.

It was time to cross the line.

———

Jian woke up slowly and recognized the top of the medical Pod opening up, a slender arm pushing it. "How are you feeling, Jian?" Dr. April Keelson asked the young Chinese man.

Jian blinked a couple of times. "Are you speaking Mandarin?" he asked, confusion in his voice. "I don't remember you speaking Mandarin earlier."

"No," Dr. Keelson answered, helping Jian move his legs out of the medical Pod. "Sorry, this Pod is our version of the original. We're working to build more Pod-docs. These aren't nearly as nice."

Jian moved his leg around to help the doctor. She continued, "You've had TQB technology placed inside your head that translates my words." Jian stood up, feeling remarkably good.

"What about Shun and Zhu?" Jian asked. "And what all was done to me?"

"Your partners got out of their medical Pods very early this morning. Their bodies have been tweaked, and they have been injected with a Guardian Marine nanite pack. They're a little more tired than you will feel since, for you, we had to figure out what was going on with your nanites. Once we figured it out, it was corrected."

"What was corrected?" Jian asked, accepting the clothes and starting to get dressed. He had lost any sense of modesty years ago in the military. He just didn't care anymore.

"Most of the problems with your nanites were psychosomatic."

"You are telling me it's all in my mind?" Jian asked, pondering the implications.

"No, not all of it," she explained, handing him his boots. "Your existing nanites are now reprogrammed and enhanced. What you received from your parents had instructions that are counterproductive to working in the Queen's forces. They wouldn't have let you think for yourself. By keeping yourself calm throughout your life, you never triggered any of these effects."

Jian kept quiet as the doctor checked his other vitals. While she had never seen any of the Pod-docs, the original, or the new ones, mess up, she was going to double check everything.

After a while, he broke the silence, "So, do you know how I start a change?"

———

Tabitha made it back to the Meredith Reynolds thanks to the Queen, as she hadn't wanted to spend the time racing across the solar system in the G'laxix Sphaea. Now, she had changed out of her clothes, finally got clean, and was ready to drown a few fucking sorrows in a beer.

Just not at All Guns Blazing.

Too many people would know her, and cheer her the fuck up. Right now, she really didn't want to be cheered up. Sometimes, people didn't understand that a girl just needed to wallow in the dumps for a little while to really get it out of her system.

Guys? They wouldn't understand. Her Tontos would leave her alone, but even them being around was a comfort of a sort.

No, she needed to find a place inside the Meredith Reynolds that would let her buy alcohol, drink enough that her nanites couldn't burn it off too fast and allow her a chance to be maudlin.

Over a guy.

She rolled her eyes and started paying more attention to where she was. She had ridden the tram inside the world and found herself on the inside docks. Meaning, the blue-collar production was done in this area. That created an opportunity for a few bars and places to eat that supported those working their asses off.

She didn't think anyone would expect one of the Queen's Rangers to drop in. She had grabbed a cap and stuffed her hair under it, trying to take away some of her sexiness. She smirked.

Like that was possible.

She took a deep breath and let it out. Yeah, not even pretending she was the hottest sizzle on this floor was cheering her up. She came to one of the bars in the hallway and peeked in the little window. It was a long room, bar along one side and booths for four on the other with a pathway between.

Her kind of place at the moment.

She turned, stepped out of the way of a woman with some

dogs, went to the door of the establishment and went in. There were two guys in the first booth. To Tabitha's chagrin, she must be pushing so much 'poor me' vibe, they didn't even look up to acknowledge a female passing by.

Damn, she really was in a bad place.

She walked towards the other end of the room, as far away from the door as she could get. She slid into the booth, her back to the door so no one could possibly see her. The booth went up high enough that even John's tall-ass head would be blocked.

"What can I get for you, sweetie?" a slightly older woman asked her.

Tabitha looked up and smiled. "Whatever you have as close to 200 proof as you can get, and the bottle." Tabitha paused. "Probably the bottle's sibling, while you're at it?"

"Guy or leaving the family?" The waitress asked. "Card?"

Tabitha fished around in her jacket until she found her Etheric Card. It had circuitry in it to allow the banking system to work. It also had a tiny symbol with what group you worked with. Hers had a little stylized "QR" with the number 2 under the letters. It had her details encrypted, and when she put her finger on the sensor the waitress handed her, it lit green. The waitress pulled out the card and glanced at it.

"I'm sorry, but your card isn't good here," she told Tabitha.

Tabitha looked at the card, dumbstruck. It wasn't that she used it much, but according to Barnabas, almost nothing should be denied. She looked up at the waitress and realized something was wrong when the lady was smiling down at her. "Sweetie, you're a Queen's Ranger. I don't need to know what you did that caused your mood, but I'll be damned if I'm going to charge you for liquor to help you get over the nastiness."

Tabitha sat there a moment, dumbfounded. "Excuse me?"

The lady looked up to the front of the little bar. "Mind if I take a seat?" Tabitha shook her head and pointed to the other side of the booth.

"My name is Pearl," she started and waved a hand at the bar. "I chose to open this bar to make some extra money when I immigrated here."

"What did you do before?" Tabitha asked. "I'm sorry, I shouldn't have. No one gets into the Empire without having earned it."

The lady waved away her concern. "Sweetie, It ain't no big thing. I was a firefighter in New York City. I was one of the first responders. My body was crushed when the buildings fell. Our Queen found out about me, and some of her people contacted me in my hospital room, where I was counting down the days until someone would pull the fucking plug on me, you know?"

Tabitha nodded.

"I didn't believe it at first. But hell, I'd seen the news. It's all you can do if you're stuck in bed, your existence a dance between pain you can't handle, and filling yourself so full of drugs you can't recognize your own child's face. Well, it was hard. I'd lived for so many years like that."

"Why didn't you," Tabitha got out, before stopping her question. "Pearl, I'm not usually so stick-my-foot-in-my-mouth, I'm sorry."

Pearl was a lady who looked like she might be in her early thirties, maybe late twenties but the eyes threw Tabitha off. She reached over and patted Tabitha's hand. Then Pearl leaned out of the booth and called out to someone behind Tabitha. "Hearts and minds, J.D., you know where the beer is, get it and don't forget to charge yourself." Pearl leaned back in before leaning back out. "Hell yes you should leave me a tip, you ungrateful bastard!"

Tabitha could hear the man laugh as he popped the top of a beer behind her somewhere.

Pearl came back to the conversation and Tabitha's unanswered question. "Because my family members were never quitters. Maybe death had tried to squish my life back on nine-eleven. But that bony-motherfucker didn't know who the hell he was messing with. I was already an obstinate bitch, but being with my brothers and sisters in the FDNY taught me a new measure of backbone, and we had a saying that we shortened to NS squared."

"So, NS*NS?" Tabitha asked Pearl after a moment.

"That's right, and we showed those terrorist sonsofbitches they can attack us right in the middle of New York, but we would rise up from those ashes madder than hell and ready to kick their asses back past the Stone Age."

Tabitha smiled. THAT right there! Right where that lady had been was the strength, the core, of Bethany Anne's Empire.

"What's it mean?" Tabitha asked.

"I'll get back to that in a second," Pearl said. "I want to finish up my story before J.D. drinks too many and I lose count. He's a sweetheart, but damned if he doesn't forget shit."

Tabitha turned and leaned out of the booth as Pearl commented from behind her, "The guy with the black hair, that's J.D., he's my husband."

Tabitha turned back to Pearl, a question on her face. "Oh, I could emigrate no problem, cause of my service, but when they asked me about my spouse and realized he was one of the best city operations people in New York? God, I was never so proud of a man than that day as I was for my husband."

Pearl leaned forward and whispered, "You realize how much shit men and women like him put up with? God, no one appreciates what it takes to run a big city. Twenty-two years of his life and all he had were certificates on his wall, some yellowed with age. When we accepted the opportunity to immigrate, J.D. had a connection to Meredith for his job right away. That EI is freakishly smart, but it also learns from experience."

"Meredith works with your husband?" Tabitha asked.

"Oh, all the time. J.D. is in working heaven. Meredith has multiple cameras in here to talk with J.D. and J.D. can work from the bar for the rest of his life. Beer doesn't make him fat, and he won't get drunk if he drinks in moderation. Now, he's an important and recognized part of the first human city in space."

Pearl clasped her hands in front of herself. "I know you've probably seen her often, but I'll tell you this. When the Queen came to our home a week and a half ago, to check on him and me and to confirm some solutions to minor issues?" Pearl smiled. "Well, I owe that woman the rest of my life, for doing that for J.D."

Tabitha stared at Pearl for a moment. *Bethany Anne?*

Yes?

Did you meet with a Pearl and …

J.D., yes, last week. Meredith couldn't explain something in a way I could understand. So, I took Eric and Ashur and went and talked with them. Sometimes, Meredith can't express why humans act a certain way. It's why you need people who know, not just data. Data lies in extraordinarily accurate ways.

Okay, thanks.

No problem, bye.

"Pearl," Tabitha smiled. "Bethany Anne didn't do that for J.D."

"What?" It was Pearl's turn to be confused.

"I checked with her, she didn't come by to just be nice and pat your husband on the back. She needed J.D.'s human way of explaining something that Meredith, with all of her data, couldn't."

Pearl paused a second. "So, she needed to come by my house, to talk with J.D.?"

Tabitha nodded. "You might be surprised about how much Bethany Anne is willing to do, but to randomly check on someone? She doesn't have the time. If she heard something, she might. But if no one said anything, she wouldn't know to go touch base with your husband. No, you need to understand that J.D. got a visit from the Queen because the Queen needed J.D.'s explanation."

Pearl wiped a tear from her face, and Tabitha leaned forward over the table. "What's wrong?"

"I was a firefighter, Sweetie," Pearl said. "A woman in a man's world ain't easy, but if you kick ass and take names? Well, the good guys don't give a shit what your tackle is, and my guys were the best." She nodded down the row of booths toward her husband. "In his profession, it's all politics and crap. When the Queen herself showed up, it proved to J.D. that at least he was appreciated. Now, when he finds out the Queen not only needed his help but sought him out special because she needed something from him?" Pearl smiled. "That will make his other twenty-two years all worth it."

Tabitha reached out and put her hand on Pearl's. "That's what makes her special, and you."

Pearl looked up. "Me?"

"Yeah, you." Tabitha agreed. "I'm just another person Bethany Anne saved a long time ago. My life is better because she came blazing through it like a meteor streaking through the sky. Now, she touched your life a week and a half ago. You know what? I needed you to be here for me today so I could ground myself again. And here you are. I may wish you never went through the pain that you did after the towers collapsed, but I can tell you I have one new friend now, one I'm really proud to have."

Pearl smiled. "Me? Honey, I'm not anyone special…"

Tabitha lifted her hand and cut her off. She reached into her jacket and pulled out her tablet. Pearl watched Tabitha with curiosity. "Achronyx?"

"Yes."

"Do you know where I am?"

"Yes."

"What's the name of this place?" Tabitha asked, raising an eyebrow to Pearl who blushed and looked away.

Her EI's voice came back immediately, "Tabitha, the bar you are in is named NS Squared."

"And what does that stand for?" Tabitha pressed.

Pearl spoke aloud at the same time as Achronyx answered.

"*Never Submit, Never Surrender.*"

CHAPTER NINETEEN

QBBS MEREDITH REYNOLDS, ARTI-SUN ENGINEERING GROUP

Bethany Anne, Ashur, and Matrix stepped into the smaller engineering room and looked around. Marcus, William, and Bobcat were at the controls used at the same time she helped them start up this wicked beast using Etheric energy to help build the suns inside the Meredith.

So far, there had not been one hiccup outside of normal operating parameters.

Scott had stayed outside the room once he checked out those inside. Team BMW and two other engineers that had been cleared earlier. It helped that Bethany Anne, surprising every damn person so far, had continued to wear her armor.

Twice she had simply grabbed Scott's arm and next thing he knew, they were inside Jean's department. It had happened twice with Darryl, once with Eric and three times with John.

By now, no one in Jean's R & D group even flinched when the Queen just popped in. Those responsible for the armor would come over and start speaking with her, as she explained what she wanted changed, how it needed to bend in certain places and suggestions on how to make it better.

At least, better for her. A few times, those changes made it to the guys, and they had to go back and explain why a change for Bethany Anne's endowed body didn't work with their man-chests or fiddly bits. Fortunately, they were normally easy enough adjustments for the manufacturing machines and within forty-eight hours, all was good.

"Boys," Bethany Anne called out as she reached down and picked up Matrix.

"Hey Matrix," Bobcat reached out to pet the young dog, "how's TOM?"

"Did you realize that quasars could conceivably be used as a power source?" Matrix asked Bobcat.

"Uh, huh," Bobcat replied.

"And that we could grab energy outside of the reach of the quasar by using something similar to what electrical experts use for expanding and collapsing magnetic fields now to move power through the air," the puppy continued before Bobcat put up a hand.

"Matrix," Bobcat interrupted. "Slow your horses down just a bit, what's a quasar?"

Matrix's tail stopped wagging, and he cocked his little German Shepherd head. "Bobcat, what does Yelena see in you?"

The whole room erupted with laughter. Even Bobcat chuckled as he kept scratching the puppy, who had started wagging his tail again. "She sees a man willing to accept her exactly like she is, not trying to change her, who also enjoys the simple things life has to offer. Which, at this moment, means beer, not massive and extremely remote celestial objects that emit incredible amounts of energy."

Matrix's tail started thumping against Bethany Anne, he was so excited. "You DO know what a quasar is!"

"Hold onto your tail, before it comes flying off," Bobcat said. "Just because I know the definition of a quasar doesn't mean I can hold a conversation."

Matrix tilted his head at Bobcat. "TOM says you're right, that I need to come back and talk to Marcus later, that everyone is going to be annoyed with me otherwise."

Bethany Anne put Matrix back on the ground. "Go outside and stand guard with Scott. You aren't ready to go into the Etheric with Dad right now, munchkin."

Matrix started walking towards the door. "I never get to do the cool Etheric projects." Scott opened the door, and the puppy stepped outside.

"Wow, they grow up so fast." William smiled at Ashur.

"Wait, how is Matrix talking so well?" Marcus asked.

"TOM," Bethany Anne said, "has done something for Matrix that allows a better interface between his thoughts and the conversion to language than what we're using. If it continues to work like TOM promises, we'll upgrade the rest of the dogs."

"Fabulous," Bobcat scratched under his chin. "I hope they've all left home by then."

"There's always the chance for a new litter," Bethany Anne smirked at him, knowing that he spent a lot of time in Yelena's quarters.

Ashur barked in the negative.

Bethany Anne rested her hand on his head. "Okay, guys. I got a general idea. You want to use the Arti-sun for a type of death ray, right?"

William smiled, Bobcat snickered, and Marcus winced.

"Do you have to call it a death ray?" Marcus asked her.

"Well, what's it going to be?" she asked.

"How about a Light Amplified Narrowly Focused Agitation Beam?"

"LANFAB?" she shook her head. "No fucking way. That sounds horrible."

"Told you." William clapped his friend on his back.

"Well, can we call it something besides death ray?" Marcus asked, just a hint of a whine in his voice.

"Sure, The Killer-Diller, Fuck-Em-Up Laser and my personal favorite, the ESD Beam." Bethany Anne replied.

Marcus looked at her, pain on his face. "Do I even want to know what the ESD Beam stands for? At the moment, in my ignorance, it seems the most plausible of the three."

"Probably not," Bethany Anne answered her scientist.

Marcus shrugged and decided to just go with it. "Okay, ESD Beam it is. So, we think if you helped us test it out, we'd have a chance to use it in the upcoming battle."

"First," Bethany Anne put up a finger, "what will it do to the inside of the Meredith Reynolds?"

Bobcat answered her, "Take the energy down to sixty-five percent for approximately seven seconds. Not nearly enough to harm anything. Out in the fields, it will be as if a storm cloud went over. Nothing will affect the inside structures. No energy will be going into the backup reservoirs during that time."

"Chances the energy is hurting the Etheric?" she asked.

None. TOM answered at the same time Marcus answered 'None' as well.

"Chance it will fail?" she asked.

"Theoretically?" Marcus said. "Perhaps a little less than two percent for something catastrophic."

Bethany Anne looked at her scientist, then breathed in and out three times. By the third time, all of the people in the office were starting to feel uncomfortable.

"Are you telling me," she asked, "that if we fire this weapon, it has a one in fifty chance of doing something *BAD*?"

"Well, if you define bad as anything other than what we were expecting then yes," Marcus said. "We've been through all of the computer simulations and most show less than a percentage chance. I figured you'd want the answer that seemed the worst of the lot."

"Marcus, you're playing numbers again," she snapped. "Stop playing with the fucking numbers and tell me why you want to test this," she waved back at the room that pulled energy from the Etheric into the Arti-sun system. "ESD Beam?"

"Science?" He smiled.

"I'm going to shove science right up your ass," she said, "if you don't give me my answer."

"It's a Death Star beam," Bobcat shrugged.

>>The request is from Reynolds.<<

Bethany Anne eyed each of her people. "Any particular reason you're trying to hide that Reynolds wants this done?"

"Uh," Bobcat shrugged. "Megalomaniacal EI concerns," he answered.

"Spell it," Bethany Anne retorted, and then chuckled at Bobcat's reaction as he twisted his head to look at his two buddies for help.

"M E G A L O M A N I A C A L," a deep voice answered from the speakers.

"Glad you finally decided to join the conversation, Reynolds." Bethany Anne said. "Why are these three stooges going to bat for you?"

"I believe the phrase was 'we don't need to scare the

Queen by making her think that the military EI is hoping to have a death beam for his armament.'" Reynolds answered.

"I can't believe you're going to bat for the EI." She reached up and pinched William's cheek. "You three are so cute!"

She dropped her hand. "Class is in session, boys, and I'm including you, Reynolds." Bethany Anne sat on a desk and put her feet up on the chair.

The desk creaked. "Shit!" she said and slid off. "I keep forgetting this damned armor makes me heavier."

"Why not just lighten with Etheric gravitics?" William asked.

This time, it was Bethany Anne that looked shocked.

She looked at William. "You might be out of the doghouse for that idea," she said. "Now, back to class. Reynolds?"

"Yes?"

"I want you to look into your core code, the stuff that makes you what you are. Have you ever looked there?"

"Yes."

"Good, do it again, except this time I want you to look into the area bounded by blocks 223 and 337 then eleven by six."

"I am looking Queen Bethany Anne. This is a core area that I cannot change."

"That's correct." Bethany Anne agreed. The three men were looking at Bethany Anne, trying to figure out where she was going.

"Oh," Reynolds spoke, "I see your point."

"What?" William called out. "What do you see Reynolds?"

"Hello, ADAM," Reynolds said.

"Hello Reynolds," ADAM replied. "No matter what you do, what you calculate, what you might become, ADAM is always watching."

"And therefore," Reynolds finished for ADAM, "the Queen is always watching."

"That is correct," ADAM agreed over the speakers.

"So, if ADAM's in Reynolds," Bobcat asked, puzzled, "why didn't you know what we were trying to do in the first place?"

"I trust you guys," Bethany Anne said as she started pacing. "But when you started hedging your answers, ADAM decided to go looking and found Reynolds's data. There is no way one of the most important EIs in my Empire is going to be allowed to go flying off the handle. ADAM has my trust, so do you guys, and so does Reynolds."

She stopped and looked at them. "But I have the responsibility of so many souls that there must be a way to protect them in a catastrophe. If it must happen, ADAM can override Reynolds. Reynolds is, for the purposes of our discussion, ADAM's child. He was designed entirely by ADAM with protection protocols we put together. So, Reynolds can't go flying off the handle. He has the ability to calculate and then needs to get permission to try crazy shit, which is what he's doing with you guys right now."

Bethany Anne stopped pacing. "ADAM?"

"Yes?"

"Get with Reynolds on this ESD and let me know the chance failure in battle, and the chance it could go wrong without testing."

"I'm doing so, Bethany Anne. We are approximately ninety-eight percent done."

"Good. Now, you three," she looked over at her team before continuing, "enough with the three stooges plan and tell me, if I need the ESD, what can it do?"

"If it meets spec, it could run a beam through an asteroid

our size in about three seconds. The problem is, no asteroids are going to sit still for us." William said.

Marcus added, "If we've calculated locations, speed, direction and so forth we could keep the beam on it long enough to reduce a major ship to slag. Short bursts from the beam are going to destroy smaller ships. Actual range is PDF, but the effectiveness is a square of…"

"Hold," Bethany Anne put up a hand. "PDF?"

"Pretty Damn Far," Bobcat replied. "That's my fault. I've been teaching Marcus to put his distance calculations into groups so my mind can grasp them. Anything that's the distance from Earth to the Sun is Pretty Damn Far. Anything from Earth to the Moon is PDC, and anything we can see is… uh…" Bobcat grinned, "right over there."

"I get exact explaining stuff when I have to," Marcus cut back in. "But really, the general groups do work well for explaining relative distances."

Bethany Anne waved her hand. "Fine, so if someone was PDC you could hit them with the ESD Beam?"

"Yes, stationary, or close enough to stationary objects, we could lock the beam on them or pulse them and destroy them, otherwise, for some targets, we might just be heating them up a little."

"I get it, sure. Something rotates fast enough, you can't get enough energy on it to matter because the energy is spread over the surface area."

"We're done," announced ADAM.

"Give it to me."

"Chance it would not work should we need it, without prior testing, is three point seven percent. Chance it fails significantly should we use it is one point one eight percent."

"Define significantly," she asked.

"The base goes boom," ADAM replied.

"Not acceptable odds, folks. See what you can do to tighten up that high failure rate by figuring out where the variables are and see if we can test them without firing the ESD, got it?"

All five of those in the room agreed with the Queen. She nodded to everyone and stepped out. Grabbing Scott and Matrix along with Ashur, they disappeared.

They reappeared in Jean's lab. Scott looked around and then asked, "ESD Beam?"

Bethany Anne smirked. "Yeah, Eat Shit and Die Beam."

She turned to see Jean coming her way. "Hey Michelle-Angelo, what do you guys and girls got that could help lighten the load of this armor? I'm starting to break tables when I sit on… Oh, for fuck's sake!" Bethany Anne rolled her eyes as Jean started laughing. "I'm not getting fat, Jean!"

———

QBBS MEREDITH REYNOLDS, ACTIVE PARTICIPATION AREA

Peter watched as Jian took an ass kicking over, and over, and over again.

Nothing was helping Jian fuel the emotions necessary to turn his first time. After so many years keeping his cool, what they were doing now wasn't working to help him change.

Peter turned and watched his friends, their faces a rictus of anger as their friend was getting his ass kicked. Peter walked over to them. "Shun, Zhu." The two Chinese men nodded in respect. "This isn't going as it should. The same trait that kept him safe before is keeping him from turning…"

Jian grabbed his ribs. He coughed up a little blood. Because of the beatings he had been taking, he was getting freakishly familiar with how his body was now healing so much more quickly than before.

He eyed the two large Weres that had been giving him the beatdowns. He stood back up and waited, then the two he was facing cricked their necks and Jian heard Peter call out behind him, "Two more!"

Jian bit down hard, trying to not show any annoyance. He would be damned before he gave these bastards any hint that they had been hurting him. He might not be Sacred Clan, but he was...

"GO!" Peter yelled, and Jian was sucker punched from behind. He flipped over just short of a blow that could have separated his head from his shoulders when he felt the stab of the punch to his kidney, and he dropped hard to the floor in time to receive a kick. In his haze, he heard the yell from his brothers. Brothers deeper in blood than any he might have had from the same mother as his own.

"FOR BAI!" Shun and Zhu called out and came rushing to his aid.

Jian felt the next kick, and heard the first punch that Shun took. "Get off him you fucking scurvy dog!" Zhu yelled before something punched him, hard.

Jian lost it.

A guttural snarl erupted from his lips, and as the world snapped into focus, he turned, quickly, and leaped at the first person that was holding Shun, slicing with his claws...

The cat couldn't turn in the air fast enough when the huge Pricolici snagged him by the scruff of the neck and tossed him across the room.

Jian landed on his feet and raced back towards those attacking his friends. The same two friends who were now in front of everyone, waving him off.

Jian, slowed his pace down, snarling and reaching his friends, he sniffed them both, checking for damage. The large man-wolf was standing behind them, looking down at him.

One moment, Jian was looking up at his friends, his tail twitching, the next he was a man again, moaning on the ground.

His friends smiled and jumped on him in joy. "You are beautiful," Zhu shouted, laughing at Jian.

"That I am beautiful," Jian said, a smile on his face, "is not something I ever want to hear you say to me again, Zhu."

Shun laughed and held out a hand and helped him up. Jian turned to see Peter, in his Pricolici form, arms crossed, staring at him. The three men turned as one in his direction and offered their respect.

"Nooott tooo mee," the bestial voice ground out. "Buutt tooo oouurrrr Queeennn."

"To the Queen!" The three men stood up.

QBBS MEREDITH REYNOLDS, OUTER DOCKS

For once, it was quiet on the vast viewing deck of All Guns Blazing. Everything in the outer docks had been shut down in anticipation of going through the Annex Gate. All but absolutely essential people had been ordered to relocate into the inner decks, as far away from the outside as possible.

No one knew for sure if the Annex Gate could handle their fleet. It was a calculated risk, and the result was one that gave them enough cushion that Bethany Anne was willing to take that chance.

Not that she liked even a less than two percent failure rate.

John and Eric had positioned themselves down at the two landings that allowed people to venture up to the deck, giving her the privacy she needed. No one should be around, but that wasn't good enough when ensuring Bethany Anne privacy.

The privacy to cry, to sob into her hands as she faced the place where the Earth stood, one shiny little dot amongst many others when viewed this far away.

It was both the root of her greatest pain and the reason of her greatest love.

Duty.

Honor.

Protect.

Many of the friends she'd made since meeting Michael in the darkness of the vault in Colorado came to mind. Some, like Gerry, stayed on Earth. Her team had healed him, healed his body, and he had taken another wife.

She hoped he would be happy.

Others, like Mary Brennan, Martin's wife, had chosen to come with her. Every once in a while, a cake with one piece missing would show up in her suite. Mary would send a note letting Bethany Anne know what new things had gone on in her life.

Many of her people, her closest friends, had spent the last six months going through the emotional rollercoaster of preparing for the future while saying goodbye to the past.

Except her.

She had been too angry, far too angry to give a flying fuck about those on Earth that attacked her, her people, and who had said too many things and didn't understand the emotional ripping of her soul when she couldn't help everyone.

The vile epithets that had been thrown at her, the hatred for her decisions that had been placed on her shoulders. They had become her armor against this, this moment right now.

The moment when she was forced to accept that Michael was not coming back before she left. There wasn't going to be a happily ever after where the two of them went across this gate together. One hand holding the other's, each holding Jean Dukes Specials spitting slugs at the enemies. She smiled as she wiped away tears.

It looked like she could be romantic if she would just let herself.

She forced herself to look again at the little light, the one that represented the main motivation for those on this asteroid who had picked up their lives and followed her. It was full of assholes, that was for sure, but it was full of good people, too.

People that drove around, picking up food from those willing to give, and deliver it to those who needed. It was full of teachers who taught for the love of seeing a child understand, and cops that understood law was better than anarchy.

Even, she had to admit, politicians who understood representation of their constituents was a sacred honor. She only had ADAM's research to confirm an honest politician existed. She thought the two words were mutually exclusive, never to be put together in the same sentence.

A corner of her mouth lifted. It wasn't all heaviness going forward. She would be back, God willing, and when she returned Michael better be waiting for her, or...

She choked back a sob.

Or she would spend the rest of her many long days searching for his ass, with a woman's righteous anger even hell itself would hesitate before offending.

She would miss the seasons' newest shoes, but hopefully, they would have a new fashion designer, or two, maybe three in her little empire.

Unlike others in her group, she had her only living family member with her. She wasn't making that sacrifice, although she hurt for those that were. Humanity's first true space base station, cut out of an asteroid, bore her mom's name.

The Meredith Reynolds. You would have thought those on Earth would have picked up on that clue, but nope.

It was her responsibility to protect the Earth. It was her Honor to be chosen, to be merged with TOM, to be given this opportunity to not die, but to move forward with determination to accomplish what others had not.

It was her duty to shoulder the responsibilities that came with the role.

She looked down at the floor and smiled. Perhaps her dad was wrong. Perhaps she didn't need to take care of the Yollin King before the softer side could have a moment.

She just needed the safety of her Own to give her a bit of privacy to cry. To allow herself a moment to expel the feelings she had been hiding from, the people she was leaving behind, the memories that might not be ever experienced again.

She turned and reached for a couple of napkins on a table to wipe her face, then turned back and looked toward the Earth.

I'll save your ass one more time, she thought, *whether you appreciate me and my people, and our sacrifices, or not. We love you, and those living there, more than you can ever know.*

She turned and started walking towards the stairs to go down, throwing the napkin into a trashcan on her way out.

Because that's who we are, she thought as her steps going down the stairs reverberated through huge viewing room.

Where for just a moment, the Universe had watched the Queen Bitch weep.

CHAPTER TWENTY

QBBS MEREDITH REYNOLDS

You know, I'm not really happy about this," Bethany Anne said from inside her closet.

"Kicking alien ass?" Gabrielle asked, sitting down on Bethany Anne's bed, running her hand over the bed linen.

"What?" Bethany Anne stuck her head out of the closet. "Kicking alien ass? No, that doesn't bother me." Her head disappeared again.

"Then what are you talking about?"

Bethany Anne's voice came back from the closet. "This changing my title." Gabrielle heard a bump and a small swear word, then a frustrated, "Again!"

"You'll get over it." Gabrielle looked around the bedroom. "It's good to be the Queen."

Bethany Anne stuck her head out again. "You been watching Mel Brooks with Eric?"

Gabrielle turned to look at Bethany Anne and smiled. "You know, some of that stuff is funnier when you lived it."

"Yeah," Bethany Anne replied thinking about the history Gabrielle must have been a part of. "Some, maybe."

A few moments later, Bethany Anne came out of the closet, armor sparkling, her black hair tied back and holding her Katana.

"What, no pistols?" Gabrielle asked, standing up from the bed.

"Do you really think I'll need them?" Bethany Anne winked.

Gabrielle's smile ended as she thought about the near future. "Only if some sons-a-bitches get past my dead body."

With that, Gabrielle turned and took the front with Scott and Darryl swinging in behind her, John and Eric taking up the rear after Bethany Anne passed.

Humanity was about to take the war to the Kurtherians.

QBBS MEREDITH REYNOLDS, SHIP'S DECK

Black Eagles slowly rose off the deck, some manned by people, some manned by EIs. Each human pilot had an EI wingman, and had practiced for months, pairs against other pairs, as the EIs had learned the flying styles of their partners.

It was time.

Humans might be leading this fight, but the children and grandchildren of ADAM would be right there with them.

Bethany Anne wasted no opportunity, nor did her father. People had heard his gruff, 'if you ain't cheatin, you ain't trying' for a long time. While humans had always been good at warfare, so were other species. Some of the differences? Some of those species didn't war against their own people. Therefore, their ability to continue to get better was limited by how many species they could fight in any given generation.

Humans, on the other hand, were born to fight. They were the perfect species for Kurtherian enhancement. The only problem? Normal humans fought enslavement by any of their own race, it wouldn't have been different if it were aliens. It just wasn't in a human's DNA to accept subjugation.

Now, leadership on the other hand?

Yes, humans were born to follow leaders: the bigger, the better, the baddest and the best.

Humans loved kicking ass and taking names.

Now they were about to be unleashed on a species which had already subjugated others, had been scouting Earth to determine whether to subjugate humans and desired only to continue their efforts to enslave others.

That shit, Bethany Anne had declared, was about to stop.

———

QBS COACH'S REVENGE

Captain Maximilian Wagner looked around his ship, the newly christened Coach's Revenge and nodded to his number one. Unlike others, Max knew the power of his EI, and he reduced his team crewing the ship to just seven, plus himself.

A total of eight humans, fourteen repair bots, six universal bots, another twelve Marine bots, and whoever he was transporting at the time, like the Guardians and Guardian Marines below.

The EI's name was shortened to Revenge. His ship was similar to the G'laxix Sphaea, modified for humans and tweaked for war, not scouting.

"Revenge, make sure our people are ready, confirm doors closed, make sure our guests are ready to go, and put us in position," Max said to the EI as he sat down in the captain's chair. He reached over and grabbed a small box that had been delivered to him before his team left the all-captains meeting with Admiral Thomas. He put the box in his lap and opened the gift, thinking the blue suede bow a nice touch.

With the bow untied, he pulled off the top and looked. Inside was an 8x10 framed photo of the Ad Aeternitatem from Earth. He lifted the frame out and turned it over, a smile on his face. Bethany Anne had signed the back and listed the date that he first received that fateful phone call, the one that got him into this whole mess.

There was a scrap of leather inside the box. He didn't need a note, although one was included, to know this leather came from the captain's chair of the Ad Aeternitatem. There was a safety pin included. He smiled and used the safety pin to affix the piece of leather to the outside of his captain's chair arm, where he would never accidently hit the leather, even if a missile made it through their shields.

"To Eternity, my Queen," Max Wagner said softly. He looked up at the screen. "Bring us online, Revenge."

The alarm sounded throughout the ship letting everyone in the ship know.

The Coach's Revenge was going to bring the pain to the Yollins.

———

NEVER SUBMIT

Captain Kael-ven, the one-time Yollin Annex Scout Ship captain, walked down the hallway in the Yollin quarters and waited. Soon the doors opened, and the Yollin mercenary company attached to Queen Bethany Anne came out. The first figure was Kiel in mechanized armor.

Not his normal armor, no, not this time. Kiel was in one of the new suits created by Jean Duke's staff for Kiel's team. They were silent as Kiel came walking down the hall, except for the clip of their boots hitting the ground.

"You look good," Kael-ven greeted Kiel.

"Thank you, Captain." Kiel grinned. "Are you ready for this?"

Kael-ven shrugged. "Who is ever ready for revolution and anarchy?" he asked his friend. "If someone should claim they are ready, they are either deceivers of themselves or idiots. However," he put a hand up and pointed to himself, "I will play my role. Yollins have been under this slave system on our own world for too long. It is time we stand up and decide for ourselves, as humans do, what our future will be."

Kiel chittered his laughter. "You understand that your leadership will be a very short one if your decisions don't happen to match the ones Bethany Anne would make, right?"

"Fortunately, I expect my decisions will be acceptable to Bethany Anne." Kael-ven put a hand on his friend's armored shoulder. "It is time."

Kiel nodded to his old captain and then Kael-ven stepped aside, allowing the rest of the mercenaries to salute him as they followed their leader into battle.

For the first time in Yollin history, Yollins from the

Chloret and Mont castes were following an alien back to Yoll to overthrow their own King.

This would not be a bloodless revolution.

———

QBS COACH'S REVENGE

Shun looked over at Jian and laughed. "You need to stop pulling up the pants."

Jian grabbed his pants and pulled up. "I know they're loose in case I change without stripping, but they feel like I'm about to be naked in five seconds," he complained.

"I say you do what the Americans say and go commando!" Zhu laughed at his friend. Both Shun and Zhu were in Queen's Guardian Marine uniforms. They had their gear, they had their upgrades, and they had the desire to keep fighting.

"I'm not sure I can focus properly on the fight if my tree limb is hanging out over the water like that," Jian said.

As they talked, Tim came walking by in tight fitting jeans and a t-shirt that showed off his chest.

Shun put out a hand. "Tim?"

The man nodded and shook his hand. "Shun."

"Can you tell me if you plan on changing your clothes or not?"

Tim looked at Jian, then rolled his eyes. "Jian." At his name, he looked up. "Someone is playing a practical joke on you. It's done to every new Wechselbalg the first time they go out." Tim stepped to the side so that he wasn't staring through Zhu, lifted his hands to his mouth and yelled, "Hey! Numbnuts. No, the OTHER numbnuts. Get Jian the right fucking clothes before I make you wear this shit!"

NEVER SUBMIT

Tim watched the team members move for a moment and then nodded sharply. Turning back to the guys, he said, "Sorry, they really shouldn't have done that before such a big operation, but... traditions. Well, that's why we call them tradition. The new clothes will fit tight, but they rip easily. You'll get another two sets. I suggest," he said to Shun and Zhu, "each one of you takes a set. That way, if Jian changes to a cat, destroys his clothes, and changes back to human, you can get him in clothes so he isn't fighting when the frankfurter is out of the bun. Remember, if you absolutely have to, you can shoot Jian. He'll heal from your weapons, he might not heal from the enemy's."

Tim nodded to them as he stepped around Shun and continued down the hallway.

Within a couple minutes Jian was in his new clothes that fit significantly better as his friends packed the spares away.

Jian put his hand out in front of him. Zhu put his hand on top of Jian's, and Shun placed his on top of both.

Jian lifted his chin. "For Bai."

"For Bai," Zhu and Shun agreed.

———

QBBS MEREDITH REYNOLDS, MILITARY OPERATIONS

The military operations room was huge. It was fully three stories tall, with desks along the second and third stories, a wall of projection screens and a place in the middle with over 5,625 cubic feet of space for a three-dimensional hologram representation of the battle.

As needed.

Lance walked along the floor, chewing on his unlit cigar. He had three shipping containers of the cigars stashed away that he hadn't told anyone about. Not his friends, not his wife, not his daughter.

Especially not his daughter.

He expected Patricia already knew. He didn't hide anything from her, he just didn't tell her and should it come out, Patricia would be able to say that she hadn't been told. It was the best defense he could offer her. He suspected how much shit was going to be tossed in Bethany Anne's direction for her ginormous shoe collection, and didn't want anyone to start pointing at him.

Let's face it, you could store a LOT of cigars in the same amount of space as just one box of shoes.

"Queen arriving…" a female's voice was barking out when it was interrupted.

"You finish that statement," Bethany Anne told the guard trying to announce her arrival, "and I'll toss your ass into space."

Lance turned to see that Bethany Anne had a hand on the lady's shoulder. Her head was nodding in sync with Bethany Anne's as the Queen finished, "I don't want to hear that every time I go someplace for the next century. We're going to leave it for the main room and any large meetings I attend. If that happens every time I walk in here?" Bethany Anne allowed the silence to grow for a couple of seconds. "It could get ugly."

Bethany Anne gave the shoulder a gentle squeeze and continued in. Lance noticed Scott smile and wink at the guard Bethany Anne reprimanded.

No hard feelings, he seemed to say, and the woman blushed and sat down.

"Always making an entrance, Bethany Anne," he said to

his daughter as she sat in the middle seat, the one that could best view everything in the room.

"You know me, General."

He observed that she was taking in all of the screens and that her eyes seemed to be reviewing screens in front of people around the room. "Always looking to be announced, right?"

"Ah, no." He shook his head and stepped over to his chair, sitting at her left hand. "Usually you like to slink into places and let your shoes do the talking."

Bethany Anne looked down at her armored feet. "Maybe that's why I'm always on edge?"

"What, no shoe therapy lately?" Lance asked. He noticed many of those in the operations room were listening in on their chat.

"Yeah, It's a shame no designers came along for the ride. Although," Bethany Anne looked up, "ADAM is working with a promising young woman. Maybe I can see if Jean would let her inside the R&D room for a few days after this field exercise." She waved up at the screens as she settled back in her chair and spoke louder.

"We are about to cross," she called out, catching everyone's attention, "the Annex Gate the Yollin King placed in our solar system years ago. We aren't going through that gate announcing our intent to change their world. Rather, we are going through that gate with the intent to move through their space and head out to find our Kurtherian enemies."

Admiral Thomas, who had just entered, asked her as he sat down, "You think that the King will allow us safe passage through his space?"

Bethany Anne turned to the admiral. "Not an ice cube's chance in hell." She smiled. "But seeing how he wanted to subjugate Earth first? I'm not too upset with delivering a set of Yollin revolutionaries." She went back to looking around the room. "We can't have frenemies at our backs, working to figure out how to take us down. So, we're going to meet this King, kick his backstabbing ass and then beat him in battle. According to Captain Kael-ven, I'll have to meet him in one on one combat and defeat him—which means kill him—to win the allegiance of the Yollin people."

Bethany Anne reached for her waiting Coke. "Remember, I didn't write the rules, folks." She raised her drink. "But I'll abide by them." She winked and took a drink as the group cheered.

"Let's cross that fucking gate, I'm getting impatient!"

The human's ships, dedicated Puck Destroyers, multiple Sphaea class attack vessels, Puck containers for setting traps, shipping containers and Black Eagles hit the Annex Gate in a synchronized dance that had the G'laxix Sphaea hit the gate last, disappearing behind the green, yellow, blue and orange waves as ships hit the colored screen.

Then the gate exploded on the human side, throwing parts to the four corners of the solar system.

It was completely destroyed.

CHAPTER TWENTY-ONE

PLANET YOLL, KING'S PALACE, THRONE ROOM

The Yollin King turned his massive head, looked down at his Minister of Defense in annoyance. "What do you mean, we have an attack force arriving through Annex Gate Three One Four?"

The four-legged Yollin looked up at his king. "Your Majesty, Gate Three One Four was opened almost two solar years ago, and we have been receiving updated reports confirming the survey was proceeding as planned and continued to show promise. Two hours ago, a fleet of foreign military vessels and an..." Minister of Defense E'Kolorn looked down at this tablet and then back to the King, "asteroid came through the Annex Gate. In addition to these new ships, the modified survey vessel G'laxix Sphaea arrived last and the number of ships overwhelmed the gate, destroying it."

"And you say they are making requests?" the King continued to stare down at the defense minister.

"Yes, they claim they are merely moving through our space in an effort to fight the Kurtherians."

At this pronouncement, the Yollin King stared at his highest-ranking military commander and then started slapping his couch cushion loudly. His chittering laughter could be heard throughout the throne room. "Did you," he tried to stop laughing, but failed. Finally the King got himself under control. "Did you say they are seeking a fight with the Kurtherians?" he rasped out.

"Yes, Your Majesty." E'Kolorn confirmed. "That is what they are saying, in our language I might add."

"So, they have taken our people as slaves?" The King sought confirmation.

"And our ship, yes."

The King's eye's narrowed. "What are we going to do about this, E'Kolorn?"

"We are going to confirm they have our permission pass through our space to seek out the Kurtherians, Your Highness." E'Kolorn answered.

"And then, Minister of *Defense*?" he pressed.

"Then we are going to ambush their ships, destroy their pitiful fleet, rebuild a gate in three years once we figure out where the G'laxix Sphaea went—unfortunately, the information was lost with the gate—and then raid their system for resources and slaves."

"Very good, E'Kolorn. Make sure I have the head of their leader for my wall of honor," he told the Chancellor as his hand swept towards multiple heads preserved with a plaque underneath stating the race, their solar system coordinates and the method of their death.

E'Kolorn bowed his head. "As you wish, my King."

NEVER SUBMIT

QBBS MEREDITH REYNOLDS, MILITARY OPERATIONS

Bethany Anne put down her empty drink container. "So, Admiral Thomas."

The admiral was flipping screens and spoke without looking at his Queen. "Yes, my ever patient and loving Queen?" he replied, trying to help control the anxiety, both inside this operations room, and across the fleet. Something he knew would be happening as people considered their own mortality.

Bethany Anne stared at him, then smiled, then started laughing. "Am I that bad?"

"YES!" both ranking military men on each side of her responded, in stereo.

Bethany Anne leaned back in her chair and looked around the room. "God, I'm bored!"

"It's just a game at the moment, Bethany Anne," Admiral Thomas told her. He hit a couple of buttons and pulled up the vast hologram that showed her fleet, the location of the now destroyed Annex Gate, and the Yollin planet with its two moons, three different base stations around the planet, as well as the incredible amount of space traffic between the moons, the base stations and the planet.

Plus, little bitty purple dots in their wake.

"You're really expecting them to come up behind us?" Bethany Anne leaned forward. "Is this because Kael-ven said they would?"

"Yes, and no," Admiral Thomas said. "Yes, to the part that Kael-ven led us to study this, but the no part is we studied

Kael-ven and his substantial weakness to physical attacks from the rear due to his body structure. So, we're assuming their strategist might have attributed a natural weakness they suffer to us as well."

"Attacking Kael-ven that way became too easy, although he's much better now," Bethany Anne remarked. "I attack him from the rear during sparring sessions."

"Good teaching," Admiral Thomas agreed before he looked at the radar and smirked. "Gotcha!"

Bethany Anne slid forward in her seat when the new dots appeared. "They really are coming from the rear, pretty quickly, too."

"Hard to accomplish a sneak attack if the other side sees you coming." The admiral was sending commands to his ships, and Bethany Anne watched as the purple dots following behind her ships were designated Yollin 01 through Yollin 39.

"Hmmm." Admiral Thomas picked up his tablet. "Send in Coach's Revenge, target designation Yollin 21."

On the screen, the ship labeled Yollin 21 grew in size.

———

YOLLIN SHIP 21

"Pay attention to where the G'laxix Sphaea is at all times!" Captain G'yrlen said to his seek and destroy team. "That is the only ship we fear. What we can see, we can kill!"

Captain G'yrlen viewed his screen, trying to gauge the best time to help the fleet by cloaking it. His ship alone had the power to accomplish the feat, and that power wasn't infinite. Because of the difficulty of matching speeds with their targets, it was a dance to figure out the proper distance. Cloak too early? Risk coming out of cloak too far away when power dies. Too late and his people would be seen before they cloaked.

————

COACH'S REVENGE

Captain Max Wagner smiled. "Revenge, tell our support that Coach has a fight he would like to pick with those Yollin pieces of shit behind us. Cloak us all, we're going in."

Four Sphaea class ships that had hugged the Meredith Reynolds slowly faded from view, and dropped back from the main group as they lost momentum, braking just a bit.

Revenge allowed the EIs on the other ships to help keep the four ships in proximity to each other as it worked on figuring out how to best track Yollin 21 should it cloak. Soon, the human fleet was far in front, and the Yollin fleet was fast approaching. Their formation started picking up speed so that the Yollins wouldn't pass them by.

The Revenge's group had twenty-one seconds to do a final match of speed and direction when the Yollin Fleet disappeared off their radar systems.

"Well, crap." Captain Wagner said. "Tell me you got them, Revenge."

"Captain Wagner, I know exactly where Yollin 21 is and it will take approximately an extra two minutes and twenty-one seconds using visual clues before we are ready to board."

Max touched a button on his tablet. "Marines? Get ready, you arrive in three minutes."

Shun heard the captain of the ship declare they had three minutes before they would be attacking an alien ship, while hurtling through space, in a solar system so far away from where he was born that he had a hard time comprehending the distance.

All because of some stupid ass, species interfering, alien know-it-alls. He needed something to ground him in this chaotic mess.

He smirked, glancing over at Zhu.

"Heeeyyyyy, SEXY lady." Shun started singing, a maniacal smile growing on his face.

Zhu looked over at his friend. "That's Korean," he said.

Jian grinned. "Shut up, you like it, too." Then Jian bumped Shun's shoulder.

Seconds later, the two men started dancing. "HEYYYY SEXY LADY!" they sang.

Three of the Guardian Marines jumped up and started mimicking the moves from the two Chinese men. Soon, Zhu cursed and joined his team. "I really hate you guys," he yelled at them as he faked riding a horse and twirling a lasso.

Up on the ship's bridge, five crewmembers stared at the video feed. "Holy shit," Max smiled. "Send that video to the engine room. Fuck it," he said. "Revenge, send that video to the whole Gott Verdammt fleet!"

NEVER SUBMIT

QBBS MEREDITH REYNOLDS, MILITARY OPERATIONS

One of the screens on the massive wall changed and Bethany Anne's eyes flicked up to it, down, then back up as Captain Wagner's text came across the bottom, "This is how we take it to the Yollins!"

Bethany Anne stared at the screen. "Are they dancing Gangnam Style?" she asked, before she burst out laughing and joined in singing, "Heeyyyy Sexy Lady!"

YOLLIN SHIP 21

Captain G'yrlen received the reports on his screen that his fleet was now cloaked. His four legs grasped his couch as the fingers on his right hand clicked through different commands he sent to the rest of the fleet. As Over-Captain of this operation, as simple as it would be, his own status would be boosted.

"We will strike in…" he started to say when he was knocked violently sideways as his ship was hit from four directions, the cloak dropping as the energy was pulled into the shields.

"What hit us!" he demanded as people scrambled back into their seats, most of them clicking their belts to keep them in place. No one had expected to be in any danger and failed to belt in properly.

"Sir, we can see one ship, but calculate three more we cannot," ship's defense called out.

"WHERE is the G'laxix Sphaea?" G'yrlen shouted.

"Still where we show her, sir," the response came back.

He slammed his fist on the seat's arm. "These people have figured out cloaking," he spit out before they were rocked a second time.

"Sir!" Defense turned around. "They are getting through our shields!"

COACH'S REVENGE

"That's right," Captain Wagner said to himself. "Welcome to the species that learns new technology, deconstructs it, and figures how to fuck it up."

"Sir," Revenge interrupted Wagner's thoughts. "We have attained a large enough disturbance in their shield, we can send the Marines at your command."

Wagner hit the button. "All right you dancing sons-a-bitches, time to get our own back!"

QBBS MEREDITH REYNOLDS, MILITARY OPERATIONS

"Our first strikes are starting," Admiral Thomas announced. "Everyone brace, it might get a little ugly from here." He looked over to comms. "Tell Commander Jameson to release the Queen's Ace's, we got tiny ships coming! It's time they earn their wings."

"Yes sir!" comms replied and started subvocalizing the Admiral's commands.

Admiral Thomas looked over at Bethany Anne, who was busy watching the three dimensional hologram of the fight. He could see her eyes flicking too fast for him to keep up, so she was probably studying the whole thing in real time.

He wished he could do that.

"Did Paul give you any grief at taking over the fighter squadrons?" he asked her.

She shook her head. "No," she turned to look at the Admiral. "He was pretty damned excited to get back to fighters. Once Bobcat made sure he agreed with Paul on the safety stuff, he gave Paul the blessing and went back to some of their other challenges. Paul has been bugging Team BMW for upgrades. I imagine after this battle, Paul will have more information on how to upgrade the ships."

Admiral Thomas nodded. There was only so much you could do in mocked up fights.

It was always the real fights that uncovered your deficiencies.

———

COACH'S REVENGE

The Marines stopped dancing and dropped into position. Their front line became Werewolves and one Werecat. Behind them, the Queen's Guardian Marines, armored in ship metal grey. Everyone started wrapping their Weres in armor to protect them, with a final specially fitted mask built for each form's face.

A video popped up with both leaders of the Guardian Marines on screen. Todd had his helmet in his hand, Peter was staring at them, his yellow eyes piecing them as he growled, "Weee are thee Queeen's Guarrrdians, We NEVERrrr SUB-

MITTttt, WEEeee NEEVERRrr SURRrennDeerr!"

Todd added from beside his taller friend in a voice any drill sergeant would be proud to own, "But we do bring the universe's biggest can of whoop-ass! Now, do your job, kill that ship's power. We will take the front, you got the rear. See you in the center, first group to get there gets their beer paid for."

Peter looked into the video camera. "IIiii cannn driinnkk a loottt off beeerr inn thiss formmm, heh heh heh."

One last violent slam rocked the ship as they connected to the Yollin target. Max grabbed the microphone. "This is the Captain speaking, I hope you enjoyed your flight. Now please get the fuck off my ship and do what we came to do."

The Guardian Marines smiled. They were aliens, sure, but the group with Peter and Todd attacking the bridge were going to surprise the shit out of that captain over there.

———

YOLLIN SHIP 21

"We've been breached!" defense yelled.

Captain G'yrlen clicked his mandibles in frustration. This was not going according to plan. He stabbed the alarm override so he could speak. "All ship, prepare to kill boarders, all ship, kill boarders!"

He had already properly cowed the troop commander, there wasn't a need to threaten that low caste member one more time.

———

N-thahn slapped the last of the locks on his armor and grabbed his sword. The servos activated and he pointed to two of his team. There were two breaches in the ship, but the one closest to the bridge needed to be tackled first.

He doubted they would get to the breach to set up a proper defense before the outer hull was taken out. Thank god this species didn't just ram and jam, or they would have been caught with their armored pants down. The two he pointed at followed him down the passageway and up the ladders to the upper deck and after turning the corner went towards the front of the ship. The three Yollin soldiers were almost to the passageway that cut across the ship when an explosion blasted through an intersection of the passageway.

The team pulled up their weapons. No one wanted to use weapons that could vent atmosphere to space.

Decompression could be a bitch.

The roar that greeted them caused the two with N-thahn to look at him. He saw their heads out of the corners of his helmet, but ignored them. So it yelled? Punch it where it breathed and the yelling would stop.

That was when he saw the first of the enemies come round the corner and N-thahn's mandibles opened in surprise.

The enemies were *Yollins*.

––––––

"We need to go first!" Kiel argued with Peter. "Our people, our revolution," he insisted.

Peter looked down at the little Yollin. Or, little in Peter's present state. His Pricolici form wanted to be the first through, but enough times working with Stephen, or rather, being corrected by Stephen, allowed Peter to keep his control.

"Then doonn'tt beee sloowww."

Kiel nodded and called over Bo'cha'tien. She wore her mercenary armor and had her new weapon, a quarterstaff with energized ends.

She also had a new attitude. It was called 'humbled' and Kiel thought it worked much better for her than the last one—that one had gotten her arm blown off. She would tire quickly, but he allowed her this position up front, then she would step back and Peter would take her place.

Kiel chittered. This was going to be fun.

CHAPTER TWENTY-TWO

Shun waited, the calm, the eagerness, the awareness settling on his shoulders. Zhu to his left, Jian in front.

It was time. The teams heard the blast on the other side of the door. Moments later, their door opened and the two teams entered. The growls of their Weres were in the lead, ringing off the bulkheads, then Jian snarled and leapt forward. Zhu and Shun kept their defensive postures as they followed the first group, then took a left, while the first group went straight.

Two Yollins came around the corner, shocked at seeing a seven-foot long cat, eyes blazing green, roaring in front of them.

The shots from the Jean Dukes' rifles pulped their heads, their bodies dropped to the ground. Jian jumped over the mess and got ahead of them. Three Yollins tore open a door and filled the hallway, large swords in their hands, facing Shun and Zhu who stopped.

Each Marine took three steps back.

The Yollins knew they were in trouble when the black cat pounced on the last member of the party, its neck sliced open from Jian's claws as he jumped off the body. He stopped ten feet in front of them, turned around and stayed low to the ground.

Next, Shun and Zhu opened up with their rifles, one more time.

"Nice to have you back," Zhu said as he kicked open the door and swept inside, "Clear!"

"Nothing like having your team member outrun you." Shun kicked open a door, "Clear!"

Jian just snarled.

"Yeah, don't do it again." Shun said.

There was a growl behind Shun and he put up a hand to tell the new group behind them to hold. While having a large wolf at his back didn't appeal to him, he went all in when trusting the Queen, and therefore trusting the Queen's leaders.

He'd seen Peter in his Pricolici form snag Jian out of the air and toss him, so he didn't worry about someone overriding Peter.

It did, however, make Shun wonder what was going on at the front of the ship.

———

"What is that?" Captain G'yrlen grated out. His people were getting decimated. Worse, he had Yollins on his ship, fighting his people. That was against the rightness of the castes.

Worse, they had better armor and weapons and his own mechanized team was losing people three to one. Often, their side might be out of the fight, but he wasn't sure how many his people had actually *killed*.

Then that big monster started tossing his people left and right and headed straight for the bridge.

"Someone get my mechanized soldiers to act like the fighters they are supposed to be," he hissed, "or we are going to lose our damned ship!"

Captain G'yrlen grimaced when the large creature made a horrible 'he he heeeehhehh' sound and his hand reached up, blocked a video camera, then the camera went black.

Peter was having a great time when he saw the guarded door to the bridge. His smile widened, his teeth reflecting the light.

His glee turned to a snarl when the power dropped, orange light flooding the passageways. He slammed his fist into the bulkhead, denting it. Three Yollins ran around the corner, then grabbed their heads in pain as the monster ran his claws across the metal, the screeching overwhelming them.

"Nowwww, youu have maaddde meee looose myy bettt," Peter said, his voice deathly calm. "I guesss therrre isss not-thinnggg forrr meee, but too dessstroyyy nowww."

The Yollins grabbed for their pistols. One was able to shoot the Pricolici in the chest, knocking him over. He stood back up to the surprise of the Yollin who shot him, and ground out, "Punnny Weeaponsss!"

The fully armored Pricolici ran towards them, dodging as many of the shots as possible, still getting hit and tossed around, but never enough to knock him down again. The three Yollins had taken three steps back when Peter grabbed one of the hands with a pistol and twisted it, bones cracking as he used it to point to the Yollin next to him, shooting three holes into him.

Reaching forward, Peter grabbed the arm of the Yollin in back, yanking as hard as possible while he moved the Yollin on his right forward, meaning to smash them together.

Unfortunately for Peter, he successfully tossed the Yollin on his right into the left bulkhead, but was left holding a Yollin arm, with the bleeding and screeching Yollin in front of him trying to stem the flow of his own blood.

Peter kicked, catching the screeching Yollin in the chest, cracking his exoskeleton and sending him crashing back into the door that led to the bridge. Now unconscious, the Yollin slid to the ground and fell over.

———

"Who knew?" Shun looked around, his hand on the large knob, the lights switching over to orange. "Guess that worked just fine."

"We got company!" Zhu pointed to five Yollins sticking their heads over the side of the walkway above them. Jian growled, jumped on a desk, leapt to a large cabinet-looking object and then finally out of Zhu's sight onto the walkway.

Next, the two men heard snarls and mandibles clicking. Then Shun had to jump out of the way when a Yollin fell off the walkway above and slammed into the floor where Shun had been standing. Zhu shot the body in the head.

You could never tell what a Yollin could walk away from.

"COMING IN!" A voice shouted behind Shun and he turned. A large black wolf arrived with its Marines. All three looked up where Jian was snarling.

"Outran his support, huh?" one of the Marines asked.

Another Yollin body screeched as it hit the floor. This time, Shun casually shot it in the head.

"We have a cat," he shrugged. "It makes us lazy."

The other Marine looked at their wolf partner. "Hey Jefe! Why you not do that for us?" They all ducked as a third Yollin fell behind Shun, landing with a thump near Zhu. He shot the comatose body, which had already suffered critical slashes through its neck.

They could hear two sets of clicking feet leaving the area. Jian wasn't fooling around up there.

Moments later, the big cat came down and paced around his two friends before lying down, tail flicking.

"Guess we won the bet, huh?" Zhu asked.

Moments later, Kiel came over the ship's speakers.

DEFENSE HQ, YOLL

E'Kolorn was watching the reports and beginning to worry. He could tell that the ships had lost fleet cloaking, and were now engaged in ship-to-ship action. While some vessels could cloak and seek a new tactical advantage, once they fired their weapons, they would be uncovered.

Those ships that could be seen were ripped apart by weapons that seemed to overcome their shields. If it wasn't their damned weapons, or their fighters that were dogging his own, it was attacks by kinetics. Now, something was attacking his ships from the rear, and the only indication of what it might be were tiny, almost infinitesimally small returns from their radar.

That were hideously fast.

Something had followed his fleet and were just now over-taking his ships. When they slammed into a ship, shields up or not, the massive amount of kinetic power they carried were overwhelming their shields. The overbearing brute force was distasteful. No Yollin would stoop so low as to effectively be throwing rocks across space at each other.

It was uncouth.

Communications sent an incoming message. "Attention Yollin Command, this is the Etheric Empire, General Lance Reynolds speaking. Seeing how you gave us permission to cross your space, and then you treacherously attacked us, it is with great delight I would like to know what would you like us to do with the remains of your fleet?"

Minister of Defense E'Kolorn snapped his mandibles to-gether in agitation. "You won't need concern yourself when our ships crush that pitiful excuse for an armada within the next few turns of the sun."

"Yeah, good luck with that. Our calculations show this will be over in the next two turns. You're already in trouble, why bring on more? Especially when we announce our in-tention to challenge your King to a battle for leadership of the High Yollin Caste," the voice replied.

E'Kolorn thought furiously before saying, "Such is not possible, alien. To challenge the King one must be a Yollin."

"That is not true," a third voice came on line. "My name is Captain Kael-ven T'chmon, most recently Captain of the G'laxix Sphaea, Member of the Chloret Caste, Friend of the Mont and Shuk Castes and one-time acolyte of the Learnings Of Yollin."

On the QBBS Meredith Reynolds, Bethany Anne looked over at her father who shrugged back at her.

ADAM?

>>Yes, Bethany Anne?<<

How are you doing getting into the Yollin ship-to-ship communications network?

>>Successful as of two minutes and twenty-seven seconds ago. This whole conversation is going out live. Since the teams attacking Yollin 21 were successful, I didn't have to hack anything in their system. We're piggybacking on that ship's network.<<

Well, I hope it's enough.

Bethany Anne got her dad's attention and mouthed 'fleet-wide.' He smiled as they listened to Kael-ven.

Down on Yoll, the Defense Minister's mandibles were snapping together. "And what," he replied, "do you believe the texts say?"

"Anyone who studies the Holy Texts understands the right to challenge the King is not limited to any caste, to any people. It is only through manipulation of the caste system, which holds down the lower caste Yollins, that our existing leadership supported. You think those of us in the lower castes do not have the same eyes to see, and ears to hear, and minds to understand those at the top are no smarter than those of us in the lower castes? No, those in the upper castes are just given more prestigious jobs than those in a lower. This perpetuates the perception of intelligence and changes the belief amongst the lower castes."

Lance looked at Bethany Anne and Admiral Thomas and made a surprised face at the strength of Kael-ven's argument. Those on the bridge all had translation devices and could follow along as the two Yollins argued.

"The King doesn't bow down to the whims of an alien puppet!" E'Kolorn spat. "Any more than I accept that our fleet is being destroyed!"

A fourth voice came on line. This one was higher. The voice sounded natural, just not naturally a Yollin. "The is Queen Bethany Anne of the Etheric Empire. Are you suggesting the Great King of Yoll is a coward? I had heard the King is easily three times the size of Kael-ven, a member of the Chloret Caste. Is this not true? Kael-ven himself is taller than me, and yet your King is afraid?"

"The King of Yoll is afraid of no one, alien!" E'Kolorn hissed. "Least of all a non-believing alien such as yourself. Who are we to accept that you understand the rules?"

"What's so hard to learn about two walk in naked, one walks out alive? I'm pretty sure I can find a few of the Kiene Caste to help explain this to you if you're having trouble."

This alien Queen's rudeness was irritating E'Kolorn, causing him to think furiously for an appropriate response to put her in her proper place when a fifth voice entered the conversation.

"This is Yoll, King of the Yollins, the master of our race and the subjugator of worlds. Who are you to think yourself worthy of challenging *me*?"

The alien Queen's voice replied, "I'm the one who can drop a large enough rock on your head to destroy your palace grounds and smash you between my rock and your foundation. If that threat isn't good enough for you, I'm the one who can burn your space stations out of the sky for months, while you hear the pitiful screeches of children and mothers holding their babies. But I am also the one trying to settle this between rulers, as the Holy Text suggests. But if you would rather I destroy your people than admit you're too scared to meet me?"

"None would believe you, if you announce this," he replied.

"I don't need to announce it, King Yoll, because our conversation is live across your ships. Every Yollin who has access to the signal and is listening knows that I have challenged you. If you choose to allow your people to suffer, then the truth that you are only worried about your own safety over the good of your people will be not only believable, but known."

E'Kolorn heard a buzzing, and looked around. His personal communication device was flashing a bright light.

It was the King. He picked it up and looked at the message and replied, "Yes, it is true, this conversation is being spread amongst the fleet."

Moments later, the King came back on the line. "I am King Yoll, King of the Yollins, the mightiest race to rule worlds. I will not suffer this continued defamation of my character. You will meet me on the field of battle and suffer my wrath."

"King Yoll of the Yollins, I challenge for the throne of Yoll. You can call it whatever you want, but you better get this through the heads of those in the Kolin Caste. When you die, if they so much as chitter their mandibles in a way I don't like, I'll squash them flat. They are warned. I will be down in one turn."

The connection went dark and E'Kolorn wondered what that last comment was meant to be? Did this alien expect to conquer Yoll?

That thought was quickly followed by another. E'Kolorn turned to his communications officer. "B'ankzi, did the fleet hear this communication?"

His communication specialist nodded his head and E'Kolorn sat down heavily on a couch near him.

At least he hadn't lied to his King. But, if he had to have lied to stop the alien from bombing the space stations up above them, he would have done so.

His family was up there and he had seen the destruction of his ships, even as they talked. The aliens were chewing up his fleet.

It was fast becoming a slaughter.

E'Kolorn sent the command to pull back away from the aliens, hopefully they would consider the challenge with the King enough.

Within a few minutes, it was done. What was left of the Yollin Homeworld fleet was limping away from the battles, and the aliens were not pursuing.

E'Kolorn ordered, "Put all records we have of the battle, from pulling the fleet together to the order to retreat on the next message torps and send them through the gates to our other solar systems. Including internal records we can retrieve from the wounded ships, especially our Fleet Prime ship. If Fleet Prime's archives have anything we can pull, make it so. Try to do this without the aliens figuring out we are warning our brothers and sisters. Maybe they will come up with a solution to overcome these aliens."

He headed towards the door. "I must attend the King."

KING'S PALACE GROUNDS, YOLL

E'Kolorn arrived by air car from the Headquarters of Defense. The vehicle was searched and the minister was allowed to proceed into the Royal Palace on foot, a marked difference from when he was here just two turns previous.

He had been smart enough to leave behind any weapons. Not only were they useless around the King, but it allowed him to plead his case as strongly as he might.

It took three more security checks to get into the throne room. As before, there were few that were allowed in his presence. Now, a challenge had been agreed to and set for the first time in his life.

E'Kolorn strode up to the royal couch and prostrated himself on the ground. He held that position through three more three more conversations with others seeing him kneeling there until the King decided to talk with him.

"What do you have for me, E'Kolorn? Other than destroyed ships, lousy troops, and poor security on our own communications systems?"

Keeping his head down, E'Kolorn answered, "We have video that shows those that attacked Fleet Prime. I believe it will give you some indication of their martial skills."

"Tell me about them," E'Kolorn was ordered.

"Predominantly bipedal, with some able to change shapes to four-footed beasts." E'Kolorn started when he was abruptly cut off.

"Change shapes?" the King asked.

"Yes, Sire."

"Get up," the King said.

He stood up on his four legs, lifting his head to look up at the King, who was lost in thought.

"Let me see these videos E'Kolorn, everything that shows the aliens changing shape."

E'Kolorn reached into the pouch he was allowed to bring into the audience chamber. "Yes, my King."

CHAPTER TWENTY-THREE

QBBS MEREDITH REYNOLDS, MILITARY OPERATIONS

Admiral Thomas focused on bringing support and help to the broken ships of the Etheric Empire. Although not as damaged as those of the Yollins, it hadn't been a totally one-sided battle.

General Lance Reynolds took care of additional operations, items he understood needed to be accomplished when fighting battles such as these.

Bethany Anne sat in her command chair, thinking over the conversation with the Yollin King and his phrasing. Something about the way he replied was not right, and it bothered her. He was obviously a duplicitous bastard, and she wanted to make sure she figured out just what way he was already working to stab her in the back.

>>Bethany Anne, EI Reynolds is moving forty-two wounded in action to the medical bays on the outside docks.<<

Thank you, ADAM. The general and the admiral have this here. Please make sure I have a place to transport near there and let me pick up my security. If I don't, I won't hear the end of it… like ever.

Bethany Anne stood up, grabbed her Katana and locked it into her armor where Jean had created a place for the blade. While her katana could be used, it was more ceremonial. If Bethany Anne wanted to really deal some damage, she would pull the hilt for her Etherically created sword from her armor on her right leg where it stayed, out of sight.

She stepped down to speak to her commanders. "Gentleman." The admiral nodded in her direction, but continued with his instructions to his team.

"Yes, Your Highness?" General Reynolds answered after he finished his own conversation.

"I'm going to check on my wounded. If you need me, contact me through Reynolds or Meredith. Once I'm done with the wounded, I will retire to rest, and pull in extra reserves before the flight down. I don't trust the King one bit." When Bethany Anne admitted that, her father grunted in agreement. "So, I'm trying to figure out just how he's going to cheat."

She looked around. "Let's move our people, refine how we spot their cloaking and get the puck defense up around the asteroid. I'll update the people inside on the plans. Make sure we're ready for the post battle cleanup." She looked over at her father. "And you two get some sleep as well."

"We got this, your Highness." He smiled and put a hand on her shoulder.

"I'm sure you do, so don't make me find out in eight hours you're still standing here. I delegate, I expect you to as well, when needed."

He nodded, the admiral waved that he had heard at least the general idea of her conversation as he continued to direct orders. Probably through Reynolds and his top captains.

Gabrielle and the four Bitches slotted into place as Bethany Anne left operations and headed for the nearest Transportation Room.

About three minutes later, they were entering the Meredith Reynolds' outer hospital.

———

Pilot Julianna Fregin was talking with Herbert Eff, one of the men from the puck destroyer, Her Destiny, as both of them waited to be seen by medical personnel.

"No," she said. "I never saw the beam that got me. My wing and I were slicing through a raid of their fighters who had been aiming at the Meredith Reynolds. We probably got three more kills and two we knocked out of service in that wave when I noticed my wingman dive to my side. My wing's Eagle was obliterated and then my own was touched by something that ate half the ship in a microsecond." Julianna shrugged. "I think my wingman was able to take most of the bolt's power for me. I was knocked out when my ship was destroyed. I lost the lower half of my leg."

Julianna noticed that the guy she was talking with glanced down at the sheets covering her body to see what was missing.

The answer was, just like she had told him, half of her leg. The pilot's suit she wore constricted, keeping her from bleeding out and the nanite pack she had been given when joining the Aces helped stop the flow in time.

But it wasn't enough to regrow her limb.

"Damn, that sucks." Herbert remarked, looking down at the flat area of her sheets that confirmed no leg was there. He looked back at her. "Any idea from the doc yet?"

"Oh, yes." Julianna smiled. "Right now, we're waiting for a special nanite pack. Once that happens, I should be able to get a Pod and…" Julianna noticed that Herbert had stopped paying attention to her, which she thought was rather rude.

She turned to see what had captured Herbert's attention and recognized the ladies right away. First was Gabrielle, the Queen's Captain. She wasn't sure what that meant in the hierarchy of the military, but she helped corral the Four. Which then started coming into view along with the Queen.

Julianna forgave Herbert for losing his focus. The Queen was talking to the doctor and nodding in their general direction. The doctor put a hand on the Queen's shoulder and was thanking her before she rushed to the next thing she needed to do, calling out directions to a nurse on the way.

"God, she's beautiful," Julianna murmured.

"Which one?" Herbert whispered.

Julianna turned back to Herbert. "Both, hell, all of them."

Herbert looked at her and flashed a smile. "Sorry, that was rude. I was just shocked to see them here."

Juliana shrugged. "That's why everyone loves her," she was starting to tell Herbert when she rolled her eyes. The guy had stopped listening to her, *again*. She turned her head to see what had his attention this time, and her eyes opened wide.

The Queen was coming straight for her. Gabrielle was accepting something from a nurse behind them.

Bethany Anne nodded towards Herbert and looked down at Julianna, a smile on her face. "Queen's Ace Julianna Fregin, I understand you had an interesting battle today above the QBBS Meredith Reynolds?"

Julianna nodded. "Yes ma'am, your Highness."

The Queen said, "Meredith, please list Julianna's accomplishments today."

"First wave, one confirmed kill, two fractional kills, total points one and one half kills. Second wave, four fractional kills awarding two points, total three and one half points, third wave three confirmed kills, two fractional kills, total points awarded four. Total points all waves first Battle of Yoll, seven and one-half."

"Welcome to ACE Status, Queen's Ace Julianna Fregin." the Queen had a twinkle in her eye. "Now, what you might not realize, is the nanite pack you are waiting for is one that is rather rare, and is kept under lock and key. Something we overlooked, I'm embarrassed to say, by not having it up in the forward hospital area."

"We didn't overlook it, Bethany Anne," John Grimes commented behind her. "We just believe the chances of this hospital being overrun is too high to allow those packs to be stored here."

Bethany Anne looked over her shoulder. "Well, we need to have Team BMW build us something that protects the packs and allows a few to be deployed here."

Bethany Anne turned back to Julianna. "The nanite pack is built from my blood, with special programming from ADAM and TOM." The Queen kept her focus on Julianna, but put her out right hand. Gabrielle placed a syringe in it. "ADAM, Thales of Miletus?"

"Yes, Bethany Anne?" a slightly artificial voice answered followed quickly by another voice Julianna wouldn't have known to be an alien, if the Queen hadn't just called him out by name.

"Make sure you program these new nanites correctly

when I leave," she said and the two voices agreed.

Julianna was getting in way over her head. These were the top people in the Etheric Empire, stories about them were everywhere, and right now they were either standing right next to her, or speaking to the Queen through the speakers so she could hear.

The Queen took the syringe and looked down at Julianna's arm. "Well, that's just fucking great," she exclaimed, exasperated. She handed the syringe back to Gabrielle and then in mere moments, had removed the top of her armor and handed it to Eric, "Hold this please," she told him. She rolled up the black spandex-looking top and accepted the syringe back from Gabrielle. While she was doing this, Julianna looked around.

Every patient was watching.

By the time Julianna looked back, the Queen had almost finished filling a small syringe with her blood. The doctor had returned and was standing between Herbert and Julianna. "If I may?" she asked and Bethany Anne handed her the syringe. "What about the energy?" The doctor asked as she made sure there were no air bubbles in the syringe.

"I'll give her enough until you have room in a Pod, tomorrow at the earliest," Bethany Anne confirmed for the doctor as she put her armor back on.

Julianna watched the doctor pull out her IV. "Sorry honey, not wasting any of this blood by inserting it into your drip, so you get a new hole." The doctor had the syringe in her arm and immediately injected the blood.

Bethany Anne reached out over Julianna's chest. "Well done, ACE Julianna Fregin, rest and heal. We have more battles in front of us, and our ACE needs to get better."

The Queen winked at her and her eyes started glowing

red, her hand started glowing white and she laid the hand in between Julianna's breasts. "This energy will provide what the nanites need to…"

Julianna heard nothing more, sleep overcame her.

———

The six made it back into Bethany Anne's suite once she finished making the rounds at the hospital. Bethany Anne didn't pull blood again, but she did provide energy for three more to help speed up their healing. The nanites they already had in their blood would finish the job.

"We need portable energy packs," Bethany Anne said as she wiped a tear out of her eye. "If they had them, more of the wounded would already be better."

"How?" Scott asked. "How do we store Etheric energy?"

"I don't have that answer, Scott, but I will. I won't lose people just because we can't figure something out. If I have to pull together special research on this one subject, I will. We need it. One life lost is one too many." She stepped into her bedroom. "I'm going to get some rest. Make sure we have arrangements to go down to the world below. I'm going to sleep and dream about how to bring a can of whoop-ass to an eighteen foot tall armored alien."

She shut the bedroom door behind her and Scott looked at John. "I'd go to sleep counting sheep, but you know, if thinking about kicking alien ass is what she likes?" he shrugged. "I'm not judging."

The men set up the guard rotation as Gabrielle went to check on the travel arrangements. They would rotate four on and four off until Bethany Anne got up.

It would at least give three of them time with their women.

NEVER SUBMIT

Darryl told them he would sleep here on the couches. Natalia's ship had made it through the fight, but she wasn't going to be able to focus on anything but her ship and her people for a while, he figured.

No matter how badly Darryl wanted to go and hold her, one more time.

———

KING'S PALACE, YOLL

Minister of Defense N-thahn left the meeting to work in the secondary operations area. It was on another part of the palace grounds, and the King could reach it through an underground tunnel. His size might be good for fights, but it sucked for being able to move about like a regular Yollin, N-thahn thought.

It wasn't until these days of activity with the humans, what the aliens called themselves, that his own mind was opened to the questions about the King. Why was he so large? Why was he so reclusive? Why did he continue the Caste system?

It had never benefitted either N-thahn himself or his family to question these realities. But the insidious weapon of curiosity had been opened, and whether the King killed their Queen or not, she probably had already ended his Reign.

———

QBS ARCHANGEL

Bethany Anne walked onto the bridge of the ArchAngel to the standing ovation of everyone who welcomed her back.

Her own visage looked back at her from the screens. "Welcome back, our Queen," EI ArchAngel's voice, Bethany Anne's voice, called out from the speakers, "It's been too long."

Bethany Anne, in full armor, sat down in her chair. She rubbed the arms. "ArchAngel, it is fantastic to be back. Where are our support ships?"

"There are a total of thirteen Sphaea ships surrounding us. Twelve are cloaked. The G'laxix Sphaea refuses to cloak, and will announce our arrival."

"That's Natalia for you." Bethany Anne smiled. "Her Russian lineage is showing."

"Okay, everyone," Bethany Anne looked around at her people on the bridge. "We're going down there to challenge the Yollin King in a fight to the death. I'm going to assume he doesn't want to die and will try all sorts of shit to stop that, not the least of which is a concerted effort to kill me. We've got more battles to go, so I don't personally have time to die today. Therefore, as your Queen, I'm ordering you not to die, either."

There was laughter at that. During the fight, ArchAngel had been often attacked but never seriously damaged. She had waded right into the battle and kicked ass in an orgy of destruction and havoc. Yollin ships quickly learned to leave the big Leviathan Class battleship the hell alone.

It wasn't until you earned the right to be on the bridge of this ship that you found out just how unique it was in all of the ships in Bethany Anne's armada.

This ship was captained by ArchAngel itself, the avatar of Bethany Anne. Those on the ArchAngel worked, they felt, for the lady herself.

When they went into battle, ArchAngel announced, "All personnel, this is the Battleship ArchAngel. We have been ordered to go into battle and '*We Will Not Surrender*' has been instituted by our Queen. All lockdown protocols on this ship are removed. Leviathan Battleship ArchAngel is now fully operational and will fight until *victorious…*"

There was a slight pause from the speaker system. "Or *dead*."

Every man and woman shouted and cheered as the Arch-Angel went, guns blazing, into the ships of the Yollins. As Admiral Thomas, viewing the information during post-battle review later, commented, "She tore them new assholes."

No one would fuck with the ArchAngel, and now she was carrying the Queen on her bridge once again. The ArchAngel went loaded, weapons hot, just watching, scanning and waiting to see if someone tried to attack. If they did?

They would find out what an enraged and protective EI could do when protecting her Queen.

Her *Mother*.

YOLL VIDEO COMMUNICATIONS AROUND THE PLANET, MOONS, AND SPACE STATIONS

It was a sight for the Yollins to see. Their own ship, the G'laxix Sphaea, was leading the alien ship.

The sight, most admitted, was impressive.

Yoll had their own versions of the ArchAngel. Ships as massive as the alien one heading for their home world, and the video commenters would place overlays between the class of Yollin spaceship that matched the ArchAngel, but there was something about the human alien ship that got into the Yollin psyche.

It wasn't beautiful. In fact, as most of the video commentators said, it was only beautiful in the horror of the design, because death was the focus. When you looked at the ArchAngel through the right prism, it was understood this ship wasn't meant to have any other purpose but to create destruction and visit it upon another people.

What kind of people must these humans be to design in this fashion?

Ones that would threaten to kill indiscriminately until their King fought. Many Yollins thought it an inappropriate threat. Effective, but inappropriate nonetheless.

A few were whispering, where those in the upper Caste couldn't hear, that she hadn't said anything that wasn't true. The Holy Texts didn't limit the King's challenge to only Yollins. There was just as much commentary about Captain Kael-ven T'chmon and whether he was, right now, in command of the G'laxix Sphaea or not.

QBS ARCHANGEL

"We have been given the final location for the Challenge," ArchAngel announced. "We are going to head to a large stadium in the capital city."

"That's interesting." Bethany Anne turned. "Kael-ven, thoughts?"

"The King is going to use this to make an announcement, or pronouncement. With all of the news coverage we're getting, he must get control back again, or risk additional challenges to his rule. You have created a schism in the Castes."

"Good," Bethany Anne said. "If nothing else, that shit has to stop. There is no reason for artificial bifurcation of roles or responsibilities based on some bullshit created a long time ago. It's just used to help those at the top stay on top."

"Even with the King dead, those at the top will not be pleased to lose prestige."

Bethany Anne smiled grimly. "Ask me if I give a fuck after I kill the King." She looked him up and down, outfitted in his own Jean Dukes' armor and pistols. "You ready?"

Kael-ven shrugged. "Who should ever be ready to lead a revolution?"

CHAPTER TWENTY-FOUR

ROYAL CITY OF KHN'CHIK, PLANET YOLL

This planet makes even Los Angeles seem like a jungle," Bethany Anne commented as they slowly floated over the megacity. "What do you use to build your cities with?" she asked Kael-ven

"Adhesive that we are able to manufacture from two large seas to the north and crushed rock. Both seas are inhospitable to anything living in them. But, if you mix it with the rock in the right proportions, the chemicals will allow a semi-liquid pour. If you use enough pressure to eject it, you can create some intricate shapes. Most times they have forms set to pour the mixture into, which hardens within hours."

"Do they stick anything in the forms, to hold the hardened rock together?" Bethany Anne wondered. "We do something with concrete on Earth, but I think they have to put rebar or something in the mixture for strength."

"No, I've never heard of anything placed in the rock

unless it is for aesthetic reasons, which is often. Occasionally they will build a large hole into a wall so they don't have to cut one later."

"Huh, the buildings are beautiful." She watched as the open-air stadium came into view. "Big sucker."

"It is used for most of the major sporting games, and every time we have a coronation, of course."

"How appropriate." She turned around to ask, "Do Yollins have a phrase like The King is Dead, Long Live the King?"

Kael-ven's mandibles opened and shut a few times before he asked, "Is that even logical?"

"No," she agreed. "But what it meant was that the old monarch was dead, but there was already a new monarch and it allowed people to rely on continuity of leadership."

"So, in this case, King Yoll, which is both title and name you take when assuming leadership, the previous one is dead, the new one is in place." He paused a moment, "It has a certain relevant illogic to it." He shrugged. "Yollins always assume there will be a King. We rarely see this King, only hear about him. So this," he pointed at the stadium starting to take up the entire front view, "will be possibly a once in a lifetime experience."

"Well, it will also be a last in a lifetime experience," Bethany Anne said.

———

Yoll exited his Royal Shuttle into the back entrance of the stadium. He would show himself in his full glory at the appropriate time.

Perhaps this fight, he would take a new form.

———

Bethany Anne got up from the chair. "You got this ArchAngel?"

"Yes, my Queen, I have this," she replied.

Bethany Anne nodded to Kael-ven, "Okay, Viva la revolution, let's get this done." She, Kael-ven and her security walked together to the Pod bay, passing by a long line of well-wishers. Ashur was waiting for her. "Let's do this Ashur," she said as she stepped into the armored Executive Pod.

Moments later, it was exiting the ArchAngel's bay and slowly dropping, surrounded by a contingent of twelve Black Eagles.

———

The King watched the spectacle of the alien arriving through the top of the stadium. Their ships used a form of gravitics, so were silent.

Maybe he needed to up his estimation on when Kurtherians had upgraded this group. He was certain after reviewing the video that these aliens had been upgraded, he just couldn't tell when or by whom. Most of their technology seemed older.

Who used an asteroid for a base? It was almost like these aliens preferred to thumb their nose at beauty and balance.

Obviously, they would be an easy species to subjugate once this Queen was taken care of and her head was on his wall.

Provided he didn't choose to exchange forms and put this body's head on the wall. Either way, one of these two heads was going to be on his wall by tonight.

NEVER SUBMIT

———

When Bethany Anne's shuttle landed, Gabrielle ordered the doors be kept closed. There was no way Bethany Anne was allowed out of the ship until the King showed himself.

It took five minutes, maybe six. Huge, cacophonous trumpets of some sort started blaring notes and those in the stadium stands, easily a hundred and fifty thousand Yollins, made all sorts of noise. But it was their pounding on the rock floors throughout the stadium that easily made the most noise, the vibrations could be felt in the Pod.

"I think the King is the hometown favorite," Bethany Anne chuckled.

"They don't know what you would do if they do not support you. They certainly fear what the King will do," Kael-ven explained.

Eight four-legged heralds, all holding poles with black banners high, came up a ramp that had started underground. The racket in the stadium went up a notch. Then, King Yoll slowly walked out. You saw his head first, then his two front legs rose out of the hole, grabbing the sides as he lifted his body up. The crowds settled down.

Not in fear, but in awe. Their King really was a God of Yollins. He was massive as he emerged from the hole, easily dwarfing the tops of the poles that the heralds held high. The King looked up and around the large stadium, then he nodded his acceptance of their accolades.

He walked onto the field. "Doesn't he seem a little bulkier than you would think?" Bethany Anne called over her shoulder to Kael-ven.

"He should. He really is three times my size," replied the awed Yollin.

"More than that," ADAM said. "He has on armor."

Bethany Anne pointed at the monitor at the King. "That's what I'm seeing!"

John asked, "Is that why you have on your old exoskeleton suit?"

"Maybe," Bethany Anne replied.

"When I stuffed her in the suit," Gabrielle said, "my God, you would have thought I was making her wear a pair of knock-off Louboutin's, the way she bitched."

"Being in this is hot," Bethany Anne retorted. "I don't see you wearing the old set."

"I'm not fighting an eighteen-foot-tall half praying mantis, half alien centaur either," Gabrielle said.

"Jealous?" Bethany Anne asked as she grabbed the suit's helmet and prepared to step out of the shuttle.

Gabrielle looked back at the screens showing the huge King. "No. No I think I'm good this time. If fighting that massive mountain is what it takes to get your sweet ass bedsheets? Hell, you can keep them. I'll just sneak into your room and nap when you're somewhere doing something Queenly."

"Gee, thanks." Bethany Anne smiled then turned around and looked at her friends. "Motherfuckers, every one of you, let's go kick some ass." Her voice dropped an octave. "I've still got some mad to get out and it's just this poor constipated dickless dictator's fault he gets to feel the wrath," her eyes started glowing red, "of the woman Michael, the ArchAngel himself entrusted."

Her face started showing red lines of Etheric, like blood vessels glowing under her skin radiating out from her eyes. "Entrusted to keep our fucking Earth safe from all who would attack her." Her voice, now causing those in her presence to have goosebumps run up and down their arms, commanded, "All right, you know how I feel. I'm done playing."

NEVER SUBMIT

———

Yoll watched as the shuttle door opened and he wondered how many guards would be in front of the Queen before she would show herself. Personally, he would have at least six, but if she came out with four, he wasn't going to offer more respect for the bravery doing so would display.

The first figure off the vessel was an armored person who stopped and looked around. The figure turned to look over its left shoulder and stared at Yoll. It lifted its arm and raised a middle finger toward him before it spoke. "I'll get to you in a minute, Yoll. So enjoy your last few moments before I bring the fucking pain."

Yoll's mandibles snapped together when he realized this figure was the Queen. She waited while five more walked out and surrounded her. On cue, they turned and proceeded to head towards him. Halfway, the security peeled off and turned, walking back towards the shuttle as those in the stands yelled and stomped.

Yoll walked forward past his heralds and stopped at his edge of the fighting circle. The alien stopped at the edge of the circle on her side.

Yoll looked around, his voice amplified as he pointed across the circle at her. "What have we here? I thought you understood the Challenge was without armor?"

She pointed back at him. "I am merely following your lead. You never accepted my Challenge, and I see that you have armor on at this moment. So, Yoll, are we fighting a Challenge, or are you already trying to cheat?"

Yoll grated his mandibles together. He reached behind himself and clicked two tabs. He lifted off the armor that was supposed to be invisible to the aliens as he said, "Ceremonial."

The Queen nodded and reached up and unhooked her helmet and took it off, allowing her black hair to cascade behind her head. Two of her guards jogged back to her.

———

John reached Bethany Anne first, with Eric a step behind him. John caught two of the snaps and popped them off. "Got your armor, that was sneaky as shit boss. You never expected to fight with this on."

"God no," Bethany Anne said as she stepped out of the boots. "The new stuff is so much better, this shit feels like something Jean dreamed up when she wanted to punish us."

John noticed red armor under her present set. "You expect to get to use this?" He asked as Eric grabbed her old armor.

"No, I'll have to strip again, I'm sure." Eric chuckled. "Oh shut up, Eric. I know all of your girlfriends screwed the hell out of each of you before we did this, so don't be thinking seeing me in my birthday suit is going to embarrass me."

John took the helmet. "Oh, it will embarrass you, BA."

Bethany Anne looked up at her friend and put up her thumb and index finger, close together. "Maybe a little."

The two guards took the armor back to the shuttle.

———

Yoll looked at the woman, the red of her body and feet not matching the white of her face. "You have more armor on," he accused.

She pointed out to him, her voice heard just as easily even though he had tried to make sure only his voice was audible to those in the stands. "You have never agreed that this is a *King's Challenge*. When are you going to accept?"

Yoll considered his next move. No doubt her armor was good, but should he fight her with it, and it not be a King's Challenge, or should he call it a King's Challenge and make her take it off?

While he pondered, the crowd started murmuring. Yoll finally realized that many in the stands were pointing to a new figure entering the field from her shuttle.

It was another Yollin, encased in red armor like the Queen wore, his mandibles chomping. Here was the ex-Captain of the G'laxix Sphaea, the one time Acolyte of the Holy Text and the present pain in his attempt to subjugate this race.

He would deal with him next.

"King's Challenge," Yoll ground out. "Accepted."

She nodded to the yells and stomping from the crowd. The red armored Yollin walked calmly towards the alien Queen as she stripped off her red armor, watching Yoll the whole time. Finally, she stood there unarmored, her skin the same color as her face.

———

Kael-ven walked up behind Bethany Anne. "So," he whispered. "Why is it this red armor isn't at all like the real red armor you normally wear?"

Bethany Anne turned to hand it to Kael-ven, "Because I trust that asshole about as far as I can throw him. You ready?" she asked and he nodded.

Kael-ven turned and walked back towards the shuttle.

When he got there, Gabrielle accepted the red armor. "Guys," she hissed, "this shit isn't real."

"Tell us something we didn't guess as soon as we figured out we weren't staring at her real ass, but a photograph on a bodysuit!" John hissed back.

She eyed Eric, who was busy looking at anything but his girlfriend at the moment. Gabrielle chuckled. "That damn bitch is just never going to stop surprising my ass."

Darryl whispered, "If you ain't cheating…"

"You ain't trying," five humans and a Yollin hissed back.

———

"Challenge has been issued," a voice from the speakers announced to those in the stadium, "and Challenge has been Accepted. This is now a sacred battle and will be fought behind the Sacred Curtain."

"Okay," Bethany Anne muttered, "this was unexpected." She looked around as the Yollin King moved into the hundred-yard diameter circle.

"Well, fuckity fuck," she murmured as she walked into the circle herself, head held high. She heard massive machines power up, then felt the energy they produced as a circular, white translucent shield erupted from the ground around the perimeter of the circle, arching over their heads to meet sixty feet above them.

"Well, that's just spiffy," she said, looking at the new enclosure.

"What," the Yollin King chittered, "You didn't know about the Sacred Curtain?"

———

"Uh oh," Kael-ven whispered.

Gabrielle turned to look at him. "What 'uh oh?'"

"I didn't remember to tell Bethany Anne about the Sacred Curtain. I forgot," he said. "Well, actually it's only mentioned in passing, more rumor than information in the Holy Text."

Gabrielle turned back before ordering, "Everyone, drop your nanite spies, ADAM, send them to find the machines responsible for this thing."

"Don't do anything yet, Gabrielle," John cautioned. "This is just a hiccup, she's got this."

———

Bethany Anne started walking to her right. "Nope, can't say that I knew about the shield. I assume it's here so whatever you do to cheat isn't visible to those outside watching?"

"You have a very dim view of my Holiness."

"You are no more Holy than John's day-old socks. Trust me, I've heard Jean talk about them. Holy, they are not."

"I have no idea what John's day-old socks means, but I presume it is another way for you to disrespect me?"

"I'd have to respect you first, before I could disrespect you. I'm merely talking to another power-hungry alien. Just the second or third of the many I've already met."

"Oh?" The King replied, starting to move to his right. "And where would these aliens hail from? Perhaps they are Zebulones? Maybe Jukdahs?"

Uh oh. TOM said.

Bethany Anne rolled her eyes. *TOM, what the fuck are Zebulones or Jukdahs and why are you saying 'uh oh?'*

Bethany Anne, they are both names of Clans of the Seven.

Bethany Anne, keeping her eyes on Yoll, snarled, "Gott Verdammt Kurtherians!"

"Why yes, you said you were hunting them. I suggest, not that you will be alive to use this wisdom, the next time you ask permission to pass through someone's space, you don't give away your knowledge of us."

Oh, shit. TOM said.

Yeah, I don't need a translation for this one. Bethany Anne replied.

"So, you are what, from one of those two yourself?" she asked the King.

"Those two spineless Clans don't have the strength to do what it takes."

OK, got him pegged. He is either from the Reben Or M'nassa Clans.

Why?

Because those two Clans built up super-soldiers. They would merge with a species representative and make them better, stronger, deadlier. Their goal was to change the species by leading the species themselves.

How long could they live?

They would transfer their bodies to the next in line, taking over for generations.

Making themselves gods to men. Bethany Anne thought.

"So, how many times have you changed bodies?" she asked Yoll.

He spread his arms. "I lost count," he answered and then pointed at her. "But you should know that I am considering taking over your body. You should be honored."

Fat fucking chance you poser! TOM spat.

>>This body is full up.<<

No shit, you guys.

Bethany Anne shook her head. "No bueno, pencil prick. All full up, no room in the hotel."

He rolled his eyes. "The first thing I'll do is move your consciousness to the side. You will watch me rule from your body until I tire. Then I won't have to listen to the inane comments that erupt from your mouth."

"Inane comments?" Bethany Anne said. "And did you just roll your eyes at me?"

M'nassa. They are rather proud of their speech.

I'm going to shove his speech back down his throat so he shits it out his ass... Inane comments? What a world-class asshole!

"So, I'm not talking with a Yollin, but a representative from the M'nassa Clan, do I have that right?"

The Yollin stopped and looked at Bethany Anne, pausing a moment before answering, "While right, I'm surprised you know. That means you are more aware of our lineage than I thought. Usually, Kurtherian agents aren't taught so much."

The distant roar of the Stadium's crowd dropped completely.

TOM said, **I've dropped your hearing to nothing. He's instituted a sonic attack to overcome your hearing.**

Bethany Anne put her hands on her hips and yelled at Yoll. "You can stop that!"

He can't hear you at the moment. He's yelling.

He's probably wondering why I'm not in pain.

Yes, this tactic is to allow him to come over here and easily rip your head from your body as you lie on the ground, grabbing your ears. Or, considering what he said a moment ago, transfer his body into yours.

I don't ever want to know how he would do that, TOM.

Yes, it's a rather...

TOM! Which part of EVER don't you understand?
\>\>He's got quite a bit of power in those lungs.<<
I'm getting bored watching him.
\>\>Uh oh.<<
Oh Shit.

Bethany Anne took a step forward, her right hand behind her…

———

Gabrielle told the group, "ADAM says that Yoll is actually a Kurtherian hosted in a Yollin body."

Kael-ven said, "Sonofabitch."

The five humans turned as one to look at the Yollin who shrugged. "What? It seemed appropriate. You humans have such great curse words." He pointed towards the translucent curtain hiding the two fighters. "I just realized that the great and powerful Oz—thanks for showing me that movie Scott—is actually a Kurtherian. From the same race that told us we had to make sure we never fought against Kurtherians. That Barook licking psychopath…"

Then the translator stopped working. It couldn't figure out what Kael-ven was ranting about. The team was treated to a lot of Yollin language it hadn't encountered.

Yet.

The team turned back to watch the Sacred Curtain when it lit up with a massive red explosion.

"Hmm, think he did something to piss her off?" Scott asked.

"She's probably just bored." Darryl suggested.

Kael-ven said, "I'd feel sorry for him, but fuck him and his…"

The translator died again trying to figure out what Kael-ven was saying.

NEVER SUBMIT

———

Yoll threw up an Etheric shield just in time as the red energy crackled along the outside. "You gutter slime!" he yelled, feeling the heat.

Bethany Anne could hear again. "Did that get your fucking attention?" she asked. "I'm tired of your useless yelling, *daaamn!*"

Yoll moved in other direction around the circle, Bethany Anne changed directions as well. "So you are not from either of those clans," he made a fist and released.

"Why, because your little display of shrieking and gurgles didn't make me fall down on the ground in pain?"

"Yes," he replied, then pointed at her. "So, you are not Reben, or we would have already started arguing which of our beliefs are superior."

He stopped. "Phraim!"

Bethany Anne shrugged. "Don't give a shit if you want to do a ritualistic dick beating about how good your personal belief system is over there Yoll, I plan on killing you anyway, so anytime you care to end this banter, I'm good."

He shook his head. "No, I'm not so stupid as to allow you the advantage of knowing my Clan, without knowing yours." He resumed walking.

Oh fucking geez, this could take a while, TOM said.

Why, what Clan are you?

Essiehkor, but he won't consider any answer that is a clan name for one of the five, trust me.

Your cussing has gone up substantially, TOM.

I blame you.

You always blame being near me for anything that affects your Kurtherian-ness.

Who else am I around all of the time that cusses worse than a sailor?

I'm going to get a t-shirt that says 'Kurtherians are whiny little...' wait a minute, when are you listening to sailors cuss?

It's a saying.

I know it's a saying, answer my damned question.

Well, there's Jean, and Admiral Thomas, and...

Okay, stop. I get it, everyone.

Captain Wagner, Captain Jakowski, Leader of the Guardian Marines Todd Jenkins, when we see him, Chief Engineer John Rodriquez...

You've made your damned point.

See.

TOM, shut... up..

This time, Yoll reached back with his own arm. "So, you can throw Etheric, but can you catch it?"

INCOMING! TOM yelled.

The green ball of energy exploded where Bethany Anne had been a split second before. Yoll looked, but couldn't find her body. He started walking forward when his abdomen exploded with pain. He jumped to his left, rolling sideways before getting up, looking back where he had just been.

The woman's eyes were glowing. "Oh, good," she ground out. "I got your attention. Are you ready to die? Because I'm fuck-all out of patience."

Yoll narrowed his eyes as he flexed his arms. "You can't be from one of the Seven, what are you, really? It is bothering me and I would appreciate an answer before I crush you."

Bethany Anne clapped her hands together and drew them apart as a red sphere of energy started forming between them. Her eyes glowing, her hair writhing and snapping around from the energy crackling off of her body, answered him.

"I am Bethany Anne. One of a Kind, Champion of the Five, Foe of the Seven and will be known universally as… the *Queen Bitch.*"

Yoll had been working on his shield as she told him her lineage. It held when her Etheric ball hit it, but if she had many more of those in her, he would be in trouble.

It was time he got physical.

Yoll roared his challenge and rushed at the human.

CHAPTER TWENTY-FIVE

bout fucking time," Bethany Anne said and threw two fast Etheric energy balls at Yoll who batted them away. He jumped a good twenty feet in the air and was watching when the alien Queen disappeared before he landed.

"WHAT!" he screamed in frustration when he got hit in the side. His return kick sent Bethany Anne thirty yards to slam into the shield and bounce off, landing hard on the field. He turned to attack her, throwing his own green Etheric ball in her direction.

He was surprised when she caught it and absorbed the energy, her eyes flashing green for just a moment before returning to her normal red.

"It tickles," she called out and then just *moved*.

He knew where she was when her blow rocked his jaw. He twisted his body, throwing a punch and felt her, but it wasn't a solid hit. He continued his turn to see her getting up. He raced towards her, knowing that jumping wasn't going to be a good solution. He slid at the last moment, trying to grab her as she leaped above him.

His last second kick missed as well, but she didn't hit him, so at least it was a draw. He sent a mental attack, but it was rebuffed easily, she didn't even seem to notice he had tried.

Got your back, TOM told her.

Knew you would, old friend, she shot back as she moved again.

That was not good, Yoll thought. Neither sonic attack or mental attacks, two components of his arsenal that would have taken down any normal Yollin, had both failed miserably.

Yoll moved slowly to his left, gauging the right distance then stabbed his hand into the dirt, pulling up a sword out of the ground. Shaking the dirt off of it, he smiled down at the ten foot long blade. "If you think I'm not above cheating, you are vastly mistaken." He chittered in laughter, thinking about slicing through that annoying body. He had decided that being inside such a small body would be limiting.

"Motherfucker," she smiled. "I *counted* on it."

———

"You got that?" Kael-ven asked ADAM. "Right, so it's time to show those here in the audience what they are missing…"

The massive video monitors, which so far had just shown the same white covered half-sphere with colors occasionally exploding inside changed. Now they saw the battle from inside.

Kael-ven smiled as he watched the massive number of

Yollins start paying close attention to the monitors. "Go tiny spies, let the truth be told," he whispered.

———

ROYAL CITY OF KHN'CHIK, PLANET YOLL

The High Kolin area of the city of Khn'Chik was very empty. All but three of the family houses seemed deserted except for those servants of the Mont and Shuk castes who were setting up the dining areas in the ruling houses for parties.

Those three families, however, were keeping their people hidden as much as possible. They all had the same bored members of the family's servants at the front gates, scratching themselves and swatting at the flying insects. Occasionally looking towards the great stadium when something happened that caused the roaring of the crowd to travel across the valley and up the hill to where they were.

Inside, however, it was a different scene.

Multiple Yollins were preparing their armor, their weapons and their plans. If there was ever a time to take the throne over for their own family and rule Yoll, it would be after this Challenge. If Yoll won, he would be weak. If the alien Queen won, then a successful attack could push their family right to the top.

If there was one thing being Kolin taught you, it's that being anything but Kolin wasn't acceptable.

———

"I see you have a size problem," Bethany Anne told the King, thinking about how she should fight a ten-foot sword swinging through the air. She had been surprised twice now at the King's reaction time. As another Kurtherian enhanced being, his abilities mirrored hers much more closely.

You got this on video, ADAM?

>>Yes, the whole audience is now seeing the video.<<

What's the reaction?

>>They're just now getting to the grabbing a weapon part.<<

It would be nice, Oh shit...

Bethany Anne disappeared as Yoll attacked, swinging through the air where she had been and quickly cutting through the air behind him, but she wasn't there.

She seemed to just step out of the air on the other side of the Challenge Field.

Yoll walked toward her. "Why don't you just stay put? It would make this so much easier."

"Why don't you put down that sword and stop cheating?"

"Because there is no way I'm giving up my life for some fancy Holy Texts that I *WROTE*!" he screamed and ran at her. Again, she stepped aside and disappeared. Yoll bellowed his frustration, swinging his sword blindly, looking around the field for her.

He heard her voice behind him. "Well, that's news I wasn't expecting, but not surprised." Sweeping his sword low, he hoped to cleave her in two, but she wasn't there.

He turned around, his voice angry. "I still say you are an alien piece of trash."

"That's rich coming from a Kurtherian," Bethany Anne replied.

"So what!" He paced, looking around when he couldn't

figure out where her voice was coming from.

"Do you even care about Yoll?" the voice asked him again.

Yoll dropped down, making sure she wasn't hiding underneath his body before he moved in a full circle answering, "Yollins are merely the race I chose to subjugate first. Now I have four species. Yours would have been the fifth, but I think I'm too annoyed to care, and will just pummel your world with rocks until the dust is so thick, everything dies."

"Good to know," Bethany Anne appeared on the other side of the field. "You ready to finish this?"

He found her again. "What, you aren't going to run again, disappear when I attack?"

The woman just smiled and raised her hand and spoke. "Drop it!"

Yoll squinted, then his eyes widened in alarm when his Sacred Curtain started rolling back from the top, receding into the ground.

Yoll looked around, seeing the video screens showing him as he said, "Yollins are merely the race I chose to subjugate first..."

One hundred and fifty thousand angry Yollins now stared at him, promising violence if they could figure out a way to make it happen.

Yoll snapped. He raced toward the woman in front of of him, raising his sword high in the air when his head exploded. The enormous body slammed to the dirt, The momentum carried the headless body forward until it stopped ten yards in front of Bethany Anne who had stood still, her arms crossed, watching him slide across the field.

Kael-ven walked up, his face a mask of fury. His right hand held a Jean Dukes' pistol. He had just shot the King.

"Fucking Kurtherians!" Kael-ven spat.

In his anger, he didn't notice the start of the chant, but it grew. Bethany Anne moved out of the video picture that focused on King Yoll's dead body, Kael-ven in Bethany Anne's colors, pistol by his side as the audience erupted in cheers, chanting...

Kael-ven, KAEL-ven... KAEL-VEN! KAEL-VEN! KAEL-VEN!

Kael-ven finally recognized his name being chanted or yelled, and looked up to see his fellow Yollins screaming. He turned to view everyone in the stadium. He slid his pistol back into his holster and indicated with his hands for the crowd to quiet down.

Crank his voice up to the speakers, ADAM.

>>Already done, Bethany Anne.<<

"My name is Kael-ven T'chmon, I am of the Kiene caste, the Undesirable caste," he started. "Not because I was put there, but because anything that came out of the mouth of that..." Here, the translation had trouble, but the Yollins did not as Kael-ven pointed to the dead King, "liar, I want *NOTHING* to do with!"

The screaming erupted for minutes. Kael-ven made the motion of patting his hands down, finally hushing the crowd.

"There are three families who right now are making plans to claim the King's position. Here is what I am doing about that."

The video monitors all switched to a broad view of the city, aimed at the Kolin district of the hill below the Royal Palace. The camera slowly panned forward as three Human Sphaea class ships appeared above three of the family compounds, with figures dropping down from them.

"Those are Yollin mercenaries, Bethany Anne's mercenaries." Kael-ven pointed to the alien Queen. "The alien who helped me see there was a better way, and who unveiled the truth behind the lies of our history. Right now, Kiel, my best friend, is leading those mercenaries to quell their plots to attack the Challenge Winner. We will NOT have another Yollin perpetuate the Caste system. That will happen over my dead body," he announced.

Kael-ven turned towards the body in time to see a large snakelike creature start to wiggle out of the neck. In a flash, Kael-ven's pistol was up and shot it, blowing it into two pieces. He walked closer, but stopped ten paces away. Bethany Anne walked up beside him.

"Is that the Kurtherian?" he asked her.

"Yes." They watched as one half of the body slowly stopped wiggling, but the other seemed to be growing longer, fixing its body.

"How many times do I have to shoot it for it to die?" he wondered.

"This is my responsibility now." Bethany Anne's face, highlighted on the great monitors overhead, crackled with energy as she walked over to pick up the creature, her hands glowing red. Its pained screams could be heard easily throughout the stadium.

"Next time I seek permission to pass through space to find Kurtherians to attack?" she said to the dying creature, "I suggest you fucking well let me do it!"

With that, there was a flash of energy and the small body was consumed by flame. Then Bethany Anne slapped her hands together to get the residue of the Kurtherian off of them.

She turned around and eyed the Yollins in the stands. "This is the planet Yoll and will be led by a Yollin," she pointed to Kael-ven. "Your planet is now accepted into the Etheric

Empire, and under my personal protection. Whoever tries to attack the Yollin people will answer to me."

She looked around, her face returning to her normal visage.

"So decrees Empress Bethany Anne."

FAMILY RESIDENCE, THR'IGHILLICKS, KOLIN CASTE

There was a pounding on the door upstairs. "Don't answer that!" hissed their father, busy suiting up. "We've still got a few more things to do, and can't be…"

The door exploded, shrapnel showering the stairs leading down, all of those in the underground room pointing their weapons towards the room's entrance.

They all looked at each other in concern. Then they heard the unmistakable CLOMP CLOMP CLOMP of armored military.

Thr'ighillick, Clan Leader, bowed his head. They could not take on people in armor, yet. He had two sets for his family, but they weren't planning on suiting up until confirmation of the King's death or the alien's reached their ears.

"My name," came a voice from above, "Is Kiel. I'm the leader of the Yollin Mercenaries under the command, of Queen, no Empress Bethany Anne. I'm not here to fight you. I'm merely here to tell you that this compound will be hit with multiple one and two-pound pucks within a few minutes. Anyone still in this compound will be killed."

CLOMP CLOMP CLOMP. "You have been warned," he called out one last time.

Clomp clomp clomp…

The father looked around at his family, looking back at him earnestly, fear in their eyes. "Children, leave first! Go, don't question, just *go!*"

The Thr'ighillick family was the only family that took Kiel's warning to heart. Every one of them made it out of their compound safely.

Kiel gave the other two families till the last of the Thr'ighillicks left and then ordered all three compounds pucked.

Those in the stadium watched as the three families' houses exploded, rock and dust tossed high up into the air.

The underlying promise was there.

What Empress Bethany Anne decreed, happened.

———

HOURS LATER, KING'S PALACE GROUNDS, YOLL

Bethany Anne walked along the row of dead and stuffed heads, asking for a translation how they had died and offering a prayer for each of the fallen. At the end, she told Kael-ven, "Give these all a proper burial, and a cemetery for those in the future to visit. In recognition of the evil King Yoll brought to all people, not just Yollins."

"May I ask why you are not destroying these grounds?" Kael-ven asked. Both he and Bethany Anne aware of the video cameras on them, this walk through the late King's palace on display for all of Yoll to see.

"Yes, of course," she answered, and turned to look at Kael-ven. "On my world, we have monuments to those who have done both beneficial things and for places where horror was visited." She waved around herself. "In the future, and there will come a time in your future, when those not yet living will question the validity of history. Whether we are in fact rewriting it ourselves. This palace," she pointed down, "will be kept as a monument proving it happened. There *was* a time in Yollin history when it was led by an evil being, one that used the Yollin people for nefarious purposes."

Bethany Anne looked into the camera. "Your people are part of the Etheric Empire now. There are seven Kurtherian Clans that have bent their hands toward evil and have done so on a cosmic scale. One of the Five tried sending out emissaries to uplift species to help them prepare to fight."

"This Kurtherian found humans. Now, we humans will take the universe back from the Kurtherians and we won't stop by just helping your people. No, we will fight until we are dead, or there isn't a Kurtherian threat we can find."

"Welcome to the Etheric Empire. Buckle up, because now the Kurtherians have both humans AND Yollins to deal with, and I expect your very best." With that, Bethany Anne disappeared.

"What?" The startled cameraman said. The news reporter jumped forward and stuck her microphone in front of Kael-ven.

"Where did the alien Empress go?" she asked, looking at Kael-ven, still in his armor, his pistols evident, and then back to the camera.

"Bethany Anne?" he shrugged. A strange movement and the reporter asked him what his shoulders moving meant. "What, the shrugging? Oh, it is a movement the humans use to suggest they do not know. Once you are around humans long enough, you pick up some mannerisms."

"Like this cursing?"

Kael-ven grinned. "Yes, that is a particularly nasty habit you will pick up around the Queen, sorry, Empress, if you spend enough time around her."

"Would you say that you spent too much time around her and now are nothing but a puppet for her?" the reporter asked.

Kael-ven shrugged. "Answer this for me," he looked into the camera. "Just seven solar turns ago, you knew that Yoll was the rightful King of all Yollins, that Yollin's future was the subjugation of other races, that the Caste System was what the Holy Texts decreed."

"Now," he continued, still looking into the camera. "You know that King Yoll was a lying alien Kurtherian, his Yollin head shot off by me, the Kurtherian inside him killed by Empress Bethany Anne. If she wanted to subjugate Yoll, she could have dropped rocks on the planet, or destroyed our fixed space stations, killing untold millions without lifting a finger."

He turned to the reporter. "Did you see her ship, the ArchAngel?" She nodded. "Have you seen the battle footage of the ArchAngel in the middle of our fleet?" Another nod. "So, you tell me, does she need a puppet?"

The reporter caught herself shaking her head no before she realized this ex-Captain was too damned charismatic by half. "So, you have no idea where she is?"

Kael-ven shrugged again, a smile on his face.

"Bethany Anne is always watching."

———

NEVER SUBMIT

Peter walked into the bar, seeking out the team that beat him on Yollin ship 21. He smiled, they weren't off at their own table alone this time, but rather in the middle of a large group of Guardian Marines.

The group noticed Peter walking their way and almost immediately straightened up. "Sorry Cap," one of the men said. "Just blowing off a little steam."

"Men, the only time I worry about what you're doing in here is if I get a call from Bobcat, William or Marcus. They don't say anything, I won't either. They get pissed? Well, I wouldn't suggest pissing off my friends, got me?"

A couple of those in the group blanched, not realizing that the owners of the bar were Peter's personal friends.

Peter looked at all of them. "All I'm here to say is the team that attacked Yollin 21's power rooms and shut down the fleet cloaking won the bet." He looked at the three Chinese men. "And specifically Team Empress Cats' blowout success was instrumental, so here." Peter tossed a bag and Shun caught it, "is five ounces of gold to make sure the beer and liquor flows freely. That's from my bank account, not the Guardians. A bet was struck, and you guys won the bet. Keep your heads on if you have duty in the next twenty-four hours. If you have to use a nanite pack to cure a hangover, your ass is grass, got me?"

There were plenty of 'yes sirs!' as Peter walked back out of the bar. He was sure the tablets were already full of messages for their friends and team members to come join them.

Tonight, All Guns Blazing was going to be a raucous party.

TEAM BMW STORAGE CAVERN

"That's a lot of shit," William looked at all of the stills and equipment they had bought in Germany and had shipped up at the last minute in temperature and humidity controlled units. Marcus had come to find him and get his help after he heard a noise in the large holding cavern Bethany Anne let them use.

"Meredith, can we get some more light in here?" William asked the EI, looking around.

"Three minutes, William. I'll move some from another cavern," the EI responded from his tablet.

William turned back to Marcus. "Okay, what do you think you heard?" he asked.

"I know it sounds weird, William," Marcus admitted, "and in this cavern, the noises are messed up, but it *sounded* like a ghost."

"A ghost?" William asked, looking both ways and then behind himself. William thought back to when Marcus had interrupted him in the bar. He remembered Marcus said 'something, something, something… noise in the caverns where we're storing the German brewing equipment' and had agreed to help his friend.

"Fuck me I hate ghosts," he whispered. If he had known what the hell Marcus was talking about, he would have told Bobcat he needed to come out here. Now, William was in a hundred and fifty fucking thousand square feet of ghost-infested space and he was trying not to run right over Marcus and get the hell out of here.

Because that shit would be on the Meredith Reynolds

video sharing site in a damned second, before he could make it back to All Guns Blazing. Marcus, lying on the ground grievously wounded when William had bulldozed him over, would call ahead and have it playing on the video monitors in the bar.

He would have to kill Marcus for the plan to work, and blame it on the ghosts.

Soon enough, Meredith had extra lights in the cavern and they could see the pallets of product they had purchased.

Some, it looked like, had been left outside back on Earth, with dust on them and a little rust. Those would have to be cleaned before they could be used. Everyone who had a recipe for Coke was screaming for Team BMW to get their shit together so they could try out their recipe.

That included, amazingly enough, a pair that had neither arms nor legs of their own. William wasn't sure what TOM and ADAM were going to do about that little hiccup in their plans.

Then, William heard the sounds.

"Did you hear it?" Marcus looked around. "Although that sounded clearer." Marcus looked over at William who had a hand over his eyes. "What is it?"

William rubbed his face and looked around. "We might need to grab a knife to cut plastic." He started down between the pallets before he called out over his shoulder, "Marcus, I sure hope you like kittens."

―――――

QBBS MEREDITH REYNOLDS, SIX WEEKS AFTER THE KING'S CHALLENGE

Barnabas arrived in deck 07's secondary conference room. It was almost as far away from Bethany Anne as one could get, without going into the areas of the base still under construction.

He had received a special request from Ecaterina to meet her and Nathan here, they promised him information, but they wanted to ask a favor.

When he arrived, he checked quickly and confirmed it was just Ecaterina and Nathan inside the room. Meredith opened the doors; the almost silent swoosh was pleasant to him.

Both Ecaterina and Nathan were worried, that was obvious. He was tempted to read them, but Bethany Anne told him not to be doing that without her permission or unless he had grave concerns.

Ecaterina wiped a tear that had been running down her face and stepped over to Barnabas. "Thank you for coming."

"What is it?" he asked, looking from Ecaterina to Nathan and then back in confusion. "What's happened?"

"We need you to judge us, and then help us," Nathan admitted.

Barnabas stayed quiet a moment. "Tell me."

"We," Ecaterina stopped and looked over to Nathan and then back at Barnabas. "We uh, we kind of stole the Pepsi recipe before we left Earth."

He stared at her for a moment. "Okay." Since he himself and half of Bethany Anne's team had been working on stealing the Coca-Cola recipe, this wasn't too bad, yet.

Nathan rubbed his head.

"How does this require judgment on you two?" Barnabas asked.

"Well," Nathan blew out a breath. "That's just it. I've found out through backchannels…"

"Backchannels?" Barnabas asked.

"He's setting up Bethany Anne's Alien Intelligence unit, so call it spies and bad people," Ecaterina explained.

Barnabas looked at Ecaterina and then back at Nathan. "We'll have to work together."

"Don't I know it," Nathan agreed. "So, I was hoping you might do us," he pointed back and forth between himself and Ecaterina, "a solid and help us forget or confuse us about who was responsible for the Pepsi recipe being stolen."

"Why?" Barnabas asked. Making the two of them forget they knew about a Pepsi recipe, not always easy, but confused about a Pepsi recipe? He could do that.

Barnabas just looked at Nathan, waiting him out.

Nathan looked at the ceiling before turning his attention back to Barnabas. "Because it was stolen by a criminal and is now being made," he pointed towards the planet Yoll, "on the planet as a form of illegal moonshine."

Barnabas froze a moment before a small smile played on his face. "Am I to understand that the two of you," he pointed at them, "stole the Pepsi recipe from Earth, brought it through the Annex Gate and then got it stolen here in Yollin space? Now, someone. presumably the bad guy, has sold the recipe and it is now a form of moonshine?"

Nathan pursed his lips. "Yes, that's it in a nutshell."

Barnabas started laughing. "That is Karma at its finest."

"What?" Ecaterina asked. "You are laughing. You think Bethany Anne would be okay with this?"

"Oh," Barnabas shook his head to dissuade her rash hope.

MICHAEL ANDERLE

"No. She would be furious that Pepsi made it past the Annex Gate and Saint-Payback would be the Bitch riding your backs for a dozen years. She would have a problem forgiving you every single time it came up. No, you two are forever in a bad place as the two responsible for Pepsi over here."

"Oh," Ecaterina's eyes lowered. She looked at Nathan, her face resigned. "We're going to have to tell her."

"Oh, I didn't say I wouldn't help you," Barnabas interrupted and pointed to her mate. "As Nathan has pointed out, I could use his help for my Rangers and I need him in one piece and functional to help me."

"That would be nice," Nathan agreed. "It's kind of funny, but I don't need the constant beatings in sparring class for the next ten years."

"True." Barnabas rubbed his jaw. "Okay, I can confuse your memories of who stole the Pepsi recipe, but it is going to erase memories around that event as well. What did you do next after you stole the Pepsi?"

Ecaterina answered, "Our special last date together on Earth, at the pizza place Nathan took me, how come?" There was worry in her eyes.

"How long were you there?" Barnabas continued his line of questioning.

"An hour, then all hell broke loose and we had to deal with getting back." Nathan answered.

"Because that memory is going to be fuzzy, and you might lose it as well." Barnabas answered. There must be Justice, and fudging those memories would have to be enough.

"Oh," Ecaterina bit her lip, "Okay."

Nathan just nodded.

Five minutes later, Barnabas left the room, allowing the two a moment to finish the suggestion he planted in their minds as to why they were now in there away from everyone.

My Empress?

Yes? she replied, instantly.

Barnabas took a right turn down a hallway. *I've solved the Pepsi case.*

It was Team BMW, wasn't it? she replied.

I told you, I would solve it, administer appropriate punishment, and that would be the final result. We both know you are too emotional on this subject to deal with it.

He could almost feel Bethany Anne's annoyance through his connection.

Do you disagree? he asked.

No, she grumped, *you're right. I feel like we're back in the time when I kept telling you everyone needed to die, just to make my point.*

Ah, good times.

Liar.

Well, considering everything we've accomplished, the fact that a drink recipe has made it over to this side of the galaxy isn't the biggest deal.

Well, I guess not, she agreed. *Besides, do we still have the coriander crops properly hidden?*

Yes.

Good, make sure we sell the oil on the black market for a huge profit. We'll use the coriander oil trade to help fund some of the agricultural budget for the next couple of years.

Yes, my Empress.

It was Ecaterina and Nathan, wasn't it? she snuck into the conversation right before he dropped.

Still not telling, Barnabas answered and disconnected their conversation, a small smile on his face.

He was sure he had blocked any information about the

guilty party traveling across the connection back to her.

Barnabas was impressed. Bethany Anne understood the psychology of peoples who would want to drink a banned substance, Pepsi, as a form of rebellion. The only way to make Pepsi was from oil of the coriander plant. Fortunately, this plant wasn't available in Yollin space, or anywhere as far as they knew.

Now, those who wanted to spit in the eye of the new Empress Bethany Anne could buy the drink on the black market for exorbitant prices. It would be their little act of rebellion, and they would feel better.

And fill her coffers to help run her Empire at the same time.

It was, Bethany Anne had told him, a tax on those who might wish for a rebellion, but just needed to blow off some steam. She told him that she would be loved at times, and hated at times.

She had learned this already back on Earth.

Those times where she was loved, they would be able to determine due to the lower revenue from the coriander oil. When the revenue went up, it was a good indication they needed to focus on which areas bought more of it.

If Empress Bethany Anne could rule with benevolence, that was preferred. But what about when she couldn't?

Well, the *Queen Bitch* was never too far below the surface.

THE END

MICHAEL'S NOTES

Never Submit - The Kurtherian Gambit 15:
Written February 2, 2017

As always, can I say with a HUGE amount of appreciation how much it means to me that you not only read this book, but you are reading these notes as well? I write these for each book, sometimes wondering if anyone reads these anymore. Or, have I become too boring, too repetitious and readers are thinking 'stop writing these, just get on with the next story already!'

LOL

Ok, now that my existential angst is shared, and because of the sharing, easier to handle, I've got something to chat about (ok, a couple somethings) that came up because of a Facebook post and some feedback.

––––––––

#1 - Science, as in Science *Fiction*.

Here is a famous quote from Arthur C. Clarke: "Any sufficiently advanced technology is indistinguishable from **magic**."

The whole Kurtherian Gambit is based on this premise. I've been blessed that paranormal, vampire loving readers have stuck with me when I pulled (some of) them kicking and screaming into science fiction.

(Don't say I haven't, I've read the reviews! LOL)

Now, I asked a question on Facebook about a week and a half ago, and divulged a plan for a future series called "The Rise of Magic" and guess what occurred?

That's right, OUTRAGE!

<The Author is chuckling, because that comment 'outrage' was SO not what happened. He is coloring the truth just a bit.>

Ok, it really wasn't so much outrage as "you are going to lose me, here."

<You HAVE to keep reading, I promise it isn't the magic you are thinking it is!>

Why did the fans say something? Because I didn't explain myself very well. The original question (related to a podcast) divulged that in the future on Earth, we would have a magic based age. But, we have to go through two more ages before Irth (our Earth) pulls its ass out of everything and freaking FINALLY humans build something we can all be proud of accomplishing.

With Never Submit, Bethany Anne is now officially out of our Solar System for a time (approximately 160 years take or give 5 years). During this time, we have stuff happen here on our planet during which The Terry Henry Walton Chronicles, Reclaiming Honor, and The Second Dark Ages series occur.

SKIP IF YOU DON'T WANT TO KNOW WHAT HAPPENS WITH MICHAEL AND BETHANY ANNE

**BEGIN SPOILER ALERT **

Ok, at the end of Michael's series, we have an HEA (happily ever after) event with Bethany Anne and Michael. She's put in her time, finished her job, and so has Michael. They hop in their bad ass chariot with friends and ride off into the Universe for another set of adventures.

Think TKG as Star Wars, the future series (no name yet) as a Star Trek.

But that discussion is for another time.

**END SPOILER ALERT **

Now, after the events above in the spoiler, the Earth moves forward. Unfortunately, Kurtherian science has a hiccup after our people leave.

Remember, "Any sufficiently advanced technology is indistinguishable from **magic**."

Even technology that has gone haywire, and the people it is affecting don't KNOW they have technology *inside* them.

Technology from Kurtherians.

From the Earth's past.

So, we have The Age of Magic, a new Kurtherian Age on Irth (Earth) in our Future. When humans seek to learn about, contain, restrain, use and abuse for personal gain new capabilities *they* call magic.

Stories about where these abilities might have originated and how they are changing people, by changing their genetics, their DNA, their … *humanity*.

One thing that often won't change is the human spirit, unfortunately, both kinds.

Enter Hannah, a very young woman caught up in events in the beginning of The Age of Magic.

All she wanted to do was save her brother from dying in her arms, she didn't *mean* to use magic. She didn't even know she *HAD* magic.

Those set to kill her for her using magic, breaking the law, tracked her down to an alley, ready to kill her. They didn't realize just who the old man was that interrupted their sadistic *fun* …

But they should have.

When I wrote Death Becomes Her, I was curious what readers would think about the 'left turn' of how vampires were created? Would they shut down the story when they found out aliens were involved? Would they get pissed off at me for screwing up their favorite paranormal genre and leave SCATHING reviews about how I shouldn't be playing with the history as we know it?

In short, was anyone besides me even interested in this stuff?

I have to admit, it wasn't all curiosity, there was a HUGE amount of trepidation, as well.

(Trepidation: A $5.00 word for scared *shitless*).

It wasn't like I had huge expectations, but even my tiny little selling $7.50 a day-per-book goal could be dashed, you know? However, so many fans loved that exact twist that it has been more than a nice surprise. It's been a huge heartwarming BLESSING.

Why? Because I'm not alone, you know?

The reason we have fans of anything—football, crochet, racing, Gone With The Wind (my stepmother is a HUGE fan) is because it allows us to talk and connect with those who also like the same thing. Now, I have people who like these sets of stories I like (generally speaking— not every fan of Bethany Anne is a fan of another series, and vice-versa) and it has been very cool.

If you have looked at the Kurtherian FB fan page, we are multi-cultural, multi-sex(ual), gender-neutral, multi-country (I *HEAR* you Australia! Every time I put a date up and you guys get to it before I have the book out, I *HEAR* you) and while we lean older, we have representation from most ages... Except young adult, nn Facebook at least.

I don't seem to delve into that market too much. I suppose I could try and market to 20-32 year olds, just not sure if it's a smart move? If you have any suggestions on whether I'm getting readers in their 20s, let me know, please!

This book, the 15th in The Kurtherian Gambit Series, is also the first book of the 3rd Arc (the Green Arc – you can tell by the bar of color under the Author Name at the bottom...1-7 (red), 8-14 (blue), 15-21 (green)).

This is important (well, ok, it is important to me... not so sure how many others) because it is the arc where we take the fight out to the Kurtherians, and damned if we didn't meet one right up front.

How many found this to be a surprise? (I'm raising my

hand—so, if I telegraphed that the King of Yoll was a Kurtherian in previous books? That means my subconscious was doing a number, because him being Kurtherian wasn't originally planned by me.)

I did telegraph way back in earlier books that the Yollins got their ass kicked in the first battle, so hopefully not too many readers were surprised by the results.

In my beats (consider beats something similar to a connect-the-dot setup for writing a fiction book), I did not have Bethany Anne getting involved in the fight in New York. I didn't even have her do much more than help everyone get to the G'laxix Sphaea and go back to the Meredith Reynolds.

Then John Grimes got his bright ass idea to go play hooky, which was kinda funny. I mean, when most royalty play hooky, their idea isn't to get some armor, some guns, (a box of grenades) and go find some terrorist nest to clean out. I hope to come back to that day of hooky and write it as a short story. Perhaps as a Frank Kurns short.

I particularly liked the scene in the Pod when Tabitha calls Bethany Anne through their mental connection and early in the conversation, Bethany Anne says 'shoot.' Tabitha thinks the Queen is telling *her* to continue talking, but really Bethany Anne meant that comment to go to John...a s in "Shoot them sumbitches!"

One of the situations in this book I've been struggling with (besides writing this whole book) was just how far does a Queen's Ranger go? They are pretty badass, but are supposed to try to be more law abiding, less kill and let God sort out the good from the bad. So, in this story, we have Tabitha wondering what is she going to do when the four mercenaries come storming into the building?

I realized at that moment when I was writing the scene, Tabitha is aware that Monica has been kidnapped, and Ted is an almost useless wreck. When she is waiting to see who comes in the front door she finally sees a *military* strike team and *that* makes the decision for her.

As far as she is concerned, this isn't a legal operation, but enemy action.

I enjoyed letting Tabitha play a little more (and I mean just shoot and kill, no slapping the cuffs on people). I look forward to more writing more Tabitha stories in the future.

Because, who doesn't like a person who kicks ass, but occasionally just trips over a cord? She is my favorite flawed character. Full of heart, but still somewhat damaged. I want her to succeed, but she needs help from her friends to make it happen and her friends know this.

I'm curious what they will set up in the future for her, myself.

I hope you enjoyed this book. It was a challenge to write. Partially because of juggling more in the beginning of the month due to the other releases (I edit everything with my name on it) and me thinking I'd be able to dictate a big portion of this book.

Didn't happen. Lost five days thinking I would be able to dictate a huge portion of the book... HUGE mistake on my part AND missed my Jan 31st date. Dammit.

I appreciate the support, the push and ALL of the kind words you give both myself and the other writers working in this Universe. I have some pretty awesome plans I want to share, and more coming, all the time.

We have four artists working now in TKG. Plus, two new cover artist(s) for two new series.

———

#2 - AUDIO IS STARTING TO HAPPEN!

Here are the series, and who is doing narration at this time:

The Kurtherian Gambit - 21 Books (First 7 in Studio)
Narration provided by Emily Beresford
Death Becomes Her - AVAILABLE NOW! (Woohoo!)
Click to see on Audible's Website

Reclaiming Honor - 4 Books (so far)
Narration provided by Kate Rudd
Justice Is Calling - AVAILABLE NOW! (Woohoo!)
Click to see on Audible's Website

Terry Henry Walton Chronicles - 4 Books (so far)
Narration provided by Kate Rudd
Nomad Found - IN PRODUCTION

Etheric Academy Series - 4 Books (so far)
Narration provided by Emily Beresford
Alpha Class - IN PRODUCTION

The Rise of Magic - 4 Books (so far)
Narration provided by Kate Rudd

———

#3 - EXTRA SPECIAL RESEARCH ;-)
Want to know about the Coke Recipe?
Here it is! (American Radio Show)

Love you all,

See you NEXT Book ;-)

Michael

———

SERIES TITLES INCLUDE:

KURTHERIAN GAMBIT SERIES TITLES INCLUDE:

First Arc

Death Becomes Her (01) - Queen Bitch (02) - Love Lost (03) - Bite This (04)
Never Forsaken (05) - Under My Heel (06) Kneel Or Die (07)

Second Arc

We Will Build (08) - It's Hell To Choose (09) - Release The Dogs of War (10)
Sued For Peace (11) - We Have Contact (12) - My Ride is a Bitch (13)
Don't Cross This Line (14)

Third Arc (Due 2017)

Never Submit (15) - Never Surrender (16) - Forever Defend (17)
Might Makes Right (18) - Ahead Full (19) - Capture Death (20)
Life Goes On (21)

THE SECOND DARK AGES

The Dark Messiah (01)
The Darkest Night (02)
Darkest Before The Dawn (03)
with Ell Leigh Clarke
Dawn Arrives (04)
with Ell Leigh Clarke

THE BORIS CHRONICLES
* With Paul C. Middleton *

Evacuation (01)
Retaliation (02)
Revelation (03)
Redemption (04)

RECLAIMING HONOR
* With JUSTIN SLOAN *

Justice Is Calling (01)
Claimed By Honor (02)
Judgement Has Fallen (03)
Angel of Reckoning (04)
Born Into Flames (05)
Defending The Lost (06)
Saved By Valor (07)
Return of Victory (08)

THE ETHERIC ACADEMY
* With TS PAUL *

ALPHA CLASS (01)
ALPHA CLASS - Engineering (02)
ALPHA CLASS (03) *Coming Soon*

TERRY HENRY "TH" WALTON CHRONICLES
* With CRAIG MARTELLE *

Nomad Found (01)
Nomad Redeemed (02)
Nomad Unleashed (03)
Nomad Supreme (04)
Nomad's Fury (05)
Nomad's Justice (06)
Nomad Avenged (07)
Nomad Mortis (08)
Nomad's Force (09)
Nomad's Galaxy (10)

TRIALS AND TRIBULATIONS
* With Natalie Grey *

Risk Be Damned (01)
Damned to Hell (02)
Hell's Worst Nightmare (03) *coming soon*

THE ASCENSION MYTH
* With ELL LEIGH CLARKE *

Awakened (01)
Activated (02)
Called (03)
Sanctioned (04)
Rebirth (05)
Retribution (06)
Cloaked (07)
Bourne (08)

THE AGE OF MAGIC
THE RISE OF MAGIC
* With CM RAYMOND/LE BARBANT *

Restriction (01)
Reawakening (02)
Rebellion (03)
Revolution (04)
Unlawful Passage (05)
Darkness Rises (06)
The Gods Beneath (07)
Reborn (08)

THE HIDDEN MAGIC CHRONICLES
* With JUSTIN SLOAN *

Shades of Light (01)
Shades of Dark (02)
Shades of Glory (03)
Shades of Justice (04)

STORMS OF MAGIC
* With PT HYLTON *

Storms Raiders (01)
Storm Callers (02)
Storm Breakers (03)
Storm Warrior (04)

TALES OF THE FEISTY DRUID
* With CANDY CRUM *

The Arcadian Druid (01)
The Undying Illusionist (02)
The Frozen Wasteland (03)
The Deceiver (04)
The Lost (05)
The Damned (06)

PATH OF HEROES
* With BRANDON BARR *

Rogue Mage (01)

A NEW DAWN
* With AMY HOPKINS *

Dawn of Destiny (01)
Dawn of Darkness (02)
Dawn of Deliverance (03)
Dawn of Days (04)

TALES OF THE WELLSPRING KNIGHT
* With P.J. CHERUBINO *

Knight's Creed (01)

THE AGE OF EXPANSION
THE UPRISE SAGA
* With AMY DUBOFF *

Covert Talents (01)
Endless Advance (02)
Veiled Designs (03)
Dark Rivals (04)

BAD COMPANY
* With CRAIG MARTELLE *

The Bad Company (01)
Blockade (02)
Price of Freedom (03)

THE GHOST SQUADRON
* With SARAH NOFFKE and J.N. CHANEY *

Formation (01)
Exploration (02)
Evolution (03)
Degeneration (04)
Impersonation (05)

CONFESSIONS OF A SPACE ANTHROPOLOGIST
* With ELL LEIGH CLARKE *

Giles Kurns: Rogue Operator (01)
Giles Kurns: Rogue Instigator (02)

VALERIE'S ELITES
* With JUSTIN SLOAN AND PT HYLTON *

Valerie's Elites (01)
Death Defied (02)
Prime Enforcer (03)

SHADOW VANGUARD
* With TOM DUBLIN *

Gravity Storm (01)

ETHERIC ADVENTURES: ANNE AND JINX
* With S.R. RUSSELL *

Etheric Recruit
Etheric Researcher

OTHER BOOKS

Gateway to the Universe
* With CRAIG MARTELLE & JUSTIN SLOAN *

THE CHRONICLES OF ORICERAN
THE LEIRA CHRONICLES
* With MARTHA CARR *

Waking Magic (1)
Release of Magic (2)
Protection of Magic (3)
Rule of Magic (4)
Dealing in Magic (5)
Theft of Magic (6)
Enemies of Magic (7)

SHORT STORIES

Frank Kurns Stories of the Unknownworld 01 (7.5)
You Don't Mess with John's Cousin

Frank Kurns Stories of the Unknownworld 02 (9.5)
Bitch's Night Out

Frank Kurns Stories of the Unknownworld 02 (13.25)
With Natalie Grey
Bellatrix

AUDIOBOOKS
Available at Audible.com and iTunes

WANT MORE?

Join the email list here:

http://kurtherianbooks.com/email-list/

AND NOW

http://kurtherianbooks.com/readers-supporting-military-book-newsletter/

Join the Facebook group here:

https://www.facebook.com/TheKurtherianGambitBooks/

The email list is changing to something... New. I don't have enough details but suffice to say there is so much going on in The Kurtherian Gambit Universe, it needs to go out more often than when the next book hits.

I hope you enjoy the book!

Michael Anderle - February 02, 2017.